The Journey of Misella Cross

A Novel

Catherine Witek

Sky Parlour Press
10575 West 153rd Place
Orland Park, Illinois 60462

Second Sky Parlour Press paperback edition November 2019

For information about special discounts for bulk purchases, please contact Sky Parlour Press Special Sales at hkwitek@comcast.net.

Cover Design by Bridget M. Hassan

Author Photo by Walter F. Piper

Manufactured in the United States of America

For my Beloved Family

"It is impossible not to conceive that men in their original state were equal; and very difficult to imagine how one would be subjected to another but by violent compulsion."

Samuel Johnson

The Journey of Misella Cross
London, 1754

Contents

Chapter 1

Prisoners huddled together in two groups on the deck of the *Seaflower*, the men, in irons, separated from the unfettered women. When the ship lurched away from the Blackfriars dock, some of the men slipped, taking their chained partners with them as they tumbled to the wet boards. The clanging of the ship's bell signaled the launch, muffling the curses of the fallen men, their shackled wrists bleeding anew.

The first mate, Amos Bristol, lunged toward them. "Get up," he screamed, "and stand quiet or you'll feel the rope's end before we reach the ocean." The cold April wind whipped the pages of the open ledger he held. "When I call your names, follow Flinty down to the hold." A scowling troll of a man in dirty muslin britches and unbuttoned shirt released the bell rope, grabbed his sawn-off musket, and limped to a square opening in the deck floor.

Some of the women wept quietly into their bunched up shawls, knowing they would never see England again and fearing what they would find in the New World. Misella Cross shed no tears, though she shivered in her torn garments. Her attention was drawn to the young girl cowering next to her, pale as death, her eyes red from weeping. She appeared to be no older than twelve and even in her brown serge convict dress, she looked angelic: her face flawless as sculptured marble, her gold-tinged hair a mass of ringlets, her delicate lips compressed in an effort to control her sobs. *She looks like me*, Misella thought, with a painful stab of recognition, *six long years ago when I, too, was forsaken.*

Misella slipped her arm around the girl's thin shoulders. "You have a friend," she whispered. "Stay next to me." The girl did not respond, her hands hanging limp, her eyes downcast.

Bristol began calling the men first. "Smith!" "Carncross!" "Move your clinkers." Two wretched-looking convicts, chained together, their shirt cuffs damp with blood, shuffled forward in unison and stood behind Flinty. After all of the men's names were called and checked off the ledger, they clanked down the ladder, following Flinty into the prison hold. They wormed their way down a narrow beamed walkway to the bow of the ship, filtered light from the deck relieving some of the gloom. A wooden barricade separated the men's quarters from the women who would be housed in the aft section.

Bare platforms constructed along each side of the hold divided the space into upper and lower levels, enough to accommodate sixty convicts in each of the forward and aft sections of the ship. Each level allowed the convicts space to sit or lie down but not to stand. The men would remain chained to their partners throughout the trip to limit the possibility of mutiny.

Flinty stood at the open doorway and shoved the men forward with the butt of his gun. "Welcome to the floating palace of His Majesty, King George," he jeered, a twisted grin uncovering the black stubs of his teeth. "You in the front take the top layer." He sniggered at the jangled efforts and the snarling curses of the men as they tried to coordinate their movements with their partners and hoist themselves up to the second tier. The remaining prisoners, equally noisy, flung themselves on to the lower levels and scooted crab-like across the planks to claim their meager space.

When they all had settled in, Flinty stepped inside and pointed to the wooden half barrel at each end of the room. "You do your business in there and no place else," he said, "if you know what's good for you." He backed out and slammed the heavy door locking the men inside.

On deck the crew diligently worked the ropes to hoist the sails; none wanted to incur the First Mate's wrath in the absence of the

Captain who had returned to his cabin. Bristol stood in front of a burly crewman seated on a small oaken barrel, a leather vest over his bare chest, as he finished plaiting the thick leather handle of a whip and began tying knots in each of its tails. "Is the cat ready yet, Logan?" he shouted, making sure all on deck heard him. "Will the Captain approve it?"

Logan nodded. Though seated, he towered over the diminutive First Mate. "Yes, Sir." He raised the leather rod in one hand and flicked his wrist, the tails whirling and cracking through the air.

While Bristol was distracted, the crew leered at the women convicts, encouraged by the bold stares from some of them.

Satisfied with Logan's work, Bristol turned to assess the women himself. He liked the spirited, pale-haired one—Misella Cross—but she had already been claimed by Captain Barclay. "Bring her to my cabin in a few hours," the Captain had muttered, "after she is checked in the ledger and settled below."

He eyed the young waif huddled next to Misella. *Could be her sister*, he thought. They looked alike, though the little one seemed cowed, untested, probably still clean. *She's the one*, he decided.

Flinty huffed up the ladder and limped over to Bristol. "All done, Sir. Ready for the doxies." He grinned at the pack of women, some of whom smiled back. A buxom redhead extended her tongue and winked at him. Flinty made his choice.

The women lined up behind Flinty as their names were called. When Bristol bellowed, "Margaret MacDonald," the frightened girl stumbled forward and fell into place, her head down, gold curls trembling. Bristol hesitated. "Look at me," he ordered. She seemed not to hear him, her shoulders drawn up around her ears as if, turtle-like, she could retreat from the threatening noise around her. Bristol stepped closer and shoved the ledger under her chin, thrusting her head up and forcing her to raise her reddened eyes to his. "That's much better," he said. With a smirk he moved on down the list.

Though Misella had been among the first in line, she slipped unnoticed to the end behind Margaret and grasped her cold hand, determined to protect her if she could.

The women followed the same path as the men down to the hold in the aft section of the ship. They passed by a recessed area in the corner, with two walls that held six swaying hammocks and a line of brass hooks. The female convicts would soon discover that the twelve-man crew was housed here in eight-hour shifts so that half the crew was on duty twenty-four hours a day. In the absence of passengers, the first and second mates occupied the two other cabins on the lower deck near the Captain's. No passengers had boarded the *Seaflower* for this trip.

Though the women's quarters were usually as cramped as the men's, this time there were fewer female prisoners, forty rather than sixty. Unshackled, they had more freedom of movement. Flinty stood guard in the doorway shooing women through and ordering them not to take the section nearest the doorway. Prodded by Flinty's musket, they quickly claimed their territories, spreading out their shawls and extra clothing from their bags to soften the boards.

When Misella reached the doorway, she saw that Flinty had grabbed the woman in front of Margaret, an older woman with a wild mass of red hair. Misella recognized her from the prison yard, Molly Parsons, sentenced for running a brothel. He cupped one of her large breasts in his hand. "Here you go, Lovey." He pushed her into the vacant section by the door. "Right up close where I can find you when I need you." She laughed and threw herself backwards spread-eagled across the plank.

Misella steered Margaret to a lower section in the back, as far away from the door as possible. She drew a large shawl from her canvas bag and tucked it around the shivering girl. "Sit back against the wall, Margaret. We'll make this into a comfortable little nest."

Misella slid into the space in front of the silent girl and began to remove the rest of her possessions from the bag, shielding them from the eyes of the other prisoners: an extra muslin dress, an embroidered apron, a hair brush, two pearl-studded combs, a small mirror, a few bars of soap, tooth cleaning powder, a bone needle and thread, wrapped pieces of chocolate, a bag of coins—all supplied by her attorney, Ben Turner, before she left Newgate.

Margaret watched her, some of the terror disappearing from her eyes. When Misella removed her worn book of psalms, Margaret cried out, "Oh, let me hold the dear thing, please." Tears welled up again in her eyes as she clutched the little book to her chest. "We had a copy of this book. My Mum would read it to us by the fire before bed, me and my little brothers." She began to sob, holding the book and rocking back and forth.

"Where are you from, Margaret?" Misella asked, her voice gentle. "Tell me about your Mum and your brothers. I never had any, only sisters."

Margaret gulped a few times and wiped at her eyes. She kissed the book of psalms and laid it in her lap. "The Highlands. My Da died at Culloden years ago when I was only five. Danny was four and the twins, Michael and Malcolm, were yet babies." She seemed on the verge of bursting into tears again, but shook her head and continued.

"We moved to London and lived with Mum's sister for seven years until my Aunt Josie died and Mum lost her job as a seamstress and Danny was sickly and couldn't work." She closed her eyes and took a deep breath. "The tailor refused to pay Mum for the last work she did, so I was to sneak into his shop and take three yards of ribbon worth three shillings and two pence, what she was owed. No one would suspect me, Mum said, because I looked so saintly."

Margaret clawed at the fringe on the shawl, wrapping the strings around and around her fingers, and choked back a sob. "B-but he caught me, and I spent a long time in Bridewell, before I was convicted. I begged the Mayor of London to give me benefit of clergy, not to transport me away from Mum and my brothers." She began to sob, her thin chest heaving. "But he wouldn't, a-a-and I'll see them naught ever again," she wailed.

Misella picked up the hairbrush and began to run it through the girl's curls, crooning softly to her, "A close friend once told me that whenever I was afraid, I should place my fingers under my chin like this and say, 'Chin up, eyes to Heaven' to help me remember we are never alone." She took Margaret's hand and showed her how to tip her chin up.

"Don't worry, Margaret," she continued. "I'll be here to take care of you. You remind me of my sister Annabelle. We'll read the book together, like I used to do with Annie." Gradually, Margaret relaxed against her, stopped her tears, and fell asleep.

"Misella Cross." Flinty's bellow woke the exhausted young girl who sat up and began to shiver again. "Step forward and follow me. Now."

Misella hid her own fear, assuring Margaret that she would return promptly. Afraid to trust that the poor, defenseless girl could fend off the thieving women around her, Misella stuffed her belongings back in the bag, all but the book of psalms resting in Margaret's lap and the shawl around her shoulders, and tied the cord around her own wrist. She wriggled out of their cave, smiled at Margaret, tipped up her chin and headed toward Flinty who flashed her an ugly grin.

Chapter 2

Misella emerged from the hold, the canvas bag clutched against her side as she struggled to gain her footing on the shifting deck. At least, Flinty had not tried to grab her or made any obscene comments when he led her up to the deck where Bristol waited scowling, the ledger tucked under his arm.

He ordered her to follow him to the Captain's cabin. Her heart thumped in her chest though she forced herself to remain calm in front of the leering crew. "Captain's bunter," one muttered with a smirk as she passed him. "Gonna ride St. George, Missy," mumbled another, "and tip the velvet?" She ignored the stares and the catcalls.

The crew and the first mate had warned the prisoners before they set sail that Captain Barclay was a harsh disciplinarian. Misella worried that he had heard how she resisted the crew members' humiliating treatment of the women before they boarded the ship; and how Ben Turner had arrived at the dock and flogged the two crewmen, one of them Flinty, with his cane.

They had to step carefully around a set of pulleys, halyards coiled like sleeping cobras, ready to hoist the remaining sails. The deck in front of the Captain's cabin was scrubbed clean and free of clutter. Bristol rapped with his knuckles on the heavy oak door beneath a polished brass plate engraved in blunt lettering, **Captain Eben Barclay**. "Enter," an angry voice barked. The first mate opened the door. "Here she is, Sir." He pushed Misella inside and closed the door behind her.

The Captain loomed behind a crescent-shaped mahogany table pushed against the wall on his left; a small oval window centered within the wall's oak paneling admitted a faint light. A fat candle flickered and hissed in a pewter bowl next to an inkpot. He glanced up, a frown creasing his broad face, free of whiskers or pock marks, and motioned to the armless wooden chair in front of the table. "Sit." He lowered his eyes. With a toss of his large head, he flipped a wayward thicket of black hair off of his forehead and resumed writing in what appeared to be a journal, one burly arm resting upon the top of the page to keep it open.

Misella eased herself onto the chair. Only the scratching of his quill, the ticking of the brass wall clock, and his heavy breathing broke the silence of the room. No sound could be heard outside the cabin—not the creaking of the sails nor the lapping of the Thames against the sides of the ship as it moved toward Dover's entrance to the ocean nor the wrangling of the crew nor the noisome prisoners in the hold. The cabin seemed a fortress unto itself, immune from the influence of the outside world. She did not find comfort in that thought, her fear mounting with each beat of the clock. She wondered if that was his purpose in keeping her waiting, if he did this to every poor miscreant that dared to break his rules.

She tried to appear nonchalant, gazing around the room as if she were merely a visitor, instead of staring at the Captain whose young and handsome face, despite the frown, surprised her. She had envisioned an older, meaner version of Flinty, portly and bearded. Instead, he appeared to be in his early thirties, she surmised, vigorous and strong. A kind of trundle bed, quite lengthy, protruded from the far wall, a print quilt tucked neatly around a generous mattress, a few pillows propped against the unadorned headboard. A long metal trunk with a carved clasp rested underneath the bed. Several brass hooks held an array of clothing, most notably a gold embroidered frock coat. A tri-cornered hat dangled next to it.

At the far end of the Captain's table a glass decanter filled with what appeared to be brandy stood behind two fat glasses engraved with black lettering. On the end of the table nearest Misella was a short wooden stand holding a massive Bible. Its presence heartened her. She wanted to reach out and open it to the place where the ribbon parted the pages, to see the passage he had read last, to find some evidence that he was a merciful man.

He laid down his quill and slammed the journal shut. He stared at her for a moment, the color and shine of his eyes like that of the mahogany table. As cold and hard, too. "You are Misella Cross," he said, an accusation rather than a statement or a question.

She nodded. "I am, Sir," her voice meeker than she intended, her breath catching in her throat.

Shoving the journal aside, he placed the quill in its holder. "Your supporter has paid for your protection." He sneered with seeming disgust, reminding her of all the people in the courtroom who had looked upon her as something inhuman. "To keep an unclean woman like you," he said. He shook his head as if in disbelief, the dark lock of hair falling again on his forehead. He tossed it back and heaved a guttural laugh. "Well, I'll take his money to deliver you unmolested to the colonies."

She looked down to hide the tears of relief that had come unbidden at the thought of kind, loyal Ben saving her once again. She did not want his charity or the obligation to love him that came with it, but facing what she now realized would be a harrowing, life-threatening journey, she was grateful. He must have arranged this at the dockside after she boarded the ship. How much, she wondered, had he paid? She feared he had indebted himself far beyond his means, and she could never repay him.

Captain Barclay poured himself a generous glass from the decanter and took a long gulp. "Leave now," he said. "Bristol will show you where you'll be housed. We can't allow you to fester down there with the other she-thieves and prostitutes, can we? I have to protect my investment."

He stood up, an imposing figure of a man, and turned his back on her. Misella arose and lurched to the door, her bag swinging from her wrist in unison with the swaying of the ship.

Bristol lounged against the railing waiting for her, his pale-gray eyes trained on the two men scaling the rigging. He stood up, straightening his scabbard and smoothing his dark jacket. "Follow me." On the right side of the ship, around the corner from the Captain's cabin, he stopped before a narrow padlocked door. He undid the lock and swung the door inward. "Get in," he snarled. He pushed her through the doorway. "You'll stay here until the Captain wants you. You're his property now." He pulled the door closed and clicked the padlock in place.

Her stomach surged. Memories of prison flooded her brain as the blackness engulfed her. She inched her way forward, bumping into wooden barrels and tripping against what felt like stacks of rope. She figured she must be trapped in a storage closet; it smelled of hemp and tea and some kind of spice, a welcome departure from the fetid odors in the hold.

Her left hand encountered a shelf. She inched her fingers along the board until they hit cold metal, a lantern. But she found nothing else, no candle or flint. She collapsed onto the humps of rope at her feet, untied the canvas bag and placed it so she could use it as a headrest. She lay down across the rope, at least no worse than raw boards, and thought about Margaret stranded below with no one to protect her; Margaret, who reminded her so much of herself when she was twelve, naive and abandoned, cast into the clutches of Sir Richard Maltby. Though she had not been able to save herself then, perhaps she could save Margaret if she could persuade the Captain to let Margaret share this space.

How different her own life might have been, she reflected, if she had found a guardian angel to welcome and protect her when she first arrived at Hawthorn Manor.

Chapter 3

Captain Barclay poured another generous draft of brandy and downed it before withdrawing a piece of parchment from his journal and reading it again.

Promissory Note

To Ebenezer Barclay, Captain of the Seaflower, in the amount of one hundred pounds sterling: 100 £ for the delivery of Misella Cross, well and unmolested, to Annapolis, Maryland, as a free-willer.

Signed this 28th day of April, 1754

Benjamin Arthur Turner
Attorney-at-Law

Barclay could not fathom why an old, broken-down barrister like Turner would invest so much to rescue a convicted prostitute. Maybe she was his daughter or, God forbid, his paramour. The Captain did not care. He needed the money; 100 pounds was more than he would earn in two years at sea. Though he knew that carrying through on this promise would be tricky and risky, he welcomed the challenge and the chance to pay off the debts his wife had left him.

Yet, he had reason to worry. Misella Cross had already been listed as a prisoner on the ledger before they left port. The transportation contract between the merchant Andrew Dunning and the justices had been struck for all of the prisoners soon after their sentences were handed out in court. If an authentic certificate of her arrival as a convict, or a legitimate death certificate, could not be produced by the governor or chief customhouse officer in Maryland, Barclay, as the Captain responsible for her arrival, would be fined 50 pounds.

He could sneak her off the ship and pay the fine with the 50 pounds Turner had given him to seal the bargain. But that would raise suspicion about him, damage his character and his reputation. He would no longer be entrusted with government contracts or trusted by any of the merchants. Everybody would wonder why the pious Captain Barclay would jeopardize his future and besmirch the memory of his late wife to benefit a filthy prostitute.

He would have to figure out a way to do this with impunity. He had six weeks to come up with a viable plan. In the meantime, he had to keep this bargain to himself. Though Amos Bristol had been nearby at the dock when he met with Turner, he could not have overheard their muted discussion amidst the pandemonium all around them. Nor could he have glimpsed the document. Barclay had made sure of that. But to explain his special attention to Misella Cross, he would have to abide Bristol's prurient interest and that of the godless, lascivious crew. Let them think that their God-fearing, Bible-reading Captain had finally succumbed to erotic temptation after the sad loss of his prim, Christian wife.

Bristol's knock interrupted this thoughts. He slipped the note inside the journal and set the book aside until he could lock them both in his trunk.

The puny first mate entered in his usual deferential manner, bowing slightly, one hand holding his sheathed sword in place. He carried that bulky thing with him at all times, as if he needed the banging of it against his knees to remind him to walk erect and speak like a man.

"She's confined in the storage closet, Sir," he barked, as if the Captain had become hard of hearing. "What's next?" He eyed the brandy, no doubt hoping to be rewarded for following orders and, from the expectant grin on his pasty face, to hear how the Captain planned to use the fallen woman. Barclay had to constrain himself from unleashing a blistering reprimand and kicking the idiot out the door—but he needed Bristol's cooperation and his bullying command of the crew. Though they all despised the posturing coward, they feared him. They knew well from experience that he would solicit the Captain's permission to punish the least infraction of the rules.

Barclay cleared his throat and made an effort to look embarrassed. Actually, he didn't need to try. He was humiliated by the role he would pretend to play. "Ah, Bristol, I'm sure I can depend upon your discretion. Yes?"

Bristol nodded his head enthusiastically, the sword flapping in agreement against his leg.

"I'll need you to bring her to me every night when you deliver my dinner, and give me a few hours before you return for her. You understand what I mean?"

"Oh, yes, yes, Sir. I certainly do." Color bloomed in his cheeks.

"I'll rely on you to accomplish this without the crew's knowledge, if possible. But if they find out or you hear any rumors, you'll spread the word that she wants to be baptized, forgiven for her sins. So in honor of my dearly departed wife, I will provide Bible instruction and baptize her when she is ready."

Bristol grinned, admiration brightening his pale eyes. "Oh, that's good, Sir. Very good. They might believe it."

"Also, make her somewhat comfortable in there—a few candles, a chamber bucket, maybe a blanket or two. And she'll need to be let out for airing once in a while, but not with the other prisoners."

"This evening, Sir? Or do you want to wait a few days until we reach the Atlantic? Let her wallow and worry in the dark so she'll be easy to teach." He laughed, his hand vigorously rubbing the sheath of his sword.

To hide his disgust, Barclay looked down and busied himself with the papers on the table. "No, this evening will be fine, Amos. Good day."

Chapter 4

Ben Turner fumbled in the pocket of his greatcoat for his office key, his hands numb from the wind that had battered him since he left the Blackfriars dock after watching Misella board the *Seaflower*. He could have hired a carriage instead of walking, but he needed to think things through. The cold weather invigorated him, clarified his thoughts, and cooled his temper. Despite his stiff fingers, he managed to insert the key in the lock, but before he turned it, the door swung open.

"Ben! Thank God you're back. I was afraid you might have signed on and jumped aboard." Charles Dunning hovered in the doorway, a rare grin relaxing his usual pained expression. "Come in, come in, man. You look half frozen. The fire roars; I'll pour you a brandy." Dunning grabbed his arm, pulled him inside, and slammed the door. Whisking the cane from Ben's fist, he began unraveling the soaked scarf from around his neck.

Ben slapped his hand away. "Why are you still here, Chaz? I didn't ask you to stay, and I'd like you to leave." He turned away, removed the scarf, unbuttoned his coat and shrugged it off, wincing from the ache in his fingers. He hung the coat on the wooden rack before slipping his hand into an outer pocket and drawing forth a small framed portrait of Misella, the only likeness he possessed. Ignoring Dunning's exasperated sigh, he leaned the portrait against the ink pot on his desk, sat down, and rubbed his hands together to create some warmth.

Looking peeved, Dunning stomped to the low table in front of the fireplace on which he had earlier deposited a carafe of celebration brandy from his own office. He poured a generous glass, picked up his own glass, abandoned when he rushed to open the door, and approached the desk. "Let's at least have a victory toast before I go, Ben. You amazed everyone, including me. A 'not guilty' verdict for murdering her child? Incredible. Thanks to you, she was indeed fortunate to be sentenced only for prostitution."

Ben stared at him with contempt before he spoke, his voice harsh with emotion. "There will not be a victory until I am reunited with her. And I will be, in eight weeks or so. I'm rendering my resignation, Chaz, and leaving for the Colonies."

"What?" Dunning slammed both glasses of brandy down on the desk, some of the liquid spilling onto his fingers. "You're joking, Ben." He yanked his linen handkerchief from his pocket and wiped his hand. He stared at Ben in disbelief. "Or you've gone mad."

"Neither. I need a change, a challenge. I can practice law in America."

"You can't," Dunning sputtered. "I need you here. You've given our partnership new life. For God's sake, let her go, Ben. You can do nothing more for her."

"I can protect her. She'll need my help to survive in the godforsaken Colonies." Ben picked up the glass and gulped down the brandy. He stared at the little portrait and spoke quietly, as if addressing Misella herself. "Do you know how those poor convicts, those indentured slaves, are treated? I've heard convincing stories from inmates at the prison about how dire their situations are. They end up worked to death on tobacco plantations. Beaten, starved, raped. If, that is, they even survive the treacherous journey across the seas." He lifted his hands, rubbed his eyes, and looked at Dunning. "I fear the law may be the only way to fight for them. And I intend to try."

He pulled himself up, leaning against his desk, exhaustion draining the color from his face. "I'll finish up here as best I can. I won't leave you in the lurch, but I will be gone within a fortnight. Now, good night, Chaz."

Shoulders sagging, Dunning emitted another deep sigh. He knew it would be useless to argue. When Ben made up his mind, nothing would deter him. Lifting his coat from the rack, Dunning headed for the door. Before he left, he faced Ben with a hint of a smile. "I do realize that you love Misella. I know she filled your empty heart after all of these years since the loss of your wife. If I or my father can help you on your journey, you need only ask. I will miss you, old friend."

"Ah, Chaz, my dear friend, I will miss you as well, but not the tussles we often had over the law, though perhaps I shall miss them, too. You sharpened my wits and often, I'm afraid, my tongue. I'm sorry for that. I hate to ask, but I do need your help one last time. I'll need a loan, if your father can assist me. A hefty sum, I'm afraid, until I can earn my way."

Chapter 5

Three days after the *Seaflower's* departure, Jack Finn entered the Fowl & Feather pub in one of London's seediest areas at midnight to meet the contact who could help him change his life. The pub seethed with activity, every table packed tight with sailors, watermen from the docks, chairmen, slaughterhouse men, bawds, whores, thieves and highwaymen, swilling their rum or beer or gin, and seeking pigeons to swindle. Finn wore a battered tri-cornered hat and yellowed wig over his dark curls, a patched and stained cloak tied over his shoulders. He was afraid to risk being seen without disguise. Someone among this motley group might recognize him and happily turn him in for a hefty reward. The warden at Newgate would welcome him back.

He scanned the crowd of stubbled, pockmarked faces looking for a sailor sporting a gold hoop in one ear and a finger-sized bone on a leather string around his neck. He spotted him wedged into a corner by the bar, staring into his pewter mug, ignoring the fiddler standing next to him who occasionally thumped him with his elbow as he wielded his bow. A drunken group, gathered around the bar, sang along out of tune. *Tell me, ye jovial sailors, tell me true, if my sweet William, if my sweet William sails among your crew?*

Jack pushed his way through the throngs milling around the packed tables, one hand holding his hat in place, the other protecting himself against random swats and shoves. He managed to squeeze in behind the happy fiddler to ask the sailor in a low voice, "Are you Quedagh?"

The man raised his eyes, his hand, missing the index finger, clutched the bone necklace in response. "Aye," Quedagh mumbled. "Say no more. Meet me in the alleyway." He pushed the fiddler out of his way. "Move your tuneless arse," he growled and plowed through the smoke-filled room, snarling obscenities at any who dared to complain or tried to hinder his progress.

Finn waited a good ten minutes, keeping his head down, sipping his bumper of cheap wine, before he squirmed through the crowd and out the door into Dark House Lane. He slipped unnoticed into the alleyway where Quedagh hunched against a brick wall. The faint glow of his pipe cast a grim halo around his pocked face.

"Come closer. Stand next to me." Quedagh kept his voice low. "How do you know Parker? Ever sail with him?"

Wary, fearing a knife to the belly or worse, Finn edged closer but kept a hand on the sawn-off musket concealed under his cape. "Met him in boarding school—my last time at Newgate. We escaped together. Never sailed with him though. Tracked him down last week at one of our old hangouts."

The pirate chuckled. "We have a few other Newgate grads like yourself besides Parker. You can have a reunion." He knocked his pipe against one of the bricks, stepped on the smoldering ashes, and slid the pipe stem into the left side of the red scarf knotted around his neck. "Did you destroy the note he sent you describing our plans?"

Finn nodded. "When do we leave?"

"Day after tomorrow." Quedagh lifted the bone medallion and unscrewed the top. He extracted a thin role of parchment and pressed it into Finn's hand. "Destroy this one, too, after you read it." Securing the bone in place, he muttered, "Until then keep your potato trap shut," before disappearing into a pack of drunken revelers weaving down the Lane.

Finn drew a wooden match stick from his pocket and struck it against the brick wall. Holding up a corner of his cape to shield him from view, he unrolled the small note. With the lit match clutched in his teeth he bent over to read:

Blackfriars dock. 9 o'clock Friday morning. Board the *Dolphin* flying the Dutch flag. No pirate flag until we're well out.

He had two days to make up his mind whether this was the safest way to reach Maryland. Once he joined the pirate crew, he'd become a criminal viewed as far more dangerous than the dandy Irish highwayman he had been in the past. Then, he had proudly considered himself a Knight of the Road, with a calling to help the poor "bog trotters" as the English sneeringly called his countrymen. Everything he stole from the wealthy Englishmen, by threat alone, he gave to those starving sod busters. Tit for tat, he believed, for a century of persecution and stripped treasure.

Joining a pirate ship, though, would be for personal reasons alone: to help himself; to rescue Misella. He had made up his mind in the courtroom as she stood dignified and unbroken despite the scorn and the unjust verdict heaped upon her. He had to find a way to follow her to America. At first, he thought of paying his way to the Colonies as a free-willer, emigrating by choice. But that was too risky. He still carried a bounty on his head for escaping from Newgate. He could put himself in the hands of a press gang who would ask no questions, but life aboard a merchant ship as a crewman would be vicious, and difficult to escape even if he did arrive alive on the shores of Maryland.

If he could reach the Caribbean aboard a pirate ship, he could manage to disappear on the streets of Jamaica, change his identity, and sail as a passenger on a ship bound for Maryland. This plan offered the best chance of success. The fear of hanging be damned!

He touched the match to the parchment, dropped them both to the dirt at his feet, and ground the ashes under his foot.

Chapter 6

The rattling of keys outside the door awakened Misella. For a moment she thought she was in her Newgate cell, with the Ordinary about to barge in waving his Bible and clutching a vinegar-soaked handkerchief to his hawk-like nose to blunt the smell and avert disease. Instead, Bristol stood in the open doorway, his sneering face exposed by a flickering candle held under his chin.

"Get up. The Captain wants you."

She struggled to her feet, her back aching. "May I have a moment to fix my dress and hair? So as not to offend him with my disheveled appearance."

Bristol snorted. "It won't matter none." He leaned against the door frame, gawking at her, his eyes glittering. "Hurry it up. The Captain's anxious for your company."

Turning her back to him, she felt in her bag for her pearl-studded combs and hairbrush. She swept the brush through her curls and hooked them back on each side with the combs. There wasn't time to change out of her torn prison dress, but she snatched up the flower-embroidered apron and tied it around her waist. She was ready to face the Captain, determined that he would not intimidate her this time as he had earlier—as the Ordinary had all those months while she languished in prison.

Once again Bristol led her to the Captain's cabin, the door slightly ajar. He bowed, mocking her, and nudged her through the doorway with the end of his scabbard. The door slammed behind her.

The Captain sat at his desk, a large glass of brandy in his hand, a pewter tray in front of him laden with a stack of cut bread, a large wedge of cheese, a pot of butter, and a bowl of sugar-dusted figs. His mouth crammed full, he motioned her to the chair without speaking.

Misella sat down, trying not to stare at the food, though she had not eaten in more than a day. Her stomach rumbled. He picked up a wood-handled clasp knife next to the tray and sliced off a thick wedge of cheese. Piercing it with the knife, he held it out to her. She slid it into her hand, careful not to touch the blade. He stabbed a slice of the bread and held that out too. She grabbed it, wrapped it around the cheese and forced herself to eat slowly, as if she were dining again at Hawthorn Manor. The figs reminded her of Sir Richard who had insisted the sugared fruit accompany every dinner. Whatever lay ahead for her, Misella rejoiced that at least she would never return to the place of her destruction.

The Captain narrowed his eyes as he watched her eat, condemnation darkening his expression. When she finished, he offered her more, glowering without saying a word. She took it and gobbled it down. He poured a small glass of the brandy and pushed it toward her. "To your health," he said with a sneer.

She shook her head, defiant. "I will take tea, if you have it."

He scowled. "Drink it. You'll need it. This is not a tea party. You will do what I say."

She straightened her shoulders. Glaring back at him, she picked up the glass and downed the liquor in one gulp. Though it seared her throat and dampened her eyes, she did not look away. He did, with a smirk, and opened the Bible. Moving the ribbon off of the page, he began to read aloud as if she were not there. Or more likely, he did so intentionally, hoping to shame her, for he chose Psalm 37, the one the Ordinary intoned each time he entered her cell.

Noisome and festering are my sores because of my folly,
I am stooped and bowed down profoundly; all the day
I go in mourning, for my loins are filled with burning pains;
There is no health in my flesh.

She stopped listening to the sonorous drone of the Captain's voice and began her own silent recitation, psalms of forgiveness and love, the ones she had learned as a child from her father so long ago. Head bowed in concentration, she did not know how much time had passed before she heard the scrape of his chair. When she glanced up, he was standing with his hands on the pages of the open Bible. He murmured something she could not hear before replacing the ribbon and closing the book. She saw no kindness in his eyes when he looked at her.

"Stand up," he ordered, his voice stern. "Remove your apron and the frills from your hair."

Now comes the holy lecture, she thought, *about purity and sanctity and denouncing the fripperies of this world.* So many times in prison she had been forced to listen to the words of the Ordinary, another Bible-quoting hypocrite. But she did as the Captain commanded, pulling the combs from her hair and looping the apron over her arm.

He drew a heavy breath. "Unbutton your bodice."

Her throat constricted; she found it hard to swallow or to speak. She shook her head, nausea churning in her stomach.

He grabbed the clasp knife, bolted around the desk, and loomed over her. "Do it, or I will," he hissed, his face heated, his eyes aflame with fury.

She closed her eyes, fear coursing through her, the combs digging into the palm of her fist. "No," she whispered, "I cannot; I will not." She felt the tip of the knife prick the skin at her waistline. With one thrust, he slashed the cloth to the neckline, severing her stays and exposing her breasts.

"Now, get out of here," he growed, backing away and throwing the knife on the desk.

With shaking hands, she clutched the apron to her gaping bodice. But she did not leave. "No," she whispered. In a strangled voice unlike her own, she spoke louder. "No. You must help Margaret MacDonald. She's innocent. She's only twelve like I was when my destruction began—the lies, the rape." She drew a ragged breath. "She needs your Christian charity, or your First Mate will rape her. Please, Sir. Move her in with me." She could say no more.

Her courage and her breath failed her as she witnessed the dark blood suffusing his face.

"Cease your prattle," he thundered. "Get out, before I forget why you are here."

She stumbled to the door and dragged it open. Bristol stood outside waiting for her, his lantern aglow in the chilly darkness.

He whistled low, his face lighting up. "Must have been a heavy Bible lesson. Hope you learned something useful." An ugly smile spread across his face. He shoved the end of his scabbard into her back and forced her toward the open door of the closet. "I have some training to do tonight myself," he boasted. "Your little curly-haired friend waits in my cabin, meek as a scared kitten."

Misella whipped around, her hair hanging wild about her face, her chest heaving. "You leave her alone," she panted. "You'll kill her if you don't. She's already half dead."

He laughed, a shrill cackle that for a moment muffled the creaking of the ship. Yanking the apron from her hands, he pressed his scabbard against her bare breasts and shoved her through the doorway. As she fell backward onto the coiled ropes, he threw the apron at her feet and drew the ring of keys from his pocket.

"The Captain will blame you if she dies," Misella screamed as he slammed the door. "He'll make you pay if he loses her bounty."

Chapter 7

Logan stiffened, his head turning toward the sounds coming from Bristol's cabin. Because of his excellent sight and hearing, Bristol had assigned him the night duty as a lookout for pirate ships or changes in the pattern of the waves which might signal an approaching storm. With his exceptional hearing, Logan at first heard crying like that of a trapped animal or a frightened child, followed by muffled screams, unmistakably human. Not cries of passion, but someone in pain. As the disturbing noises continued, Logan, confined to his post, could do nothing but clasp his hands over his ears and wait for it to end.

Inside his cabin, Amos Bristol stood half dressed, his breeches slipping, and leaned over the inert body of Margaret MacDonald, his hands gripping her thin forearms. "Wake up," he snarled, jiggling her as if he were shaking the remnants from a sack of tobacco. The skin around her eyes had darkened; blood trickled from her mouth. He wished he had laid her shawl underneath her before the attack. He hadn't thought this through. Her sobbing had excited him, her pleading as he pulled her filthy dress up over her battered face, her screams as he tried over and over again to gain some traction. Seeking release from his frenzy had consumed him. But now, her blood—there was so much of it—soaked his cot, and he couldn't rouse her.

Hours ago, he had ripped her shawl from her fingers as she held on tight. He was surprised by how strong she was for such a wisp of a thing. Now, he grabbed the shawl from the floor where he had flung it. Returned to his senses, he worried about her condition. He remembered what Misella had screamed at him earlier. If the little convict died, he would face severe reprimand from Barclay, maybe even lose his position on the ship.

The Captain prided himself on his delivery record. He had never lost a prisoner since he began running convict ships to the Colonies. An unusual record. Though he had wide latitude from his merchant contractor to do as he pleased once they set sail, he refused to cut costs on food and water when buying supplies or deprive prisoners of their fair share as so many other Captains did to line their own pockets. Bristol had never understood the Captain's reluctance to take advantage of the situation. What did it matter if they lost a few of these thieves and murderers during the journey, these human serpents who did not deserve his charity?

Bristol was biding his time until the day Barclay retired, when he could take command of the ship and conduct the transportation business his way. But that promotion he had worked so hard for might be in jeopardy if this little thief died, and he was blamed for her death. He would have to make sure that didn't happen.

Rolling her onto her side, disgusted by the mess she had made, he wrapped the shawl around her tucking the ends between her legs to absorb the blood that still seeped out of her. He would have to deal with cleaning up the cot later. For now he was anxious to get her back to the hold where she belonged without anyone suspecting him for her condition. Only Flinty, who had brought her to his cabin, knew where she had been—he could trust Flinty. And Misella Cross knew, of course. He regretted now taunting her earlier about the little convict waiting in his room, but he wanted to let her know who was boss, who controlled what happened to the prisoners. He wanted to scare her.

Securing his breeches around his waist, he opened the door a crack and surveyed the quiet deck, inky black thanks to the moonless night. Extinguishing the lantern next to his bed, he scooped up the bundle and held it out in front of him to avoid contamination. He crept out of the room and hovered by the doorway until his eyes adjusted to the darkness. Logan's huge shadow emerged, standing guard in front of the wheelhouse. Bristol would rather have Flinty handle the problem, but he couldn't risk taking the time to rouse the off-duty Flinty. "Logan," he called, his voice low. "Come here."

Logan hesitated for a moment, wishing he could ignore the brutish tadpole, but knowing he had better follow the order. He moved through the darkness with ease and stood in front of Bristol who shoved a bundle into his arms.

"Take this down to the hold and leave it on the floor outside the doorway to the women's section. Then hurry back to your post. And forget where you found her. Understand?"

Logan grasped the bundle in one arm, nodded, and proceeded to the hatch to make his way down the ladder. He could tell that the small girl in the shawl was alive; she struggled to take small gasps of air, followed by a moan before she struggled to breathe again. He could not see her face, but her head, covered in a tangle of curls, lolled backwards over his arm. He did not want to leave her unattended, but if he carried her inside and woke one of the women prisoners to help her, he would be blamed for her condition; Bristol would force him to take the blame.

He cursed Bristol, but he knew the price he would pay for defying him. He still bore the scars on his back from the beating Bristol administered when he resisted his order to flog poor Jamison on their last journey. The bold Irishman had called the First Mate a tadpole in front of the crew, and Logan had chuckled. When he refused to obey the order, Bristol made him join Jamison, each of them shackled to the bowsprit one after the other while Bristol flogged them until the sweat poured off of him and the old cat o' nine tails broke apart. He enraged Logan further when he ordered him to fashion a new, stronger whip and to have it finished when they set sail this time. Logan understood the warning.

Feeling trapped now, disgusted by his own cowardice, Logan laid the girl outside the door as gently as he could and returned, heartsick, to the deck.

Chapter 8

Unable to sleep that night, consumed by nightmarish visions of Margaret, helpless in Bristol's cabin, Misella relived her own sordid past. If only she had been plainer-looking like her sister Elinor, less vain and naïve, less dutiful and more able to resist her mother's dreams for her, if only she had known about men like Sir Richard, or Amos Bristol, skilled at deflowering innocent girls.

She did not see the Captain nor Bristol the next evening which worried her. Instead, Logan, the brawny maker of the cat-o-nine-tails, unlocked her door at suppertime, and set a tray of food on the floor.

"Where is Bristol?" she asked. "Why isn't he here?"

He ignored her questions. Watching her with smoldering eyes, his arms folded across his broad chest, he motioned for her to pick up her chamber bucket and join him. She lifted the handle with care and stepped on to the deck behind him. He nudged her forward without speaking.

The massive sails, fore and aft, billowed and snapped above her, the sky a wide and cloudless slate. Her breathing quickened; the salt-laden air chilled her as she inched forward to the railing.

The waves mocked her, furious, alive, lashing the ship with angry slaps, spitting their cold spray into her face. She gasped, her breath deserting her as it had the day she almost drowned. That terrible day when Isobel, Sir Richard's spiteful daughter, shoved her deep into the sea, knowing her fear, knowing she could not swim, determined to dispose of the upstart Misella, the little beggar who threatened to replace her in her father's affections.

Misella shuddered at the memory. In one swift move, she emptied the bucket into the churning waves, and leapt back, colliding with Logan who stood like a wall behind her. "I beg your pardon," she mumbled, embarrassed by her show of naked fear before this seaman who lived on the water.

The wind increased and the timbers groaned. She shivered without her shawl and thought about Margaret as the sky darkened and night began to close in. Logan tapped her shoulder and nodded his head to indicate that her outing was finished. "Please," she said, "can you tell me about Margaret MacDonald, the young prisoner? Gold curls? How is she?"

He shook his head, glowering. "Your time is up," he mumbled and pointed at her closet. She took a one pound coin from her pocket and held it out to him. "Please. Bring me any news you can about her, and I'll give you more." He snatched up the coin without looking at her and shoved her forward.

Chapter 9

Two weeks after the *Seaflower* sailed, Ben Turner entered the spacious office of Charles Dunning's father with trepidation. He hated what he was about to do—become a shameless beggar dependent upon his partner's disowned father.

Andrew Dunning came around from behind an enormous desk covered with ledgers to greet Turner and shake his hand. Red-faced and shifty-eyed, a robust man, much stockier than his slender son, he wore a richly embroidered velvet jacket thrown open over a ruffled silk shirt, a gold chain looped across his ample stomach. "Glad to finally meet you," he said. "You're the reason my son has spoken to me after five years. I gathered from our brief conversation that he idolizes you. He told me your visit was important."

He yanked on the gold chain and withdrew a jeweled watch fob, clicked it open to glance at the time, and returned it to his pocket. "In a bit of a hurry right now. What can I do for you? My son mentioned you need a loan?"

Turner reddened and said, "I need three hundred pounds to reach America and establish a law practice. I will pay it back within a year.

Dunning frowned. "Hmmm. Nice cane you have there."

Turner wished he had left the cane behind, though he needed it to avoid tripping on the cobblestoned streets. It was his one luxury—a rare piece of polished hawthorn crowned with a silver lion's head.

He had paid a fortune for it. He imagined what Andrew Dunning must be thinking. *Why doesn't the beggar sell the cane to get the money he needs?* Turner shuffled his feet and mumbled, "Arthritic knee. The cane helps me keep my balance." He thought of Misella already two weeks into the journey on this man's ship, and swallowed his pride.

Dunning continued, "Quite a hefty sum. I'll need some assurance that you'll be able to pay me back." He rubbed his chin, closed his eyes as if deep in thought, and then opened them wide to pin Turner with a cold stare. "Of course, you'll have to sign a Promissory Note, but that large a loan might be pretty risky for me. I mean you can't guarantee what will happen in the Colonies. You could be wiped clean within six months, find it too difficult to earn a living there." He took the watch out and swung the chain back and forth as if the action was helping him make up his mind.

Turner knew Dunning was stalling for effect, relishing the discomfort of the supplicant made to grovel before him. Three hundred pounds was mere pocket change to this scoundrel who made his money off the backs of the poor convicts who suffered on his ships. He began to understand why Chaz had disowned the insufferable lout, wanted nothing to do with him. He also realized what a sacrifice Chaz had made in agreeing to help him. He owed his partner unending gratitude for this. If he had anyone else to tap for the money, he'd turn his back and walk out. But he had to reach Maryland, and soon.

"Here's what we'll do," Dunning said. "I'll add a clause to the Note indicating that if you haven't paid up by the deadline, you will return promptly to my son's law offices and earn the money back that way." He smiled without a shred of warmth. "That is if Charles will take you back. But I guess he would if I asked him to."

The nerve of the man rankled. Turner struggled to maintain his temper; his hand closed tight around the lion's head. But he nodded in agreement.

Dunning returned to his desk to pick up the Promissory Note already detailing the terms he pretended to think through as they spoke. He invited Turner to sign below his own signature. After the signing, Dunning opened one of the drawers and removed a lock box from which he extracted a fistful of coins, counting them one by one and dropping each coin into a small muslin bag. He picked up the bag, bouncing it up and down in his palm a few times. "Heavy," he noted, as if he knew Turner had never held so much money at one time.

"Now," he continued. "You can book passage today, if you wish, on one of my many merchant ships headed to the Colonies. The *Mary Anne* departs from Blackfriars next Tuesday morning, arriving in Annapolis sometime in late July. Thirty-five pounds for a shared passenger cabin. Can you afford that?" He chuckled, amused by the flash of anger in Turner's eyes.

Turner bought the ticket, his lower lip clenched between his teeth, his face hot, as he drew forty pounds from the bag.

Dunning made an elaborate show of giving him five pounds back. "*Bon Voyage,*" he said. "I hope to see your money, not you, in the near future."

Ben scowled. "I can assure you that is my hope as well," he said, thumping his cane on the floor. He resisted the urge to throttle the stiff-rumped sharper with the cane on his way out.

Chapter 10

Logan unlocked Misella's door late the next day to deliver her dinner. In the dim light of the doorway she saw him slip something from inside his leather vest and drop it on the tray before he slid the tray across the floor to her. He stepped back before she could speak and slammed the door shut. Misella opened the lantern, struck the flint and lit the candle. Her tray sprang into view. Next to the slice of bread and chunk of cheese lay her book of psalms, its cover stained with blood. Her heart pounding, she snatched it up.

She flung the cover open. Across the title page Margaret had scrawled, *I want to die.* "Oh, Margaret," she cried out. "What has happened to you?" Frantic with worry she wanted to pound her fists on the door, scream with fury, attack Bristol with her bare hands, but she knew that would only cause more trouble for both of them—and probably for Logan, too. Instead, she opened the book of psalms and prayed.

Far into the night, as the candle melted to a stub, she read until she heard the padlock click open. She sat up and shoved the book beneath a coil of rope as the door swung open.

Logan's huge frame filled the doorway. He tossed her a scrap of paper and eased the door closed. The candle sputtered, about to go out. Misella grabbed the bit of paper and leaned closer to the meagre light, barely able to decipher the few scribbled words: *Tell the Captain.*

She lowered the paper to the last of the flame. It flared for a moment and then disintegrated into the melted wax.

Chapter 11

Jack Finn scanned the blue glass of the Atlantic spread out before him. He marveled at the vastness and at the fact that he experienced it from the deck of a pirate ship. A Dutch sister ship on its way to the Caribbean shimmered into view on the horizon.

"Hoist the pirate flag. The *Argyle* lies ahead." Quedagh lowered his eyeglass and shouted at Parker and Jack Finn to grab the pulley and bring down the *Dolphin* flag. Together they yanked the rope as fast as they could, untied the *Dolphin* flag and replaced it with the skull and cross bones. "We wait until the last minute to make the switch," Parker told Finn. "Fool the lookout until it's too late for them to get away. They'll try to outrun us, but Quedagh won't let them."

Finn's heart pounded with fear and excitement on his first encounter as a pirate. Parker and some of the others had trained him for weeks, but he would watch the first attack by staying close to Parker to learn the routine.

Quedagh, a skilled ex-navy officer, served as the gun captain in charge of the cannon, a critical post as timing the shot was crucial. As the pirate ship gained on the *Argyle,* he gave the order for the gun crew to move the loaded cannon into firing position. At the precise moment of a downward-rolling wave, he shouted to Parker, "Light it now."

Parker struck a hemp match and lit the powder in the vent.

"Jump back," they both screamed at Finn, and he stumbled backward just in time to avoid the recoil as the ship rolled back up, crested the wave, and the ball roared across the *Argyle's* bow, flames igniting her rigging.

"Grenade," Quedagh yelled to the gun crew as they closed to within twenty-five yards of the disabled merchant ship.

"Watch this," Parker said. "We send them another warning. When this lands on her stern, they'll be terrified, and we can board her without a single shot from them. We'll loot whatever we want from the scared buggers. Like taking a sugar tit from a baby." He lit the cloth fuse of the grenade and lobbed it towards the other side of the deck where it exploded in a burst of fire. The rest of the gun crew picked up ropes weighted with grappling hooks and heaved them toward the ship, anchoring it so they could draw the vessel close enough to board her.

Led by Briggs the quartermaster, the boarding party—some armed with rapiers and pikes, others with cutlasses clenched between their teeth—climbed over the railings of the captured ship. A few pikemen stayed on the deck of the pirate ship in case any crewmen from the other ship tried to board her. Finn had gone aboard empty-handed behind Parker because he needed more training with handling the knives. He knew how to use a sawn-off musket and a pistol, the weapons he relied on during his highwayman days, but he was inexperienced in the kind of hand-to-hand combat pirates needed. Only the toughest pirates, those who had proven themselves as vicious fighters, joined Briggs.

Finn watched the action from the quarter deck, noting how Parker and the others intimidated the Captain, the crew, and the trembling passengers who all willingly gave up their goods without a fight. Most of the pirates' time was spent rounding up the booty: gold, silver, rum, weaponry, navigational tools and maps, soap, candles, sewing tools, galley utensils and medicines which they loaded into burlap sacks and hurled across to their fellow crewmen on the *Dolphin* or slung over their backs when they departed the denuded vessel.

When Parker joined him on the quarter deck, he instructed Finn. "You saw us interviewing the Captain, crew, and passengers." Finn nodded. "We learned that the Captain had not mistreated anyone on board. That's why we won't destroy the ship and will leave him some provisions, enough to keep those aboard alive until the ship reaches port. We also invited skilled crew members to desert and join us instead, but none from this ship would. Sometimes they do. Barrett and Horner joined us that way."

He asked Parker why they hadn't captured any of the women passengers to bring on board.

"The Captain will not allow it," Parker grumbled. "I wish we could, but the Captain says they bring bad luck and cause fighting among the men. So we wait until dock time to find us some doxies—and homes for our plug tails." He grinned. "Those are the best times," he said with a wink.

Finn was surprised. He expected the pirates to be more ruthless, but much of what he experienced with the pirate crew had changed his opinion of them. Used to working alone as a highwayman, he was learning how to work with a group of pirates united in a common enterprise. They called themselves "Robin Hood's Men." Honor among thieves, Finn surmised.

Briggs was in charge of dividing the booty equally among every pirate aboard. First, he doled out mugs of rum, and they all drank a toast to celebrate another victory, slamming their empty mugs on the table and shouting "Huzzah."

He handed Quedagh the Captain's own pistol taken from the vanquished ship. "This is for you, mate, because you saw the sail first."

Two of the men each picked up a burlap bag and dumped the contents on the table in front of Briggs. Gold and silver pieces of eight spun and glistened before them. The counting began. Each man received an equal share of the money, which stunned Finn. He reaped a fortune, far more than he ever had during his highwayman days.

The looted finery from wealthy passengers was handed out next to anyone who sought exotic clothing—satin and silk shirts with ruffled fronts and cuffs, velvet coats and breeches, fine silk stockings, and even fancy shoes with pumped-up heels. Their leader, Captain Kerry, was given first pick, and he chose his favorite fancy outfit. "For Jamaica," he said, slipping on a gold velvet jacket and preening. "A sun god for the ladies of the Caribbean."

When offered his pick, Finn took a more demure blue velvet coat, a pair of ivory silk britches and a matching silk shirt to wear when they reached Jamaica. He would need this kind of outfit to pass as an English gentleman.

Quedagh, drunk on rum, threw an arm around Jack and Parker. "Next time, my brother sailors, the student goes over the rails with a cutlass in his teeth. Prepare yourself, Finn. You and Parker here, you old prison rats, will work together when we catch the *Mary Anne.* She can't be more than a day or two ahead of us. Got that sweet bit of information from the *Argyle's* Captain—thanks to a little prompting from the blade of my cutlass pressed to his throat."

Finn bristled with pride at Quedagh's confidence in him. If the next raid went as smoothly as this one, he may not have to use his cutlass at all.

Chapter 12

As dusk turned to darkness, Flinty rapped twice on the door of Bristol's cabin, their signal when an emergency required a hurried, clandestine meeting between the two. Bristol swung the door open, grabbed Flinty and pulled him inside.

"The girl is dead, Sir," he muttered. "Some of the bitches are riled up."

"God be damned!" Bristol slammed his fist against the closed door. "Go back and tell the bitches to settle down. Take the cat whip as a warning. We'll have to give the little thief a decent burial—and I'll have to inform Barclay." Bristol picked up his belt and clasped his sword around his waist. Deep in thought, he rubbed his hand along the case. "Tell the women we will have a service for the 'sweet thing' right away. Ask them to donate a decent frock to bury her in, and make them clean and prepare the body."

He opened his travel trunk, rummaged around, and drew out a piece of muslin. "When they're done, have them wrap the girl in this and bring her up to the deck. I'll join you there after I see the Captain." Flinty grabbed the cloth and slipped out of the room.

Bristol waited, taking long swigs of rum from his flask. When he thought enough time had passed to bring the body on deck, he put on his dress jacket, took a deep breath, and left his room. He hoped that Barclay was alone in his cabin—God forbid, not with Misella Cross. He hadn't seen her in a few days, not since that blasted night with the mewling kitten. After that unpleasant confrontation, he assigned Logan the job of watching over the she-wolf for the Captain. He wanted nothing more to do with her. He knocked quietly on the door of the cabin and entered at Barclay's command, relieved to find the Captain alone reading his Bible.

"Well, what is it, Amos? Haven't seen you lately. You must be busy. The crew giving you a hard time again?"

Bristol nodded. "Not the crew, Sir, taking care of some unpleasant business with the prisoners. Ah, I'm sorry to inform you that one of them has expired—Margaret MacDonald, a young thief we picked up from Bridewell, mentally unstable, Sir. She suffered from severe melancholia, refused to eat, spent her days crying, screaming, and making a terrible ruckus for the other prisoners. Tried to jump over the railing once during the on-deck airing."

Barclay slammed the Bible shut and stood up. "What the devil? Why wasn't I informed earlier about her condition?"

Bristol swallowed and cleared his throat, his hand moving up and down his scabbard like a small rodent eluding capture. "We didn't want to bother you with this, Sir. Thought she was just acting out, looking for attention and sympathy from the others. I had no idea it would end this way. We have her ready on deck for burial. But I can take care of that, Sir. No need for you to bother."

"I—will—bother," Barclay snapped, the color rising in his face. He kicked the chair out of his way, toppling it to the floor with a loud bang. Bristol jumped and stepped back, fear coursing through him. The Captain looked ready to attack him.

"I will see the body. And I will conduct the burial service." He lifted the Bible from its stand, yanked open the door, and stormed from the room, slamming the door behind him as Bristol attempted to follow. His heart beating wildly, Bristol exited the cabin, trying to compose himself for the service.

Flinty and Logan stood guard over the wrapped body laid on the deck in an empty space between two barrels. The Captain placed the Bible on one of the lids. "Unwrap the body," he ordered. Startled, they both looked to Bristol as he joined them and stood next to the Captain.

"Is...," Bristol's voice cracked, and he cleared his throat again. "Is that really necessary, Sir? She's not a pleasant sight—the self-starvation and all—not pretty."

Barclay ignored him. "Unwrap the body, now," he ordered looking at Flinty.

"Right away, Sir." Flinty bent over to begin removing the muslin, but Logan nudged him out of the way, squatted down, and carefully untied the pieces of twine holding the cloth together. He folded back the shroud exposing Margaret MacDonald's body covered with a white shawl donated by one of the prisoners, Molly Parsons.

"Bring that lantern here," the Captain ordered Flinty who slipped the lantern from its hook and held it over the body. Barclay frowned, disgust clouding his expression. A mass of blond curls framed the alabaster face of a child marred by several bruises that lined her jaw and encased her closed eyes. He lifted the shawl to expose her entire body. "God's blood," he muttered when he saw the contusions that covered her upper thighs and stomach.

Bristol spoke up, his voice quivering. "I warned you, Sir, didn't I?"

The Captain held up his hand in warning to silence him while he carefully replaced the shawl. The poor thing looked somewhat familiar, but he couldn't recall having seen her before.

Guilt and sadness flooded through him as he realized this was the girl Misella Cross had tried to save. He should have listened to her. The thought of her made him stare more closely at the innocent young face in front of him. *My God,* he thought, *an uncanny resemblance. This child could be her sister.*

He lifted the Bible and murmured to Logan, "Replace the shroud and gather her up while I recite the burial prayer." Throughout the short service he tried to keep from thinking about the idea that had flashed unbidden into his mind. He loathed Bristol and what he had done. He wished he could string him up for this himself, make him suffer as he must have done to this poor child, convict or not. The bastard could have chosen any one of the older female prisoners willing to satisfy his needs.

But as repugnant as the idea was of extracting a payoff from this ugly affair, the poor, dead girl offered him a solution to his problem, a way to fulfill his promise to Turner to deliver Misella safe and free to the Colonies. Even worse, he realized he would have to enlist Bristol's help to accomplish it.

Disgust with himself raged through the Captain. He felt trapped because of his own greed and the foolish promissory note he had signed. But he had given his word; he had to deliver on his promise which meant that not only must he refrain from punishing Bristol for his murderous behavior, but he also would have to make him an ally in the plan.

When Logan heaved the body into the water, the Captain struggled to keep his composure, to control his temper and his voice when he told Bristol to follow him to his cabin. "We need to talk, now."

Chapter 13

Without a candle to light, Misella languished in the dark, her canvas bag in her lap. She felt around inside and withdrew her money sack. She intended to pay Logan when he came to take her to the Captain tonight. She owed him for all he had done. The sound of hurried footsteps outside must be his. The key turned in the lock, and she stood up to greet him.

The door swung open letting in some dying sunlight. Bristol stood in the doorway, a grin on his face. "Time to see the Captain," he chortled.

Her stomach heaved. She choked back the tears that she refused to let him see. She wanted to scream at him, but she needed to see the Captain and feared Bristol would stop her if he knew what she planned to do. When she showed Barclay the book of psalms with Margaret's blood on the cover and her desperate words inside, she felt confident that he would reconsider and move Margaret into the closet with her, out of Bristol's vicious clutches. She grabbed her canvas bag, the book of psalms tucked inside. "I'm ready," she murmured and followed the monster out.

She trailed the whistling Bristol to the Captain's cabin, appalled by his nonchalance but unable to rebuke him. As soon as Bristol closed the door of the Captain's cabin, Misella fumbled in her bag and removed the book of psalms. "Look what that monster has done to Margaret," she cried, laying the book on the table in front of Barclay.

"You have to do something, move her up here with me right away." She opened the cover and thrust Margaret's words in front of his face.

Barclay pushed the book away. "Hush," he said, his voice harsh. "Not another word. You will keep quiet and listen. It is too late. Margaret MacDonald is dead. Buried at sea this afternoon."

Misella's face crumpled, tears flooded her eyes and coursed down her cheeks. She shook her head back and forth. "Oh, please, no," she choked. "She was so lost and innocent, a delicate child who needed protection—my protection," she sobbed. She confronted him. "And yours!" She spat the words at him.

The Captain's expression showed no sympathy, his eyes cold, his words clipped and hard. "Stop your caterwauling. Here is what you are going to do if you want to avoid what happened to Margaret and survive this journey. You will from here on, without the crew's knowledge, become Margaret MacDonald. A death certificate will be created for the prisoner Misella Cross who died of a fever and was buried at sea."

Misella, stunned into silence, sank onto her chair, dropping her canvas bag, the coins inside clinking when the bag hit the floor.

"Only First Mate Bristol and I will know about the switch. Your routine will continue as usual until we reach the port of Annapolis where suitable plans for you will follow."

Bile rose and burned in her throat. Her face aflame, fury igniting her words, she lashed out. "You…and that monster. You're a team," she screamed. "You didn't care what happened to Margaret. You were helping him." She stood and grabbed the book of psalms from his desk. "This is her blood." Her voice broke. She shoved the book into his hands. "See what you have caused," she cried.

Shocked by the accuracy of her words, Barclay hesitated, overcome for a moment with guilt and repulsion. He did appear to be colluding with Bristol. He should have heeded her warning; he could have stopped him. He hated himself for taking advantage of Margaret's death in order to help himself. But Misella, this murderess, attracted to the cheap glamour of prostitution, she would benefit as well from his plan. He could convince Gretchen, his dead wife's sister, to take Margaret—a petty thief still young enough to be saved with biblical intervention—to work at her boarding house in Boston, but never would she consider a filthy prostitute.

Who was Misella to make him feel guilty and heartless? She had no moral right to blame him. "That's enough," he thundered. As if to underscore his command and restore his authority, the ship's bell sounded. Clang! Clang! Clang! The signal for an approaching storm.

In the heat of their battle, neither the Captain nor Misella noticed that the ship had begun to pitch more than usual. She grabbed on to the desk to keep from being thrown to the floor. Her canvas bag bounced madly across the boards, disappearing under the Captain's cot. His legs apart, knees bent to steady himself, the Captain gained his bearings. He extinguished the candles, and darkness enclosed them like a fist. Lightening flashed at the oval window as he made his way to the cabin door and wrenched his rain cape off of the hook. The ship creaked and the wind howled. "Lay down on the floor against the far wall, and stay there," he ordered. Fighting with the door, he opened it despite the wind, escaped to the deck, and either he or the wind slammed it shut behind him.

Thunder pounded the heavens open, and torrents of rain tore at the window. As the floor dipped and rose, Misella dropped to her knees and crawled, terrified, to the Captain's cot. Grabbing the quilt, she wrapped it around herself, and lay trembling against the wall next to the cot. The ship heaved, she heard the crew shout, the ocean roar—and the dark blade of memory cut through her mind.

Twelve years old again, dressed by her mother like a porcelain doll, she waited in their fishing shack for Sir Richard to arrive and take her away—against her will. She did not want to go, but she knew it would do no good to cry anymore. She had tried that for days, but her flood of tears had met with sunny platitudes from her Mother about her soon-to-be-elegant new life, and dark, brooding silence from her Father. His betrayal cut into her heart more deeply than did her mother's. She had been sure that he would never let her go. But he had abandoned her when she needed him most.

Chapter 14

The Captain struggled toward the main mast, the First Mate bent over beside him, both of them blasted with sheets of rain. The ship reeled, timbers creaked; crewmen shortening the sails clung to the rigging like wild monkeys; the horizon tilted on its side. The crew fought to see in the inky blackness without the benefit of torches or candle lanterns, relying on sporadic flashes of lightening to illuminate the position of the trimmed sails. Shouts of "Sail ho" or "Look out" or "Watch the stern" penetrated the thunderous air around the two as they joined the frantic men.

A fierce gale lifted a wall of water that exploded across the bow, slamming the Captain to the deck and somersaulting Bristol like a mad contortionist against the rails. "Bring down the sails; bare the poles now," the Captain shouted to the crewmen swaying from the rigging. "Hang on," he bellowed, as he clutched a coil of rope wound around a wooden post. Seawater streaming down his face and blurring his vision, he scrambled upright. "Point her into the waves," he yelled to the helmsman. "We'll ride it out."

The ship labored through waves that overran the decks and seeped into the hold where the prisoners, damp with salt water, rattled in misery, vomiting in place, unable to reach the necessary tubs which sloshed their contents into the seawater pooling in the corners of the slatted floor. As they tossed like bobbins on their wooden planks, the men moaned and cursed; the women cried and prayed.

Molly Parsons untied the scarf tethering her waist to her bed slat and staggered upright. Hanging onto the post, she gathered up the pile of rags she had accumulated and yelled, "Listen to me, Slammakins. You survived prison, you can survive this." She made her way down the aisle, swaying and tossing damp rags into each cubicle. "Stop your howling. Clean yourselves up; we're not animals."

On deck Logan, the strongest of the crewmen, was charged with pumping out the water from the bilges at the bottom of the ship. He struggled, not only battling to hang on against the wind and the relentless pounding of the waves but also to turn the windlass pulling the water up the wooden tube from the bilges and into the channel that diverted it overboard. Yet he found some comfort in his backbreaking task, this Sisyphean activity that freed his mind from dwelling on the death of Margaret.

The storm continued through the night until dawn when the sky emerged, a cold flat slate, drained and docile—the crewmen, too. Chilled and wet to the bone, gray with exhaustion, they raised the sails once more before heading below to the galley for breakfast.

As he hauled himself back to his cabin, the Captain told Bristol, "Do not disturb me for at least twenty-four hours, unless the ship sinks."

Bristol, who had forgotten his rain cape but not his sword, limped after him, his jacket a sodden mess, the sword drooping from his waist. "What about the…woman?"

Barclay turned to face him, his eyes dead and cold. "Forget about her." He opened the cabin door and closed it behind him before Bristol could manage to look inside.

Misella sat pressed against the wall, his bed quilt wrapped around her, her head resting on her drawn-up knees. Her head snapped up when the door closed, her hair disheveled, her reddened eyes unfocused. "Father," she cried, "you're here. Why did you send me away with Sir Richard? You were supposed to protect me. You knew what he was—you knew."

She began to sob, rocking back and forth. "He ruined me. His daughter tried to drown me. She wanted me dead. I am dead, like my poor Lily, my baby. I couldn't save her." Her sobs increased to a keening wail. She beat the floor with her fists.

Stunned by the spectacle of this crazy outburst, the likes of which he had never before witnessed, all Barclay could do was resort to giving orders. "Stop it," he yelled. Have you lost your senses? The storm is over, just a brief squall. Stand up."

She shook her head over and over. "No, I won't go. Not with that rapist Sir Richard. Not to Lady Miriam's den of horror. Not back to prison," she screeched. "No, I'd rather die." When Barclay uttered a brutal obscenity and stamped his foot, she looked up and realized her present surroundings. Kicking off the quilt, she raised herself to her knees panting, "I am Misella Cross. I…am…not…Margaret."

Barclay reeled back in alarm, his exhaustion replaced by fear that Misella may actually have lost her senses and with them, any chance for him to carry out his plan. He had never experienced such raw emotion and did not know how to handle it. His wife, passionless and proper, never exhibited strong feelings. Even when he had confronted her in a rage about the money she had given to her sister, Gretchen, without his permission, nearly bankrupting them, she bowed her head and endured his tirade. Indeed, he had never seen her shed a single tear, not even when she lay silent and dying in child birth.

Faced with this incoherent, mad woman in front of him, he did the only thing he could think to do—he grabbed the bottle of brandy and a glass from his desk and filled it. Crouching down to where Misella had collapsed in a heap of quilt, he grasped her shoulders and sat her upright. "Drink this."

She shook her head. He tipped the glass and drank half of it himself. "Please," he said softly, "take a sip. Tell me, please, about Sir Richard. I want to know how you came to be on my ship."

His words dragged her back to the present; the softness in his voice shocked her into submission. She gulped the brandy and handed him the glass. She wiped her eyes with the edge of the quilt and took a deep breath. "The letter," she murmured. "Sir Richard's letter to my mother when I was a child of twelve." Her eyes filled again with tears. "Like Margaret," she moaned. "But Margaret remained innocent of any wrongdoing, and I did not."

She sat up straighter and brushed away the tears. "Sir Richard was my mother's distant cousin, the heir to her father's estate. She convinced him to adopt me in exchange for money to support our destitute family—and to give me a better life. For years, I blamed her and my father for abandoning me. Perhaps I still do.

"A better life—what a sad joke. He trained me from the day he took me away, flattering me, appealing to my vanity. Oh yes, I was a vain little know-nothing, so easy for him to lure me with his attention, to play me against his plain-looking daughter Isobel who hated me—with good reason—to ply me with secrets and jewelry and promises."

She took the refilled glass the Captain offered her and downed half of it, her eyes filling again. "He…he…finally finished what he set out to do. And when I was with child—his child that he bid me to abort, my poor Lily—he abandoned me to a penniless existence on the streets of London."

The Captain reared back in disgust and infinite pain, remembering the shriveled, lifeless body of his own new-born son. He stood up with effort, his weary bones creaking, and sat down on his cot. His voice hardened. "A capital crime for which you should have hanged. How did you receive a lesser sentence?"

She shook her head, almost spilling the rest of the brandy. "No, no," she whispered. "I didn't abort…or murder the baby." She raised her voice and looked at him with defiance. "Despite Sir Richard, I bore a daughter, Lily, and she lived for eight months…until…a terrible accident. She died, crushed by the wheels of a carriage."

Without stopping or weeping, she told him everything. "I was a ward of Lady Miriam Bentley, but she sent me to debtor's prison. I refused to stay there and endanger Lily. Lady Miriam left me no choice except to work for her in her high-class brothel in order to pay the debt. After I had met Ben Turner, an attorney, I sought his help when I was falsely accused of throwing Lily to her death. He defended me at my trial. I was found innocent of murder but sentenced to seven years indenture for prostitution."

Barclay listened without interrupting, taking the glass from her hand and finishing the brandy. When she stopped speaking, he set the glass down on the floor, and rubbed his eyes, exhaustion overwhelming him. "I believe," he rasped, his voice harsh, "that the

Crown does not prosecute prostitution as a crime. How, then, could you have been convicted and sentenced for a non-crime?"

She did not hesitate to answer him, refusing to be intimidated by the accusation in his tone and the doubt in his eyes when she looked up at him. "A double verdict, common enough in His Majesty's courtroom. And a jury determined to convict me for the only crime of which I was guilty, not murder, but the other—which I have never denied. Thanks to Ben Turner and the defense he crafted to save me from a trip to the gallows. The Court wished to make an exception in my case, to punish me and their enemy agitator, Ben Turner."

The Captain, too weary to think, yearned for rest and escape from the cloud of unwelcome emotion that overwhelmed and confused him. He needed to replenish himself with sleep before he could process all of the information she had shared, before he could decide whether to believe her outlandish story. With effort he arose. "That's enough for now. You'll return to your room and receive further orders in a few days when we reach port. I won't see you again until landfall."

Chapter 15

Jack Finn lounged against the railing of the upper deck, welcoming the breeze that cooled his face and lifted the loose ends of the scarf tied around his head like a turban. His cutlass lay atop the coiled stack of rope next to him, grappling hooks protruding from it like quills from some maritime porcupine. The sails ballooned above him as the *Black Dagger*, its pirate flag flapping in the wind, skimmed across the fraught waves to reach its target. He was ready to confront the *Mary Anne*, their final raid before heading to Jamaica for needed supplies and merriment.

He felt once again the exhilaration of his highwayman days, but the anxiety as well—the tightening in his chest, the trembling in his limbs. Not fear, though. He refused to let himself be afraid. He had a mission that compelled him to set aside any thought of danger, or any twinge of conscience. He thought only of Misella and what he needed to do to reach her.

The pirates were well armed, with a crew, they knew, three times larger than the merchant ship they were about to overtake, a vessel smaller than theirs. This Quedagh had learned from the *Argyle's* Captain, which meant, no doubt, a small passenger list, or perhaps no passengers at all. The only obstacle they might face was if the ship had a guardian with her for defense, a companion naval ship much better armed. But their own Captain Kerry had dismissed that possibility. "They'll not bother with the expense to protect such a piddle of a ship," he asserted. "No worries. Let her fly, men." The Captain was right. The *Mary Anne* emerged, a lone speck on the horizon, surrounded by nothing but turgid blue as far as the eye could see.

They closed on her quickly, and even though the first cannon shot missed its mark, they gained on her before she could defend herself. After the second barrage of grenades lobbed onto the deck created a firestorm, fear seemed to render her crew helpless. They gave up in terror without a fight. Finn joined Parker and the rest of the boarding crew as they scrambled over her rails with blood-curdling yells.

Waving his cutlass, Finn barked questions at two trembling crewmembers who leaned against the ship's unused cannon, their hands raised in surrender. "Have you any passengers on board? Where are they?"

The heavier one, his eyes sweeping the swarming deck, shook his head, his dank hair falling across his pocked face. But the skinny one next to him, his teeth chattering, bowed at the waist and blurted out, "Only two, Sir. Hiding in the Captain's quarters." He pointed toward the stairway to the lower deck. "I can show you where they are."

Finn smirked and shook his head. "I'll find them myself. You two stay right here." He signaled to a couple of pirates whirling around nearby and asked them to keep an eye on the two crewmembers. He found Porter rounding up the guns and ammunition left untouched on the quarter deck by the vanquished crew. "Captain's quarters," he shouted and pointed down. "Two passengers. I'll meet you there." Porter nodded.

Pirates swarmed the lower decks, herding the crew into docile groups of bystanders, watching in terror amidst the pirates' menacing threats, screams and curses as they helped themselves to whatever bounty they wished. The ship's Captain, dragged from his quarters, encountered a sword-swinging Briggs who barked, "Down on your knees and go to prayers for with this knife I'll be your butcher." The Captain dropped to his knees. "Where are the passengers?" Briggs demanded. "You have two listed in your log."

The Captain, unintimidated, muttered, "I do not know. If they are not in their quarters, you'll have to search the ship for them."

One of the pirates charged with ransacking the passenger quarters approached Briggs. "Empty, Sir. Nothing there but the beds."

Briggs pressed the blade of his sword against the Captain's throat, drawing a thin line of blood that trickled onto his ruffled shirtfront. "You'd best tell me where they are, Mate, or I'll have to finish off you and your crew one by one until I find them."

Grimacing, his teeth clenched, the Captain nodded. Briggs eased the pressure on his throat; the Captain swallowed and rasped, "Trap door, under my rug."

"Get to work," Briggs ordered the pirates milling around him. "Bring them here and any booty you find hidden with them." He removed his sword enough so that the Captain dared to slump back on his heels and sigh with obvious relief.

"Don't get too comfortable yet," Briggs warned. "We will strike without mercy if you or they should try to resist any further." The Captain nodded vigorously to show he understood and intended to cooperate.

Finn arrived outside the Captain's quarters just as Durkin, Briggs' favorite henchman, dragged a portly passenger in a torn ruffled shirtfront and dusty britches forward and dropped him in a quivering heap at Briggs' feet. "No problem with this one," he said. "Still working on the crazy one—a fighter. Be right back."

Sounds of a scuffle and cursing emanated from the Captain's rooms. Durkin yelled, "Blast your mangy hide, you old fool. Give us that cane or we'll have to hurt you." A howl to rouse an army followed by a resounding whack, grunts and a scream preceded the appearance of a red-faced Durkin, a cane in one hand, his cutlass in his teeth. With great effort and much huffing, he managed to haul a large, disheveled bear of a man out of the Captain's quarters and shove him toward Briggs. Dropping the cane, he held tight to the rumpled collar of the man's jacket and removed his cutlass from his teeth before gasping, "The bugger refuses to release his bag of coins, Sir."

The scruffy passenger clutched the folds of his brown doublet together over a mound underneath from which thin leather strands snaked out and wrapped tightly around his ample wrist. Sweat creased his brow under the wispy ends of tousled gray hair that fell over one squinting eye. The other eye stared down with cold malice at the Captain hovering beneath him. "Judas," he spat. Scowling, he eyed Briggs. "You'll have to kill me to get this bag, Sir. By God and His Majesty the King, I will never surrender it."

With a bellowing laugh, Briggs raised his sword ready to strike. "Happy to accommodate you, my Lord."

"Wait!" Stunned, Finn rushed forward. "I know this man. Ben Turner. He's a barrister from the King's Court. He can be of use to us."

As Jack had done at first when he recognized Turner, Ben Turner gaped in wordless astonishment at the image of Jack Finn. He could not comprehend how the courageous Finn who had vowed to help Misella Cross in any way possible could be standing before him now attired as a pirate, a gangster against the Crown.

Briggs laughed. "How pray tell, young snipper snapper, can this bloody Kingsman possibly do anything for us?"

"His glib tongue, Sir. He knows the law and can twist it to fit our needs. Why . . . why he defended a young woman recently in a famous child murder case before the Court. Managed to get her acquitted. It was all over the papers. You must have seen it or heard his name." Finn kept talking, thinking as fast as he could. "He could help us in Jamaica. Provide a convenient and respectable cover for us—negotiate for supplies, act as our agent, quell any suspicion, handle any bank transactions for us as if we were a normal merchant ship."

Briggs looked skeptical. "But how could we trust him. Look at him. He's a wild man. He'd renounce us the first chance he had."

Finn shook his head. "Let me talk to him alone for a minute. I can convince him to do this for his own good. He wants to reach America. He'll make a deal to help us if we can help him. I know it. Let me try."

Briggs glanced around at the others. "What do you say, men?" Some nodded in agreement; some shrugged their shoulders.

Porter spoke up. "Finn's a good man, a man of his word. I'll vouch for him."

Briggs nodded and lowered his sword. "One minute."

Finn grabbed Turner's arm and steered him to the railing where they could talk. "Work with me on this and trust me," he muttered to Turner. "This is the only way for both of us to reach Misella. We dock in Jamaica in a few days. You and I will stock the ship, and before she sails again, we'll disappear, hide, and book passage on another bound for Maryland. "

Turner blanched, his voice rising, "I'll not give up my money or my cane."

"Just temporarily—to me. As part of the bargain. Insurance for us. I'll tell Briggs I'll keep them until after you have done what we need you to do in Jamaica. It's the only way you can stay alive now."

Turner frowned but agreed. "A pirate! God and the King forgive me."

Chapter 16

"Land Ho!" The young lookout lowered his eyeglass and shouted out again before sprinting down from the Crow's Nest, his bare feet flying, unhindered by the rigging. "There she is, Mate, look for yourself." He thrust the glass into Logan's hands and pushed him toward the railing. "It's America on the horizon. I seen her!"

Logan grabbed the glass with eager hands, anxious to see for himself that his hellish nightmare of service would soon be over—six long years before the mast of the *Seaflower* had left him exhausted and demoralized. The adventure he had convinced himself he might find despite his entrapment by a press gang had turned into a life of misery in service to the monster Bristol. Escape from him had fueled his days and nights with enough hope to keep both him and his dream alive of finding freedom in the New World. He planned to disappear into the bowels of Annapolis, as many had done before him—unhappy sailors and indentures who viewed the town as their gateway back to England. But Logan knew he would never go back and risk being pressed into service again. He would stay in the New World.

Word of land on the horizon spread quickly bringing excitement that rippled throughout the ship. Logan informed Bristol, who took the good news to the Captain.

Barclay ordered him to begin the process of preparing the prisoners. "You know what to do. Bring them on deck in small groups, clean them up, and give decent clothing to those who need it. Leave the chains on the men until landfall when the sales to landowners will begin. And bring the prisoner 'Margaret MacDonald' to my quarters now."

She entered his cabin with a trace of stubborn hope in her heart and a ghost of a smile on her face. "Good morning, Captain Barclay. It seems a happy coincidence for me that land was sighted today, on July 1st, my nineteenth birthday."

"Sit down and be quiet," he ordered her in a firm voice. She hesitated for a moment seeming confused by his threatening demeanor and harsh tone. He raised his voice. "You do as I say without uttering a single word. Do you understand?" Barclay was determined to deal firmly with her; he would allow no theatrics or fits of temper from her this time.

She drew back, nodding in agreement, and sat down. She had braided her hair, and wore her customary garment, the bodice stitched haphazardly together. Reed-thin, with her face scrubbed clean and her hair in pigtails, she looked presentable enough, he thought, and could pass as the young prisoner Margaret.

"We will make landfall in a few hours," he said. "I wanted you to know how you are to behave when that happens. I have arranged for a buyer who will bid for you when the selling takes place aboard the ship after we land. Acting as servitor for Gretchen Dobbs, he will purchase the indenture of Margaret MacDonald at my suggestion, instead of a random female convict. Mrs. Dobbs had pleaded with me by letter before I left England to deliver an appropriate indentured servant to her on my next journey. You will remain on board and travel with us to Boston where you will be delivered for service to the Dobbs Boarding House."

Misella gasped. "B-Boston? No, I can't. I have family there—my father, my sisters. I told you about that, how he abandoned me years ago. Sir Richard told me that my father had found employment in Boston, though he never wrote to me himself or tried to visit me. What if they see me there and recognize me? No, no."

"Stop," he thundered. "Do not argue. It's not likely that they would even know you after all of these years—or that your paths would cross. You will not be allowed to wander around Boston. You will be a prisoner, and Mrs. Dobbs will treat you as one. She is a fiercely devout Christian woman, hence your change of identity. Never would she agree to take on a filthy, child-murdering prostitute; she might very well have heard of you, if as you told me, your trial was widely publicized. But Margaret's situation, poor, young, unjustly convicted, will appeal to her sense of Christian charity. She will consider it her duty to convert the naïve sinner."

Barclay flipped open the journal resting on his desk and withdrew the Promissory Note signed by Benjamin Turner. He turned it around so that Misella could read it. "Because I have given my word to your lawyer friend, you will only be interred at the Boarding House for less than a year. On my return journey to London, I will meet with Turner, give him the letter which you will now write in your own hand, and receive payment for your freedom.

"Then when I return to Boston, I shall buy your indenture from Gretchen Dobbs and you will be free. At that time you can go searching for your father if you wish. Though I do understand why you want to avoid any contact with him, even if you can forgive him. So much has happened to you, he may find it difficult to accept you as you are now."

Misella noted in stunned silence the amount Ben Turner had agreed to pay for her safe passage and freedom—a shocking 100 pounds sterling, no doubt, more than a year's salary for a barrister. She knew she could never repay him; she would be indebted to him once again for her very life, a burden of gratitude she could never escape. He had given her no choice this time. She looked up at the Captain. "And if I refuse to write the letter?"

He stared back at her with the same contempt and coldness he had shown the first time they met. "Then I will write to Mr. Turner and absolve our bargain. And you will join the other prisoners up for sale to the highest bidder among the plantation owners seeking fresh blood in their tobacco fields and barns—or as breeders to propagate their work pools."

She shivered and closed her eyes, thinking about her past life: forced to succumb to Sir Richard's demands, abandoned penniless on the streets of London when she finally refused to cooperate, cast into a sordid life of prostitution. She could not bear the thought of doing it again. Bowing her head she whispered, "I agree."

"A wise choice," he said and tore a blank page from his journal. He placed the sheet in front of her on the desk, told her to pull her chair closer, and set a quill and pot of ink before her. "No need to mention your change of identity; I'll explain everything to Turner when I see him in London. Just a brief note to let him know you are well and will be released in Boston as soon as the debt is paid. And sign it Misella Cross."

She nodded, dipped the quill in the ink, and began to write, *Dear Kind Sir....* She recalled the last note she had written to him before she was transported, refusing his offer of marriage as a way to annul her sentence. She could not marry him; she did not love him. "I must accept my original sentence," she had written then, "if I am to have any chance of achieving the serenity and salvation I so desperately seek." How confident she had been that she could become the strong and honest woman she dreamed of being in this new world beyond the seas. How foolish and naïve to believe that she could find a new beginning. She was naught but a spineless puppet, forced once again to live a lie.

Chapter 17

On the first of July, eight weeks after leaving England, the *Seaflower* reached Annapolis. After several tries, the wind having increased and whipped up the waters of Chesapeake Bay, the ship managed to squeeze in and dock at the wharf beside another merchant ship. As the best port of entry from the Atlantic in the Bay area and a major center of the tobacco and slave trades, the waterfront teemed with activity. Freight from the other ship filled the holding area on shore, a large square of logs tethered together to keep the goods from sinking in the mud—casks of wine, barrels of tea leaves, stacked wooden boxes of spices, salt and sugar.

Slaves and servants dressed alike in striped ticked trousers and loose linen shirts labored in the July heat hauling barrels of tobacco leaves up the gangplanks onto the emptied ship for its return to England. The *Seaflower* would have to wait a day or two until the dock cleared and the other ship launched before the vessel could begin its own deployment of cargo. In the meantime, the prisoners on board would remain in the hold, the men chained, until the time to unload arrived.

Tempers flared in the stifling heat onboard the motionless ship. The crew with nothing to do but mill around the deck begged to go ashore. Bristol, strutting on deck and steaming in his full regalia, screamed, "Shut up, you mongrels, unless you want a flogging." He stopped in front of Logan who leaned on the railing, his back to

Bristol, scanning the shoreline with hope-filled eyes. "Turn around and look at me."

Logan stood and faced him, towering over the fuming little tyrant. "Yes, Sir," he said. "At your service, Sir!"

Bristol glowered. "Are-you-making-fun-of-me?" Before Logan could respond, the crimson-faced First Mate yelled so all could hear, "In case you were, here's what we'll do. You will remain on board the entire time we are docked. You will not go ashore with the others. Is that clear?"

Logan blanched, his heart in his throat, his disappointment visible in the slump of his shoulders. "Won't I be needed to heft the tobacco barrels aboard, those headed for England, Sir? I can handle more than two crewmen together."

Bristol smirked, dismissing him with a flick of his wrist. "Oh, I think the crew are men enough to handle the work themselves. Isn't that right, mates?"

Flinty blurted out in a loud voice, "Yes, Sir! We'll do it alright, won't we boys? We done it before without Mr. Colossus."

The rest of the crew mumbled in agreement without looking at Logan who, despite his mounting despair, could not bring himself to apologize or to beg this little runt to change his mind. He would have to escape in Annapolis somehow. He'd have a better chance here than when they docked at Boston's much busier wharf with British soldiers around. Whatever the cost, he could not bear to remain any longer in bondage to this warped man. With feigned obeisance, he addressed Bristol. "Yes, Sir. Whatever you say."

Panting in misery, Misella roasted in her airless closet, the heat unlike any she had ever experienced before in England. She had done everything the Captain asked of her. She could not understand why she was kept a prisoner, made to suffer like this. Why was nothing happening? Her only decent gown was soaked through with the heat, her braids coming undone, her hair hanging in damp strings from her dripping forehead.

When Bristol flung open her door and ordered her to join the Captain in his quarters, she jumped up with relief and scrambled out onto the deck hoping to find a breeze. Instead, she was confronted by a wall of heat that stopped her breath and a piercing sun that tore the sight from her eyes. She stumbled after Bristol with her eyes shut until she could open them again inside the Captain's stuffy cabin.

When her vision cleared, she saw the Captain seated with quiet authority at his desk, a glass of brandy in hand, addressing a slender gentleman dressed in black, a wide-brimmed hat in his lap, sitting in the chair she usually occupied. He arose, hat in hand, while the Captain remained seated. "This is Mr. Briar," Captain Barclay said, "Mrs. Dobbs' servitor from Boston. He wished to see you before the selling of prisoners takes place onboard tomorrow so he will recognize you in the crowd of female convicts. He will bid first, select you, Margaret MacDonald, for Mrs. Dobbs, pay the bounty, and return immediately to Boston. He will meet us again when we dock there and transport you to Mrs. Dobbs boarding establishment."

Misella tucked wayward strands of hair behind her ears, trying to look meek and presentable, and nodded to Mr. Briar who stared at her with cold, deep-set eyes, his thin face dry, no sign of any moisture, his features pinched with distaste. He turned to Barclay and said in a gravelly voice, "She will have to do. Good day to you, Sir, until the morrow." He donned his Pilgrim hat and without another glance at her left the cabin.

Barclay, perspiring profusely, unbuttoned and fanned his shirt a few times, finished his brandy, and said without looking up, "Mrs. Dobbs is my widowed sister-in-law, and Mr. Briar is one of her boarders, nothing else. You will find them both difficult to please. Do not attempt to impress them or solicit their good will as you have done with me. You will not find any. Just work hard, keep your mouth shut, and your head down. You can manage that for a few months, can't you?"

Misella nodded, and then realizing he still wasn't looking at her, murmured, "Yes, Sir." She hesitated for a moment before asking, "Could I please be allowed to stay on deck? The closet is so hot. I fear I may melt away before tomorrow comes."

He slammed the glass down. "Did you not listen to what I just said? You are still a prisoner, and you will remain so until I'm rid of you in Boston and my time of giving you special treatment is over. Until then, you will carry on as usual. Bristol is waiting for you outside."

As she headed to the door, she noticed what she assumed was sadness and regret in his eyes, even a hint of tears, as he watched her leave. *Perhaps, against his will, he will miss me*, she thought. *He may have come to admire me after hearing my story, to see me as a fighter, and to realize I was not a prostitute by choice.* The thought comforted her and gave her hope for the future.

Chapter 18

The women prisoners appeared on deck first, led by Flinty. He ordered them to line up along the railing of the quarter deck. "And shut your traps," he snarled. Bristol stood waiting, Misella at his side, before pushing her into the line near the front. A haggard-looking woman on her left sneered at her and muttered, "So Captain's little whore ends up with the rest of us."

Bristol whacked her across the face with the log book. "Shut up," he muttered through clenched teeth as the Captain stepped on deck followed by a group of gentlemen, some dressed in fine linen jackets and wide-brimmed straw hats, others, clearly overseers, in planters' garb of ticked trousers, loose jackets and felt hats.

"Gentlemen," the Captain said, "we'll sell the women first, ten pounds for each, and then we'll bring up the men at twelve pounds per prisoner. After you have chosen what you need here, Flinty will take them down to the lower deck and hold them until you have made all of your purchases. Take as much time as you need to check out these healthy specimens." Flinty waved his pistol back and forth as a greeting and to reassure the buyers that he would control the prisoners under his watch.

Mr. Briar, wearing the same black suit and hat, pushed his way forward and grabbed Misella's arm. He yanked her out of line, telling the Captain, "This one will do," and thrust a ten-pound note into his hand. The Captain nodded and motioned to Bristol to record the sale in the log book. The ship's owner, Andrew Dunning, would check the log in London on their return to make sure he received all of the money due to him from the sale of the slaves. A leering Flinty, brandishing his pistol, used the butt of it to shove her toward the lower deck stairs.

When she looked back, she saw the buyers helping themselves to the women, pulling them out of line and feeling their arms and torsos and shoulders, forcing open their mouths and checking their teeth, lifting their dresses and squeezing their thighs. She shuddered, relieved that she escaped the mauling, but furious that she must witness such violations and know she was powerless to do anything about them.

Flinty hurried her back to the closet, dangling the Captain's keys in front of her and grinning. He unlocked the door and said, "Your quarters, Madame." He grabbed her breast and gripped hard as she moved past him. "Sorry you had to miss out on the fun up there," he said.

She slapped his hand away. "Sorry for you when the Captain finds out," she said.

He laughed, his black-stained teeth an emblem of his soul, she thought to herself. "That's funny," he said. "The Captain doesn't own you anymore."

Her chest tightened, and she struggled to slow her breathing as Flinty locked her into the hot, airless closet, her own private hell. So much worse than her stone prison cell at Newgate. She almost wished she was back there. At least her cell had been cool and spacious enough so that she could move freely—and she could breathe.

Flinty was right, though. Why should the Captain care what happened to her? She wished he did care. She had witnessed his tender side during the storm, when he listened without interruption to her story, the shine of tears in his eyes when she described Lily's death. She felt closer to him in that moment than she had to anyone in a very long time.

But he had not cared what happened to Margaret, and Misella could not ignore that cruel fact. She and Margaret were nothing but chattel when they boarded the ship, and both of them still were, she carrying Margaret's name. She collapsed in despair onto the coiled ropes, longing to be the young innocent girl she used to be sitting with her father in front of the fireplace reading the psalms together on a cold, windy night.

She thought with regret and ineffable sorrow of her mother whom she had blamed most for giving her away. Not until the birth of her own daughter, Lily, had she begun to understand her mother's decision and come to realize why she gave up the daughter she loved best—because she wanted her to have a better life. A mother's sacrifice, gone terribly awry for all three of them.

Chapter 19

When the sales were finished and all of the prisoners had departed the ship with their new masters, the loading of tobacco barrels began. Though not allowed to exit the ship, Logan helped to lug the barrels to the storage area once the struggling crew hauled them on board. Originally, he had decided to wait until well after midnight to sneak away, after all the crew had returned from their respite on shore and had bedded down for the night. He knew from past experience that Bristol and Flinty would both be drunk enough to pass out until morning. But early in the evening, as the Captain was about to disembark for his own evening entertainment, he found Logan prowling the deck.

"Not going ashore, Logan?" he asked.

Logan shook his head. "No, Sir, not this time.

"Guard duty, eh? Too bad." Barclay hesitated for a moment and then withdrew a ring of keys from his pocket. "Take my keys," he said, handing them to Logan. "Use the key to the storage closet and release Misella Cross. Let her wander around on board and cool off for an hour or so. Then make sure to lock her in and put the keys back on my desk."

A new escape plan taking shape in his mind, Logan responded, "Yes, Sir, I'll be happy to do that for you."

He watched for several minutes until he was certain the Captain had disappeared into the ghostly blur of the fogged-in waterfront.

Lantern in hand, he lowered himself down the steps into the silent hold to retrieve his few belongings thrown together earlier in his stained canvas bag. He paused at the open doorway of the women's section, eerily empty though the stench of unwashed bodies and unemptied necessary tubs prevailed. It would not begin to dissipate until the next day when the crew scrubbed everything down with lye and vinegar to prepare for the next group of prisoners to accompany the *Seaflower* when she returned to Annapolis in early October. He would not be on it.

He startled Misella when he threw open the closet door and held up the lantern. She cried out and jumped up. But when she recognized Logan, she sighed in relief. "Thank the Lord. I thought you were Flinty or Bristol."

Logan shook his head. "I'm leaving, Miss, and I need your help. I intend to desert the ship and disappear in Annapolis. I need you to do my assigned chores on board after I'm gone to give me more time. Will you do that?"

Misella gasped, but didn't answer immediately. If she helped Logan escape, she became his accomplice, subject to the same punishment as he if he were caught—hanging. Yet, he deserved her help for the risk he had taken in retrieving her book of psalms and his efforts on Margaret's behalf. She owed him her trust and his chance for freedom.

After a long few seconds, when Logan added in a pleading voice, "Please, Miss," Misella responded, "Yes, I will do it—because you helped me when I needed to find out what had happened to Margaret. But you will be in danger. You could lose your life if you're caught deserting."

Logan snorted. "I don't care. I have no life here. Follow me, and I'll explain what you need to do." He waited as Misella took several deep breaths of cooler air and wiped her face with the edge of her sleeve.

"In one hour, light the candles in the lanterns on the decks and the two near the gangplank so the crew can find their way back." He handed her a pocket watch and a tinderbox of sulfur-tipped matches. "Ring the ship bell every hour after that. It will be heard all along the waterfront and signals that I am standing guard. I'll show you how. As soon as you hear footsteps or voices on the gangway, return to your closet and close the door. It will have to remain unlocked, but no one will notice that or discover I am gone until morning at least. They'll all be in a drunken stupor until sunrise. I'll return the keys to the Captain's desk before I leave."

She followed after him and watched carefully as Logan showed her what to do. "That's it," he said, throwing the strap of his bag over his shoulder. "Thank you for helping me."

Misella took his large, callused hand in hers. "I'll miss you. And I'll worry about you. I pray that you find help and peace wherever you may go. Stay safe."

Logan nodded. "I wish the same for you," he said, "and hope that we might meet somewhere again in this new world." He moved quietly down the gangway and disappeared from view. He avoided the log road into the town and instead trod through the surrounding muddy fields which silenced his footsteps until he reached the woods. They were further then his earlier surveillance from the ship had suggested, and he feared he may have lost his way in the darkness, but the smell of hemlock and the clutch of branches raking his cheek, reassured him. With confidence, he lit a candle.

He forced himself to keep moving through the dense cover the trees provided, as far inland as possible before daybreak, before he could afford to rest and decide where to set up camp. He would need to find a source of water, a stream or brook, and he knew he risked the chance of being found by poachers hunting for escaped slaves or convicts or deserters from ship or tobacco plantations.

Logan was right that none of the drunken revelers would notice that he was missing when they returned to the ship. Even the Captain, who had imbibed more than usual after meeting a few retired seamen at his favorite waterfront bar, paid no attention to whether the crew had all returned. He was certain that they would if they wanted to receive full pay for this journey when they docked in England. He found his keys safe on his desk, fell into bed and slept undisturbed until an irate Bristol pounded on his door late in the morning.

"One minute," he roared. Head throbbing, he stood up and wrapped the quilt around his naked torso. He stumbled to the door and flung it open. "Why are you bothering me now? Forget what I said about an early morning start. We can wait to launch until this afternoon."

Bristol looked ready to explode or maybe he already had, Barclay thought. His shirt hung open wrinkled and untucked over stained trousers. For once he had neglected to wear his jacket or his belted sword or to grease his hair in place. His face slick with sweat, dark circles underlining his bloodshot eyes, he panted, "He's gone, deserted. Can't be found anywhere."

Barclay dragged him inside and closed the door. "Who? What are you talking about? Make sense, will you?"

Bristol took a deep breath, his hand on his heart. "Logan," he almost sobbed. "That scum of the earth. He's escaped. I have to find him right away. He knows too much. I'll teach him a lesson like he's never felt before."

"Calm down, will you? What time did you learn he was missing? I saw him last night before I left. He seemed docile enough and resigned to staying onboard and keeping guard." Barclay glanced at the keys lying where he had checked them the night before. "Wait. What about Misella. Where is she?" His voice rose in alarm. "Did he take her with him?" As that possibility hit him with blind force, the Captain picked up the keys and threw them at Bristol, panicked by the thought of what he stood to lose if she had disappeared. "Go check and see if she's there," he barked. "Right now, and bring her to me. Did you hear me? This minute. Now," he bellowed, as a shaking Bristol picked up the keys and fled.

By the time Bristol returned with a frightened Misella in tow, the Captain had donned his shirt and taken a brisk shot of brandy. Bristol had regained a bit of starch in his spine and at least pretended to look composed. "The door was unlocked, Sir. She claims she did not know that or she might have tried to escape, too."

The Captain eyed Misella with cold suspicion. "What do you know about Logan's escape?" He leaned closer, his temper beginning to flare, his voice straining with suppressed rage. "What did you do? What did he tell you? You'd best answer me truthfully."

Misella managed to suppress her fear, determined for Logan's sake to present a calm demeanor. She was emboldened and encouraged by the late discovery of his absence and the knowledge that he had gained several hours of travel already. "Logan unlocked my door sometime soon after sunset," she began in a quiet voice, "and told me he had your permission, Sir, to allow me time on deck to get some fresh air. While he stood guard, I walked around the deck, observed the stars emerging in the velvety, purple sky, and tried to view the waterfront, though the fog had moved in low by then and I couldn't see much. But it was lovely to be out for a while, and I was grateful."

"Never mind the pretty twirl of words," the Captain exclaimed. "Just tell us what Logan did."

She nodded and continued, "He returned me to the closet, though I begged him for more time. I said no one would know since all were gone, but he was firm and told me I had to follow orders. He closed the door and that is the last I saw of him. How could I know that he had left it unlocked?" The Captain seemed convinced and relieved that she had not escaped. He poured himself another brandy and told Bristol to take her back and lock her in until they reached Boston. "And have the crew ready the sails. We'll leave within the hour."

Bristol gasped. "We must set up a search party. Immediately, Sir, to find Logan and bring him back."

The Captain scoffed. "He's been gone for hours. Maybe halfway to Philadelphia already. We'll not find him so easily. And we can't waste any more time pursuing such a fool's errand. We have to launch this afternoon to reach Boston by Wednesday morning. I'll not delay departure any longer."

Bristol sputtered in frustration. "But we need him on board, Sir. He does the work of two men."

"Find somebody to replace him when we're in Boston. Or find two, I don't care. There are bound to be some poor, unhappy buggers who will want to work their way back home to England."

Bristol could not let it go. "I swear I will find him no matter how long it takes me. I will make him pay dearly for defying me. And God and the King will bear witness to my quest; he shall never escape justice or my wrath."

For once Barclay was unable to contain his contempt for this paltry little worm, especially since he no longer needed his compliance in handling Misella's situation. She would soon be safely deposited in Boston. Barclay shot a withering look at his agitated First Mate and lashed out. "Forget the bluster, you miserable coward, and just do your job on my ship. You will follow my orders. If you can't do that, you will be replaced. Do you understand?"

Bristol's head jerked back as if he had been struck in the face. He blushed a deep crimson and stuttered, his voice cracking, "Y... yes, Sir, of course. I...I do understand. You know that you can count on me, Sir. I'm at your disposal at all times."

Barclay turned away and slammed his glass on his desk. "Then get out of here, both of you. I don't want to see the likes of either one of you until we reach Boston Harbor."

A frantic Bristol shoved Misella back toward the closet. "Hurry up, bitch. I have searching to do on shore before we launch."

Back in her prison, her mouth dry, her mind thick with distress, Misella seethed with anger for missing an opportunity she might never have again. She could have escaped with Logan. She should have insisted that he take her with him. But when she calmed down and her breathing slowed, she recovered her senses. Escaping with him would have put both of them in serious jeopardy. She took comfort in knowing that Logan had gained several hours of travel time because of her.

Chapter 20

A smiling Captain Barclay, happy to have reached his final destination, scanned the busy wharf as the *Seaflower's* crew hitched the hawsers into place and pulled the vessel close enough to the dock to accommodate the gangway. He didn't see Mr. Briar anywhere in the crowd. If the servitor failed to pick up Misella by the time the crew finished unloading the tea, Barclay would have to make the trip himself to Gretchen's, a meeting he had hoped to avoid. He had not spoken with her since she left England ten years earlier, an unlikely spinster bride with her decrepit Calvinist minister seeking religious freedom in America. The Captain's own young wife had been devastated by the departure of her older sister whom she feared she would never see again.

Left in Boston with nothing after her husband died, Gretchen had survived by opening their small church rectory as a mission home for Presbyterian boarders, thanks to the financial help from her younger sister. Barclay had reminded Gretchen of that help when he wrote to inform her that his wife, her only sister, had died in childbirth. He hoped she might consider repaying the loan, but she had never responded.

He reminded her again of the loan when he sent her a quick note with Mr. Briar before the servitor left the dock in Annapolis. He told her that the young, indentured servant he had chosen for her was a poor child unjustly convicted of a minor crime, a lost soul who needed saving. He asked her to send the servitor to pick up the girl when they docked in Boston on the following Wednesday morning. Mr. Briar had refused to take Misella with him when he left Annapolis, but he had promised to meet them at the wharf in Boston. Something must have prevented him from keeping his promise.

His patience worn thin and his light-hearted mood shattered, the Captain bellowed to his First Mate, "Bristol, bring Margaret to the gangway. Make sure she has everything with her. And be quick about it." He stomped back and forth in front of the gangway, searching in vain for a glimpse of Briar's dark Pilgrim hat among the motley group of dock workers loading boxes onto horse carts.

After Bristol delivered Misella to the gangway mumbling, "Here she is, Sir," he departed quickly, fearing another verbal attack from the frowning Captain.

Misella stood meekly, her head bowed as if by the weight of her hair braided into a large coil at the nape of her neck. She wore her flowered apron over her faded brown dress, cleaned and mended as best she could. Her canvas bag swung freely from her wrist, its original contents much diminished.

The Captain's mood softened when saw her demure and ready to comply with his wishes; he cleared his throat before he spoke. "Mr. Briar appears to have forgotten to meet you, so I'll take you to Mrs. Dobbs." He buttoned his dress jacket and donned his tri-cornered hat.

She nodded her head but she did not trust her voice to speak, confused by the emotions raging through her: fear of what lay ahead, relief at her release from this prison ship, yet unfathomable regret about leaving Captain Barclay. This vision of him in his dress uniform, the sun bouncing off the gold buttons of his jacket, dazzled her, probably, she thought, because she had never seen him this way before. And she realized that she might never see him again.

"We'll take a carriage," he said, "as it is too far to walk on such a hot afternoon. You will follow me, please." He preceded her down the gangway and pushed his way through the crowd to a line of carriages parked near the dock. He chose one of the newer coaches, told the driver the address, and asked the price of the round trip.

Satisfied with the amount, he withdrew the money and paid him upfront. The driver opened the carriage door, placed the step stool, and moved aside. Removing his hat, the Captain ducked his head and stepped up inside before half turning to see if Misella was behind him. "Quick now," he said, "I have much to do today."

Misella hesitated, remembering that day so long ago, her first journey in a carriage alone with Sir Richard Maltby. How far she had traveled since that fateful day and how far she had fallen. She had told the Captain everything; he had heard her story. Did he yet blame her for her fall from grace, still view her as a fallen woman, she wondered. She tried without success to swallow her tears. Not wanting to annoy him, she averted her gaze as she sat down across from him. Without a word, he placed his folded handkerchief in her lap and continued to stare out the window at the bustling street.

She picked up the soft, white handkerchief, the initials EB embroidered in silver thread at the corner, and blotted her cheeks. "Thank you," she murmured, gaining control of her voice and reaching out to return the handkerchief to him.

"No, keep it," he said, glancing at her before facing the window again, "until I return. You will have to be brave a little longer, I hope just three months, before I can return and relieve the burden of your indenture."

But she was not Margaret, the naïve, untested child. She was Misella who had learned well over the past six years the fallacies of hope and the foolishness of trusting empty promises. She doubted that she would see him again.

Neither spoke during the rest of the journey. The carriage bumped its way down cobblestoned streets, stopped repeatedly by loaded horse carts or scurrying foot-travelers. As the crowds thinned, the carriage clattered onto a slatted log road at the edge of town. The driver stopped in front of a small wooden building with a faded white steeple. A single peony bush in full pink bloom overran the rough-hewn steps leading up to a set of double doors with black metal handles.

Misella waited for the Captain to exit the carriage before she stepped down and followed him up the planked sidewalk. She stood behind him as he pounded with a closed fist on the door. He was about to knock again when the door flew open, and a scowling Mr. Briar confronted them. "Do you think this a home for the deaf?" he blurted before recognizing the Captain. "Oh, it is you. Here so soon? Strong winds, then? I thought you were to arrive tomorrow."

"Wrong," the Captain grumbled, "I distinctly told you to meet the ship today. And I must return quickly, so let's get this over with. Where is Gretchen?"

Mr. Briar did not apologize. He opened the doors wider and with a sweep of his arm and a slight bow, he signaled them to enter. "If you will wait in the parlor, I will inform Mrs. Dobbs of your presence." He ushered them into a small, dark room. A single candle in a pewter holder flickered on the mantle. Mr. Briar drew back the heavy curtain on the room's only window so that the dying sunlight could somewhat illuminate the rest of the room. "Do sit, Captain," he said, gesturing to a plain, hardwood armchair next to the fireplace. He ignored Misella.

"Mrs. Dobbs is in the garden collecting greens for our dinner." He hesitated, a flush creeping over his boney face, before hurrying on. "I mean she provides dinner for all four of us, her boarders—original Church members, deacons of her husband's before his untimely death. I will get her for you," he mumbled as he left the room.

Misella stood just inside the doorway next to a long, altar-like table that held a series of pamphlets fanned out in front of a massive Bible resting on a short, metal stand. She thought this seemed more a prayer room than a parlor since it contained only a few unadorned wood chairs and a line of wooden kneelers pushed against the opposite wall.

The Captain rose to his feet as a tall, gangly woman appeared like a shadow in the doorway, wisps of gray escaping from a tight cap of hair parted severely down the center and wound loosely into a bun over each ear. A gray muslin garment draped her emaciated figure, cinched at the waist with a braided leather belt. A large metal cross hung from a chain around her neck and rested flat against her chest. She glided into the room, her black slipper shoes soundless on the planked floor. "Ebenezer," she said, "after these many years, Our Savior has allowed us to meet again and heal our differences."

"Hello, Gretchen," the Captain said, grasping the claw-like hand she held out to him. She had aged far beyond her forty years, but still retained the stern, religious demeanor he remembered from ten years before when she had departed for the Colonies. "I've forgotten any differences we may have had in the past. Gracie's death annihilated all of our silly squabbles."

Mrs. Dobbs sniffled, her voice choking. "Dear Grace. How sorry I was that I could not be with my baby sister and her wee one at that terrible time." She sniffed again. "But God had other plans for me."

The Captain nodded. "And for me, I guess." He glanced at Misella. "But enough of the past. I am grateful that you have agreed to accept Margaret MacDonald's indenture."

"In Gracie's name, I have agreed to do this favor for you. I cannot pay her anything, you understand. She will earn her keep here but that is all."

"Yes, of course, she understands that, don't you, Margaret." He turned to her, standing by the table in silence. "Come here and meet Mrs. Dobbs." As she stumbled forward, he grasped her hand, and turning away for a moment from Gretchen's needle eyes, he pressed a few coins into her palm, aware that she might need them to survive Gretchen's wrath until his return. He folded her fingers into a fist.

Misella looked at him, sudden tears welling up in her eyes, not for herself but for him. She wanted to tell him how sorry she was for the loss of his wife and child. Not knowing if she was expected to bow or curtsy, she did neither and simply murmured, "How do you do, Ma'am. Pleased to meet you."

Mrs. Dobbs sniffed again and stared at her with pale, watery-blue eyes. "You will start in the kitchen right now. I hope you know how to cook a simple meal. If not, you will learn right quick. The pantry will serve as your lodging." She sneered at the muslin bag gripped in Misella's hand. "Is that all you brought with you?" When Misella nodded, she said, "Well, you won't find anything here that you can steal, Miss Lightfingers."

"Margaret was unjustly accused of theft and sentenced unfairly as I explained to you in my note," the Captain said, clenching his jaw. "She will not give you any trouble."

"Humph," Mrs. Dobbs snorted. "We shall see." With that she bid the Captain good-bye and hoped to see him again before the seven-year indenture ended. "You can let yourself out, can't you? My boarders will be returning soon for their dinner." She turned to Misella. "Come along, Miss Margaret Lightfingers. You have work to do."

Misella looked back at the Captain before she followed Mrs. Dobbs through the doorway. "I'm sorry," she murmured, "about the loss of your wife and baby."

"I'm sorry, too," he replied softly, "about Margaret."

"Thank you," she said aloud, "for your kindness." She remembered her final vision of Jack Finn, as she boarded the *Seaflower*, who offered his symbolic gesture, the one he had taught her to use years ago whenever she felt afraid: "Chin up; eyes to Heaven." Placing two fingers under her chin, she raised it high, giving the Captain a sad smile as she left the room.

Chapter 21

Finn managed to haul Ben Turner over the rails and onto the pirate ship before it departed the disabled *Mary Anne*. He left it to Quedagh to explain to their Captain why they had returned with Turner. Assuring a concerned Parker that he could handle the snarling cripple, he steered Turner to the vacant prison cell on board and ordered him to sit down on the room's lone wooden stool. He drew Turner's bag of coins from inside his blouse and tossed it in his lap. "Keep this hidden somewhere on your person; otherwise your money will be confiscated and shared with my fellow pirates as Robin Hood did with the rest of his men."

"Robin Hood's men, my good eye!" Turner spat out the words, clutching the bag in one hand and standing up again, brandishing his cane in the other. "Pirates are thieving louts that terrorize decent men."

Losing his temper at last with the pig-headed barrister, Finn raised his voice. "A pirate is saving your life right now, not your so-called decent men! The Crown, your fellow Tories, the wealthy noblemen and merchants who feed off of the rest of us poor sods? Raping, pillaging my Irish homeland until we must scrape the very earth with our bare hands in order to survive? They're cheating and ruining their own countrymen. If you truly believe them to be decent men, why do you rail against them in your court of law? Why defend the likes of Misella Cross if you think so highly of their kind and so ill of these men who fight, as she did, to survive?"

Turner set aside his cane and sat down heavily upon the stool. "We are a nation of laws, Sir," he said quietly. "Not always fair laws, I agree, and Justice is often held hostage, I know, but we will not release her by sinking to the level of common criminals. No, Sir. If you want to change our laws, you have to work by degrees within them, gradually. Changing people's minds takes time and patience and tenacity." He rubbed his eyes for a moment. "I admit I often forget that. I lose patience. I'm quick to anger as I fear I was too often with the injustice done to Misella Cross."

Finn's voice softened. "You saved her life, Sir, with your masterful defense."

Turner shook his head. "I'm afraid not. My anger and disdain for my fellow barristers resulted in her transportation sentence on a trumped-up charge. It was done to punish me for my hubris, my lack of courtroom decorum, the disrespect I failed to keep in check. And the irony is she must pay the price, perhaps with her life in that god-forsaken place…" His voice cracked. He slipped his hand inside the pocket of his vest and withdrew the small portrait of Misella that he kept there. "I must do what I can to help her now."

"So must I," Finn said. "May I hold that, Sir, for a moment?" Finn took the portrait Turner handed him and stared at Misella's beloved image. She wore a heart-shaped locket around her neck that he recognized from their last days spent together at Hawthorn Manor—a proud neck, uplifting her head, her serious eyes gazing forward, her lips parted as if to speak.

Finn closed his eyes, swallowing the lump arising in his throat. When he was able to speak, he said, "The two of us must work together again as we did during her trial. We will find her. You have done all you could to keep her safe. I pray that Captain Barclay has kept his side of the bargain you made on her behalf."

"Amen," Turner murmured, returning the portrait to the safety of his pocket.

Chapter 22

Though July, the hottest month, had arrived, trade winds tempered the heat along the Southeastern coast of Jamaica which welcomed the pirate ship, now flying the *Dolphin* flag. While giant bamboo grasses threatened to overtake much of the shore line, a stand of tall, graceful palm trees waved their flat, green arms as if in greeting. A range of mist-covered mountains stood watch in the distance as the ship sailed boldly into the principal port of Kingston to stock up on supplies. Upon reaching the land mass, the helmsman maneuvered with care around the Palisadoes and the Port Royal lagoon to the landward side. The pirates in camouflage clothing, looted from respectable passengers, threw ropes to the landing crew standing on the Kingston dock.

Finn had convinced Captain Kerry to let him accompany Ben Turner to the merchant house where Turner would act as the *Dolphin's* negotiator and purchase essentials for the ship—much needed water, meat, sugar, yams, molasses and rum.

"He will preserve our cover," Finn assured the Captain, "and help us avoid raising the suspicions of any British patrols. Turner is a new face here, and so am I. We won't run the risk, as other crew members might, of being recognized from past visits to the island or from dealings with the merchant house staff."

The Captain agreed but issued a stern warning. "He's a clever one that swivel- eyed Gollumpus. I have no doubt he is a boot-licking

Loyalist. He could betray us in a lick with one flick of that wayward eye. You'll have to watch him every minute; don't leave him alone. And return to the ship immediately when you finish at the merchant house. Don't stop anywhere else. We'll be watching you."

Finn nodded his head. "I'll keep him in line. He'll listen to me. I know how to handle the old bumper." In truth, though, he worried about how he and Turner could disappear on the island long enough until the dogged Captain ordered the ship to leave without them. Pirates swore an oath to loyalty punishable by death if they broke that vow, and they considered desertion the most egregious betrayal. He would feel more confident if he could escape alone without having to drag the headstrong, half-blind Turner with him. Not to mention the challenge he faced in convincing Turner to dress his part by donning the fancy finery confiscated in the ship's raids.

The battle commenced as soon as Finn entered Turner's cell, a pile of velvet and fine lace in his arms. Turner arose from his makeshift cot already fully dressed in his shabby brown coat, wrinkled britches, and worn cotton stockings. "That outfit will not do, Sir, if you expect to pass scrutiny as a barrister for a wealthy Dutch merchant." Finn spread the finery across the cot: a claret velvet jacket and britches, embroidered vest, white silk shirt with ruffled cuffs, a starched neck cloth, and silk roll-up stockings. He placed a pair of black, patent leather pumps on the floor and then drew an enameled snuff box from his pocket and put it on top of the jacket. "I'll be back shortly when you are ready to disembark."

Turner picked up the snuff box and flung it across the room. "No, Sir, not on your life or mine. I'll not play a powdered fop for anyone. I left England to escape men you want me to impersonate. I'll dress as myself. If you want to convince the customs officers at the merchant house that I am legitimate, then give them an honest picture they'll be more likely to believe. If they see me trying to strut around stiff-rumped on those foot grippers, they will think me nothing but a sharper."

Controlling his temper, Finn picked up the snuff box and confronted Turner. "I know you detest pomp and play-acting as fakery beneath your high standards." He lowered his voice. "Given our mission, our escape depends upon you playing along. We must dupe our adversaries. Haughty displays of wealth and frippery impress the people here just as they do at home."

"I will not succumb to such rank foolery. You are right that it is beneath me. I have spent my life fighting against the very people you want me to become—defenders of greed and inhumanity." Turner shook his head and thumped the floor with his cane. "No, Sir, I cannot do it. I will negotiate as myself."

Finn took a deep breath. "Misella is the reason you began this venture, isn't she? If you hope to complete this journey to find her, you will need to listen to me and follow all of my instructions without question. Otherwise, Sir, we remain on this ship, pirates forever, or return to England in chains to face hanging, and neither of us will ever see Misella again."

He threw the snuff box onto the cot. "I'll return in ten minutes. You can let me know your decision then." He slammed the door behind him, but hovered outside the room listening for a few minutes. He took comfort in the grumblings, the snorting, the racket, the unexpected cursing that emanated from inside, for he knew Turner realized he had no choice but to accept the challenge.

When Finn reentered the room later dressed in his own finery, Turner was a sight to behold. His face, a shade darker than his jacket, shone with perspiration. His neck, trapped in the starched white cloth wrapped around it, thrust his chin up as if he already wore a noose. The vest covered his girth adequately so the ill-fitting jacket could remain unbuttoned; the lacy ruffles extending from the cuffs fluttered over his large wrists. At least, the britches, stockings and shoes seemed to fit. He stood, tilted slightly forward, with his legs apart, grasping his cane with both hands as if afraid to move. Breathing heavily, he gave Finn a withering look.

Finn whipped a powdered wig from behind his back and plopped it on Turner's head. "That will do it," he said, straining to keep his composure and not laugh at the bizarre vision before him.

"Damnation, you jolly dog," Turner snarled. "You've turned me into a Capon. This had better work or by God, I'll see you pilloried if it's the last thing I do."

"We'll make it work, my friend, I promise. Trust me. I want to succeed as much as you do—to find Misella and help her."

Chapter 23

The port area of Kingston buzzed with activity. Hordes of half-naked slaves, the men in pantaloons, the women in cotton skirts, their waists cinched with ropes of woven sawgrass, carried baskets on their heads. They snaked single-file up gangplanks to merchant ships awaiting delivery of sugar, coffee beans, and bananas. Horse carts, their wooden wheels planted in the sand, awaited passengers.

As Finn and Turner made their way down the *Dolphin's* gangplank, Turner stumbled in his shiny pumps, cursing and clutching his cane. Finn took pity on the "trussed up Capon" and hired a horse and cart to transport the two of them to the merchant house though it was an easy walk of a few blocks. Climbing into the back of the wooden box cart proved more challenging for Turner than the walk might have been. Finn helped him jump in and squirm into a sitting position with his silk-stockinged legs hanging over the back edge of the cart. Finn hopped up next to him and handed him his cane.

Wheels creaking, the cart bumped along the uneven packed sand until they reached the dirt road. Scattered along the roadway, wood houses, not much bigger than the cart, rose above them on stilts, their rooves thatched with palm leaves. The road widened as they neared the merchant house, a sprawling whitewashed building that commanded their attention. As the cart approached the building, Finn extracted a sheaf of paper from the inside of his velvet jacket.

"You'll do the talking in there," he told Turner. "Give this to the staff at the desk. After you negotiate the price, I'll give you the money. Once they have marked this list paid in full, they'll take the order to the warehouse in back and begin the process of loading their carts to take to the wharf. We'll accompany them to the warehouse and oversee the loading to make sure everything is included. At this point, I take over and do the talking. You'll remain silent."

Turner nodded, the wig slipping sideways over his good eye. He batted at it, his starched ruffled sleeve almost knocking it off before Finn grabbed hold and eased the wayward wig back into place. "I hate these blasted things," Turner grumbled. "They plagued me constantly in the courtroom. I never wore them anywhere else."

Finn helped him exit the cart, hanging on to him with both hands until Turner gained his footing on the stone pathway leading to the stairway of the merchant house. Turner slapped his hands away once he had his cane set, but Finn kept one arm locked around his as they made their way up the steps and into the main room.

They waited in line behind a richly clad plantation owner who took his time negotiating the sale price of his latest sugar crop. When he finally finished, he bumped into Finn as he turned to leave. He ignored Finn, but bowed to Turner and removed his broad-brimmed straw hat. "My apologies, Good Sir, for the delay. Are you here from the one of the ships, by any chance—to buy goods? You'll find an excellent price for sugar."

Finn answered for the scowling Turner. "No problem, Sir. Thank you for the advice." Turner snorted and remained silent. As the gentleman departed, Finn whispered to Turner, "You see? Dress like an aristocrat, and you'll be treated as one."

"By a lying, overbearing sycophant, you mean," he muttered, tugging his wig back in place again as they approached the agent behind the desk.

Finn introduced his master to the agent and told him their mission. Turner took over at that point, handed the list to the well-dressed native and stated that they needed these items delivered immediately to the wharf. He wrangled with the agent over the prices, especially the sugar price which he refused to pay until the price was lowered to the original price per pound the agent had offered the plantation owner for his crop. "If you want to sell us all of these goods, you will have to lower that price," he insisted over and over again until he wore the agent down and received the price he wanted.

When the sale was final, they moved on through the back doors to the open warehouse, a jumble of wooden boxes, kegs and fat canvas bags stacked haphazardly on the packed earthen floor. Each, however, was carefully labeled with its contents. Directed by the agent with the list in hand, bare-chested natives, some only in loin cloths, worked in the suffocating heat loading wheeled carts. Brown bodies slick with sweat, they would haul these carts to the wharf and load their contents onto the ship.

When all of the contents were loaded, Finn told the agent, "Have your man with the first cart give the list to the ship's overseer sitting dockside at a little table, and be sure to tell him that we will wait here at the warehouse until the last cart has left." The agent nodded. "Oh, and Mr. Turner and I will have some time to spend ashore until returning ourselves to the ship. Since he is a British subject, he is interested in visiting the British military headquarters here on the island. Do you think you could round up a horse and cart to take us to that location?"

"Yes, of course," the agent replied, "but be forewarned, the headquarters are temporary at the moment, set up in an abandoned warehouse a few blocks inland. Don't expect an elegant reception."

"No, that's fine. Mr. Turner believes he has an acquaintance who has been stationed here and would like to pay him a visit." Finn ignored the look of surprise on Turner's grimacing wet face as he wobbled in obvious distress on his black pumps. When the agent left to find them a horse cart, Finn explained his plan thus far to him in a hushed voice. "We'll be expected soon at the wharf, and if we don't show up, the Captain will send a few henchmen to the warehouse to look for us. The safest place for us right now is British Headquarters—they won't go there. When we don't return by late afternoon, I'm hoping the Captain will think that you have betrayed us, given me up as a pirate to the Brits, exposed the ship's cover, and asked them to transport you to the Colonies where you were headed."

Turner looked perplexed. "Is that what you want me to do? Do you think me a Judas to betray you along with the others? If I do that, you'll be hanged for sure."

"No, of course not. We'll have to maintain our cover with the military, too. You, the English barrister working for the Danish merchant who owns the *Dolphin*, and I, John Barron, your assistant. I'll have to use an alias in case any of the Brits have heard of me from my highwayman days. We can't risk telling them the truth, about the pirates seizing the ship and forcing us to help them, for a day or two until after the ship has departed and is out to sea. The Captain will not wait. If we haven't shown up soon after the delivery, he'll leave. Of that I am certain."

"And then what?" Turner fumed. "I'm forced to roam around like this?" He yanked at the neck cloth, now damp with sweat, and stamped one heel in disgust.

"We have no other choice," Finn argued. "You have your cane; I have your money, and a small amount of my own. We can replace your clothes later. I've left everything I owned on board, too, including most of my money. It has to appear as if I thought we would return."

"And what do we do until morning, pray tell, my fine plumed friend?"

"I haven't thought that far ahead yet. Let's get to the headquarters, out of harm's way, and I'll think of something while we're there."

Turner scowled, his face a shiny mask of misery. "By God and the King, I hope your plan works."

Chapter 24

On the evening of her first day as Mrs. Dobbs' indentured servant, Misella knelt in the boarding house parlor on one of the wooden kneelers, the room feebly lit with the help of a few random candles. The four boarders, including Mr. Briar, occupied kneelers behind her; they all faced the front table where Mrs. Dobbs stood erect in front of the Bible droning from the New Testament in her high-pitched voice. Misella's knees and back ached from having to maintain a rigid position on the hard kneeler. Her stomach growled, still half empty after their meagre supper. She slumped forward a bit, resting her torso against her clasped hands.

"Up straight, Miss Lightfingers," Mrs. Dobbs rasped. "We'll have no swaybacks here."

Misella forced herself upright. She craved sleep; even the straw mat on the floor of the pantry appealed to her now. With Mrs. Dobbs breathing over her, pinpoint eyes alert to her every move, she had prepared their supper of fish head stew and salad greens from the garden. She thought about Elinor, the older sister she had not seen since leaving home. Elinor, who used to cook fish head stew for their family. Jealous Elinor who envied her and hated her for being the chosen one, Sir Richard's protégé. If only Elinor could know that Misella was not the lucky one after all.

Glaring at Misella with her needle eyes, Mrs. Dobbs raised her voice, "***He who steals must steal no longer; but rather he must***

labor, performing with his own hands what is good, so that he will have something to share with one who has need." With that she closed the book. "Take heed, Miss. We will be watching you closely to make sure none of our belongings disappear. Isn't that so, gentlemen?"

Mumbling their agreement, the boarders shuffled to their feet and pushed their kneelers to the wall. Like a flock of crows, they moved together to the doorway in their faded black suits. "Before you leave," Mrs. Dobbs told them, "I'd like each of you to draw up a list of chores that you need done by our servant here and give them to me tomorrow. She will be available to do whatever you want her to do."

Mr. Briar stopped, allowing the other three to proceed through the doorway. He waited for Misella to move her kneeler to the wall before he spoke to her. "You will bring a pot of tea to my room in ten minutes," he ordered, squinting at her as he slipped his glasses into the side pocket of his jacket. "You will knock twice before you enter." He hesitated for a moment. "Is that alright with you, Mrs. Dobbs?"

Mrs. Dobbs looked startled. She retrieved her Daybook from the table and clutched it to her chest. She blinked her eyes several times and took a deep breath. "As you wish, Mr. Briar." Bending down, she blew out each candle in the branched candleholder next to the Bible stand. "To the kitchen, Miss Lightfingers," she snarled, sweeping from the room ahead of Mr. Briar who hastened after her.

Misella felt like crying with frustration and fatigue. It was late, and she was exhausted. She missed the ship, as foolish as that thought seemed, but at least there she did not feel so alone and abandoned as she did here already. She missed the Captain and his kindness, though he often tried to hide it. And Logan, too. She could not bear to think of Jack Finn—too foolish a yearning. She had decided on the ship that she must put him out of her mind once and for all. No more useless woolgathering about what might have been.

Mrs. Dobbs appeared in the doorway. Her screech cracked the air like a whip. "Are you hard of hearing as well? Get thee to the kitchen now!"

Misella wiped her eyes with the edge of her apron and hurried out to the hall, following Mrs. Dobbs' rigid back through the dining area and into the kitchen. Like a gray whirlwind, she flung open a cupboard, grabbed a tin of tea, and banged it down on the table. Spinning around to grab the tea kettle off of the stove, she bumped into Misella who hovered close by. She slammed the kettle into Misella's midsection. When the poor girl cried out and tried to catch her breath, Mrs. Dobbs screamed at her. "You stupid little thief. Do I have to show you how to do everything? Do you know how to make tea?"

"Yes, ma'am," Misella wheezed. "I—I do."

"Then do it. Put everything on the tray and take it to Mr. Briar's room immediately."

"Which room is his, ma'am? I have not yet been upstairs."

Mrs. Dobbs sneered. "You're such a smart girl, aren't you? Maybe you can figure it out." She picked a lighted candle holder off of the table, leaving one behind for Misella. "Be sure to blow this one out before you retire. Leave it here. Do not take it into the pantry with you. You'll be able to scramble around in the dark—like you did in prison."

Misella dragged herself up the stairs to the second floor, the tea service and candle holder bouncing on the tray in concert with her heavy footsteps. She hesitated on the landing to study the string of four closed doors. They all looked the same, though the room at the far end of the hallway was set slightly apart from the other three. She surmised that the dour Mr. Briar might want as much privacy as possible, so she approached this room, rested the tray on her hip before releasing one hand, and rapped twice on the door.

"Enter."

Mr. Briar, clothed in a long, white night shirt, sat hunched over a large desk covered with papers, a fat candle sputtering nearby on a pewter plate. An empty stool stood next to his chair. A narrow cot, resting against the far wall beneath a large wooden cross, comprised the room's only additional furnishings. He did not look up at her. He gathered some of the papers together to make room for the tray. "Pour my tea," he ordered, "and sit down next to me."

Misella poured the tea and set the cup and saucer on the desk. Uncomfortable with the intimacy of this side-by-side arrangement, she moved the three-legged stool to the corner of the desk and sat down. Face flushed, eyeglasses glittering in the candlelight, Mr. Briar glared at her. "Move the stool back where it was," he said and waited, sipping his tea, while she did as she was told.

"Now then," he continued without looking at her, "Captain Barclay told me that you are literate. I will be dictating my treatise on God's law and the sins of the flesh, and you will write what I tell you. We will meet like this every evening for two hours." He placed a few blank pages in front of her along with a pot of ink and a quill. "Do you understand?"

Misella's shoulders slumped; her eyes burned as she forced herself to keep them open. "Yes, Sir," she murmured picking up the quill.

Mr. Briar dictated the first sentence, "Let us consider the duty that God's law doth require of us." After Misella had scratched out the words exactly as he had intoned them, he leaned down, his eyeglasses inches from the page, his breath warming her hand, and reviewed what she had written. Nodding his head, he sat up and continued: "Purity of mind and body, our goal; prayer and penance, our weapons, armor, as it were, to protect us from the constant temptations of the flesh."

He seemed unaware that his knee had pressed against her; his leg began to shake up and down as his voice rose, "Even secret concupiscence is a sin according to God's holy law..." He stopped and waited for her to finish writing. "...a law sharp as a sword which can pierce the most protected corners of the heart. Hereby, we shall be made fearful to offend though it be but a momentary thought."

She scribbled as fast as she could to keep up with him, but before she had finished, he pushed his chair back, his hands clutched together in his lap, his head bent.

"You may go now," he croaked. "Leave the tea things."

Though less than an hour of her required time with him had passed, Misella, relieved and thankful, stood quickly without saying a word, grabbed the candle from the tray, and fled the room. She had endured this kind of hypocrisy and false preaching before from the Ordinary in Newgate prison. She knew from experience that over time the threat to her safety would escalate, that Mr. Briar would act on the impulses he tried so hard to control, and that he would blame her for his subsequent transgressions. She had to find a way to avoid this unhealthy duty he had thrust upon her.

She hurried down the stairs to the ink black kitchen. Leaving the candle here, unlit as Mrs. Dobbs ordered, would force her to wander in the darkness, find the pantry door, open it, and crawl along the floor to locate the straw mat.

Instead, she carried the candle with her into the pantry, set it on the shelf next to a stack of plates; undressed; folded her gown, stays, and petticoat; placed them on top of the root vegetable box; donned her makeshift nightdress; unbraided and brushed her hair; and retrieved Captain Barclay's handkerchief from her canvas bag before extinguishing the candle. She laid down, the handkerchief pressed to her face, inhaling its scent as she fell asleep.

Chapter 25

Five weeks after the escape from Jamaica, Ben Turner leaned against the railing of the naval ship, the *Lancaster*, surrounded by a cheering group of petty officers and midshipmen as the port of Annapolis came into view. He wore a cast-off "working rig" donated to him by the ship's Captain before they boarded the ship, a simple unembroidered frock coat with muslin britches. Though he still sported the white silk stockings he had arrived in at the Jamaican British headquarters, he had scrapped the pumps for a pair of the Captain's old leather slippers.

Finn pushed his way through the crowd of sailors. Brandishing Turner's cane in one hand, he joined Turner at the railing. "You forgot your cane, old man," he said. "Those slippers won't work so well on the cobble-stoned streets of Annapolis. You'll need this until we can buy you decent shoes."

Turner breathed deep, stood up straight, threw back his shoulders and grinned at Finn. "I don't think I'll need it here. I'm a new man, Finny. After weeks of walking the deck in this fresh pure air, in the company of these fine youngsters, I'm as spry as a spring lamb." He threw an arm around Finn. "I am ready to conquer the New World. And find Misella Cross. You and I together."

Finn bowed his head and closed his eyes for a moment. Lifting his head, he thought to himself, *Chin up; eyes to heaven*, before answering Turner. He could not match Turner's exuberance, his glowing confidence and twinkling eyes. His Irish sense of foreboding prevented him from celebrating too soon. He dared not hope too much that reuniting with Misella would be easy or even certain. "I'll hold on to the cane for you," he said. "You may need it when we disembark. We should go below and gather our things."

In truth, they had very little to bring with them. Turner refused to take the fancy clothes he had abandoned as soon as he had boarded. Finn, however, wanted to change out of the outfit he wore throughout the trip, a simple frock coat and britches borrowed from one of the petty officers. When he landed in Annapolis, Finn would do so as an English gentleman in all his plumed finery, accompanied by his own barrister. He smiled to himself at the irony of such a transformation.

Upon exiting the *Lancaster*, they secured lodging at a public house recommended by the Captain, Reynolds Tavern near the Harbor. "Separate rooms," Turner insisted. "I've had enough of sharing my every move with you for the last seven weeks. I'll pay the price for a little privacy, so I can grumble and talk out loud to myself whenever I want to. And dress as I choose!"

After settling into their rooms, they met in the tavern downstairs to have lunch and plan their search for Misella. Spooning his soup with care to protect his ruffled shirtfront and velvet waistcoat, Finn dithered about how best to proceed. "We need to settle in here, find some means of support. Get to know our surroundings and meet people. Ask questions. If we don't succeed in locating where she is, we will have to wait and confront the Captain of the *Seaflower* when he returns in the fall."

Turner wiped chowder from his chin and threw the napkin on the table. "No, Sir," he said, "I do not intend to wait until then to find Misella. I will go to the custom house this afternoon, alone, as an attorney representing the ship's contractor, Victor Dunning, and ask to see the transportation contracts from the ship's recent landing."

Finn shook his head. "What good will that do? The listed contracts won't tell us where she is now, or reveal whether the Captain kept his part of the bargain. She could be anywhere in the region, trapped on some godforsaken plantation. Buyers come from all over when a ship comes in, some as far away as Boston."

Turner's voice rose, his face reddening, his good eye shooting sparks at the young, prinked up dandy sitting across from him in his stolen finery. "At the ripe age of fifty, my boy, I believe I have a bit more experience judging people than you—at least twenty-five years or more. I trust the Captain to have kept her safe, arranged her freedom, and honored his promise. But with your shady background, honesty is not a trait you'd know much about."

Finn bristled. "I've done all I could to save your miserable, swivel-eyed hide," he snarled. "If not for me and my 'honest' efforts to help you, your bones would be lying on the ocean floor by now or swinging from the gibbet at Tyburn. I've had enough of your canting and complaining. Maybe it's time for us to go our separate ways." He slapped his napkin on the table and stood up.

Turner looked sheepish. "I'm sorry, my boy. That was ungrateful of me. I am anxious to find Misella, and I know that you are, too. I do need your help, and I hope we can continue to work together. For her sake…and for mine."

Easing himself back into his chair, Finn calmed down. "I respect your insights and your knowledge of the law…and your devotion to Misella's well-being. I have never doubted that. Look what we've achieved so far—you and I. We will find her."

Making a point of grabbing his cane from the vacant chair where he had laid it, Turner stood up. "With my bad knee, I'll need this for my walk to the custom house. You were right about these cobble-stoned streets, a bit of a challenge for a swivel eyed, old toast like me." He winked and smiled at Finn. "I'll meet you back here in an hour or two, Finny. Wait for me."

Chapter 26

Ben Turner navigated the cobblestoned street with care, thankful for his cane, and that the customs house was a short walk from the dock. A tall brick building, one of the oldest in Annapolis, the house was fairly deserted now that all in-coming ships had cleared out of the harbor. Turner made his way up the broad wooden steps to the portico flanked on both sides by a single white Palladian column. He was tired and hot after negotiating the two-block walk over uneven cobblestones in the heelless slippers. His knee and ankles throbbed. After finishing here, he intended to buy himself some decent lace-up shoes.

The cool, quiet lobby provided instant relief. He approached the clerk, an older, neatly dressed gentleman standing behind a long counter stacked with papers; book-laden rows of shelves stretched along the wall in back of him. Shuffling through a stack of papers, the clerk didn't speak, but he acknowledged Turner's presence by raising his index finger to indicate that he was almost finished. Turner leaned on the counter, happy to rest for a minute and catch his breath until the clerk set aside the stack, looked up over his wire-rimmed glasses and asked, "What can I help you with, Sir?"

Turner removed the copy of his law license from his pocket and placed it on the counter. Introducing himself as Victor Dunning's emissary from London, he said, "I am here to check the transportation documents from the *Seaflower's* last arrival, sometime in late June or early July, I believe.

Seeming alarmed, the clerk removed his glasses. "Is there a problem, Sir? The ship's Captain should provide a verification copy to the merchant when the vessel returns to England. I can assure you we are very careful about documenting the arrival of all contracted prisoners. Parliamentary law, you know."

Turner nodded. "Yes, I do know. It is not a problem on your end, to be sure. Mr. Dunning asked me to do a quick follow-up check. Some question about numbers and the payment schedule. He wants to be certain that all assigned prisoners he contracted for were included and no unpaid stragglers added at the last minute." The clerk frowned, looking unconvinced. "You know how some of these rich merchants are," Turner continued. "Afraid they might be cheated out of a few pounds."

The clerk smiled knowingly. "I understand. That document probably hasn't been filed yet. Give me a minute to look through some of these current ones." He pulled a stack of papers forward and began riffling through them. "The *Seaflower*, you say?"

"Yes, that's right." Turner, trying to appear nonchalant, picked up his license and returned it to his pocket, relieved that the clerk had not noticed the expiration date. He had not bothered to have it renewed before he left because he would need a new license here anyway. He asked the clerk checking the papers one by one, "Out of curiosity, does the document indicate to whom each prisoner was sold?"

"No, it doesn't indicate buyers. That's a different recorded procedure. Those documents are kept at the courthouse." The clerk pulled out one of the papers. "Ah, here it is, Sir." He placed the document in front of Turner.

Turner was heartened to hear that he would be able to search for that information later if it so happened that she had been sold because Captain Barclay was unable to keep the bargain.

The ship's name and date of arrival in port was inscribed in bold lettering at the top of the page. The alphabetized list logged the name of each prisoner, date and location of incarceration, date of sentencing and a brief notation of crimes committed. Turner leaned close, squinting his good eye, and scanned the first page quickly, then flipped to the second page which contained the list of female prisoners. He located Misella's entry and gasped, the bold letters easy for him to see.

Misella Cross, 2 April 1754; Newgate, 8 April 1754; prostitution----DECEASED, Buried at Sea, 2 May 1754

His cane clattered to the floor. He grabbed hold of the counter and leaned heavily against it. "No!" he exclaimed, "This cannot be."

Startled, the clerk stopped inserting pages into the book files and hurried around the counter. "Are you all right, Sir?" He stooped and picked up the cane. "Let me help you to a chair."

Turner pulled out his kerchief and wiped his face and his eyes. "This heat gets to me at times," he mumbled. "Shocked to see that a prisoner was lost under this Captain. I know he has a pristine record on deliveries. Can there be a mistake, perhaps? An error in the logbook?"

"No, Sir. The numbers are always correct, and the prisoners are all accounted for as soon as a ship arrives. The Customs House and the Captains of these vessels are required by law to keep accurate records."

Turner bowed his head. "I see," he said quietly.

The clerk hesitated, looking somewhat troubled, as if debating whether to say any more. "You are correct, Sir, that the death of a prisoner has never happened before on Captain Barclay's ship. Another odd thing happened," the clerk continued. "The ship's First Mate rushed in here, the morning after the prisoner sales, red-faced and breathless, to inquire whether anyone had seen a crew member who had deserted. A giant of a man, he said, by the name of James Logan. Though desertion is a common problem on these ships, it had never happened before on Captain Barclay's watch." He shook his head back and forth and shrugged his shoulders.

Turner took a deep, shuddering breath, reached for his cane and turned away from the counter.

"Let me help you down the steps," the clerk offered in a gentle voice, concern evident in his expression. "I'll arrange a carriage for you."

"No, no," Turner countered, "I'm fine. I can make my way back with my cane. Very kind of you. And I do thank you for your help. Good day." He tried to stand as upright as he could, his cane grasped firmly in one hand. With slow, uneven steps, he made his way to the door and left. He stood under the portico for several minutes, collecting himself, disbelief raging through him. Pain squeezed his heart. He had not felt such despair and desertion since Tetty's death had left him a widower many years ago.

Defending Misella, helping her, loving her had given him new life and a renewed sense of purpose that had slipped away as the years passed. What did he have to look forward to now? A void. Nothingness. Except the difficult task of informing Jack Finn that his world had also contracted to none but a vacuum.

Chapter 27

Jack Finn returned to the Tavern after spending a couple of hours checking out the shops in the area. He found a cobbler's shop for Turner that offered a selection of ready-made shoes with sturdy heels and laces, and bought a pair for himself. At a local tailor shop, he had ordered himself an everyday suit. He asked both shopkeepers about employment in the area but didn't receive any leads.

He spotted Turner sitting at a far corner table beside the empty, cave-like fireplace draining his glass, with a fat bottle of what looked like brandy and another glass in front of him. The bar was uncrowded this early in the afternoon, and Finn wondered why Turner chose to hide himself in the corner. He suspected that the heat and the walk back and forth to the customs house left him exhausted and in one of his black moods. The brandy, Finn knew, would only make it worse, so he prepared himself for some snarled accusations and complaints.

But when he reached the table, Turner spoke in a subdued voice. "Hello, Finny. Join me in a drink." He poured a generous amount into the extra glass and pushed it across the table. "Hot out there, isn't it? Where did you go?"

Finn held up the box. "Found shoes for me," he said putting the box on the floor next to his chair. "If you like them, we can go back and get you a pair."

Turner shook his head. "Not now." He refilled his glass and carefully set the bottle down. "I have something to tell you—about

Misella." His voice cracked, and he swallowed a few times. "I saw the transportation document. Misella died on the ship and was buried at sea."

Finn jolted back in his chair. He set his glass down before he had taken a drink, spilling some of the brandy onto the table. "What are you talking about, old man? Maybe you didn't read the list carefully with your half-blind eyes. I'll go back with you to look again."

Turner closed his eyes and lowered his head. When he looked up again at Finn, his eyes flooded with tears, he said, "I'm sorry, Jack. This is difficult for both of us. But there was no mistake. I pressed the customs house clerk about that. He told me Misella's death was especially notable because Captain Barclay has never lost a prisoner on his ship for as long as he has been in the transportation business."

Finn shook his head, the shock taking away his breath for a moment until he was able to speak. "What was the cause of death?" His voice caught in his throat. "Barclay was paid to keep her safe."

"No cause was listed. The clerk told me something else, but I was only half listening. Now, though, I remember his words, and I am beginning to wonder about Barclay and his promise. The clerk said another unusual occurrence happened soon after the sale of prisoners took place on the ship. The ship's First Mate rushed in to the customs house the morning after the sale inquiring whether anyone in the customs house had seen a crew member who had deserted, a large man by the name of James Logan. Though desertion is a common problem on these ships, it had never happened before on Captain Barclay's watch."

Finn frowned, picked up his glass and drained it, and slammed it down on the table. "We can't wait for Barclay's return in October. I'll find Logan and make him talk." He grabbed the bottle and poured himself another full drink. Glaring at Turner, he declared, "That's what I intend to do, and I won't stop until I find him. Will you join me?"

Turner shook his head. "I understand, my boy. But that won't bring her back." He sighed deeply. "While waiting for you, I have pondered my own situation. I fear I must return to Old England. There is nothing for me here now, and I have a debt to repay." Sorrow and immense regret showed in his face and shadowed his words. "I pray that Chaz will take me back when I show up on his doorstep, an old fool—a half-blind beggar."

Finn cursed, anger curdling his words. "So you just give up. The brilliant barrister retreating like a cowed mongrel. You sought justice for her once. You owe it to her to find out what happened to her and why."

Turner slowly shook his head again. "No," he said. "But there is one thing I can do for her. I can go to Boston before I leave and try to find her father and sisters. I want them to know her story; I want them to remember her as I will—a woman of enormous courage and strength and grace."

Chapter 28

Misella spent a sleepless night tossing on the straw mat in the windowless pantry, contemplating how to handle the problem of Mr. Briar. She would have to be clever enough to convince Mrs. Dobbs that Mr. Briar needed her to help him in place of Misella. She thought about how Ben Turner had handled his adversaries in the courtroom when he mounted her defense, especially against her nemesis, Isobel.

He had used flattery and sympathy to disarm Isobel before challenging her misconceptions about the guilt of the accused. Misella was determined to find a way to do the same with both Mrs. Dobbs and Mr. Briar. She would need to convince them first of all that she was sincerely penitent for her crimes. She could start by quoting the psalms at appropriate times—she knew most of them by heart, thanks to her father who taught them to her when she was a child—and reading the Bible as often as possible. And asking them both, especially Mrs. Dobbs, to help her return to her Christian faith. Only when she had made up her mind to become a saint in their eyes did Misella finally close hers and get some much needed sleep.

She arose before sunrise, lit the kitchen candle, and put on the tea kettle. She placed her worn copy of the psalms on the table under the candle, ignoring the stained cover and the flyleaf, and opened it to Psalm 32: *I acknowledged my sin unto thee, and mine iniquity I have not hid. I said, "I will confess my transgressions unto the Lord;" and thou forgavest the iniquity of my sin.*

She prepared a pot of oatmeal and set the wood ablaze in the cast-iron stove. She murmured the words as Mrs. Dobbs bustled into the kitchen. A look of surprise transformed the scowl on her face.

"What's that you're muttering?" she asked. She glanced down at the book of psalms and snatched it up, leaning into the light to see what trash Misella might be reading. "Where did you get this book?" she demanded, her voice sharp. "Did Mr. Briar give it to you?"

"No, ma'am," Misella murmured. "This belonged to my dear Father who insisted long ago that I memorize all of them. I struggled to do that before he died, but have only gotten as far as this one. He always carried this book with him and had it in his jacket pocket when he died at Culloden." Misella raised a corner of her apron, seeming to wipe her eyes, and prayed that Margaret would forgive her lie."

Eyebrows raised, Mrs. Dobbs noticed the stained cover and opened it to see the scrawled words *I want to die* on the inside. She glanced up at Misella with a glint of tears in her eyes. "Your father fought at the battle of Culloden?" she asked, a softness in her voice Misella had never heard. "My father and brother died there, too." She rubbed her hands slowly back and forth over the cover and closed her eyes for a moment. "We were of the Duncan clan," she said with pride. When the teakettle began to steam, her eyes flew open, and she put the book back on the table.

"Enough of the melancholy," she said briskly, a scowl enclosing her face again. "Get busy. We have much work to do today." She pulled a paper from her apron pocket and handed it to Misella. "You will start with this list as soon as you finish the breakfast service." She was about to leave the room, but turned back as the darkness beyond the small kitchen window began to dissipate. "Was Mr. Briar satisfied with your work last night?"

Misella lowered her gaze and, in silence, began to fiddle with the paper, folding and opening it, in an effort to appear embarrassed.

Mrs. Dobbs raised her voice and stepped closer to Misella. "What did he say to you? Answer me, Miss, and tell me the truth."

Misella sniffled and covered her mouth as if trying to hold back tears. She gulped a few times and then blurted out, "I don't think he likes me. He thinks I'm too slow. 'Slow-witted,' I think I heard him mumble more than once. 'Not like Mrs. Dobbs.'"

A hint of a smile relieved some of the tightness of Mrs. Dobbs' face. "He will come to his senses soon enough and realize he needs my help. When he does, I'll release you from that chore." Seeming almost cheerful, she said, "Carry on," and darted from the room.

When Mr. Briar entered the dining room for breakfast, dressed in his black suit, he bowed to Mrs. Dobbs and ignored Misella. He remained silent after the long grace before meals said on this morning by one of the other boarders. His voice was harsh when he asked Misella to refill his tea cup halfway through the meal. Her hands shaking, she spilled a little of the tea on his place mat. He scolded her, "Stupid girl. Watch what you are doing."

Mrs. Dobbs smiled. "Have patience, Mr. Briar. The girl is doing the best she can. With my help, she will improve."

Chapter 29

Upon arriving in Boston, Ben Turner rented a room for the night at an inexpensive inn on Water Street near the harbor. "Do you happen to know of a fisherman around here named Johnnie Cross?" he asked the wizened inn keeper, bent over the wooden reception counter, his gnarled hands gripping the edges. The old man chewed his plug of tobacco, his weathered brow wrinkled in thought.

"Nope," he said. "Can't say that I do." He spat a brown string of liquid into a metal can resting on a stool next to him. "Ask down at the harbor. Those fellas would know."

Turner thanked him and headed for the harbor, grateful for the sturdy new shoes he wore and to Finn for showing him where to buy them. Not that the streets in Boston were any easier to navigate than those in Annapolis. The closer he came to the harbor, the more he felt he could be back in London approaching the Thames: the surrounding area clogged with brick row houses, streets teeming with horse-drawn carriages, push carts, locals on horseback, and pedestrians in a hurry.

The briny smell of fish enveloped him as he stepped onto a long wooden pier. A second pier further down housed larger sailing ships, their folded sails inert while they docked. A few ships in the distance with sails furled moved out of the harbor, their country of origin flags snapping to attention in the wind.

Turner accosted a young fisherman in patched britches and a damp-looking plaid shirt as he emptied a minnow bucket at the side of the pier. "Can you help me, lad? I'm looking for Johnnie Cross, an old friend of mine. Do you know him?"

Squinting in the sun, the young fellow shaded his eyes and looked at Turner. He set the bucket down. "Sure do. I work for him," he said. "Pilot one of his fishing boats."

Startled, Turner introduced himself and explained that he hoped to surprise his friend whom he hadn't seen in years. "Not since he left Portsmouth, England. Could you direct me to where he lives?"

"Sure could," the young man answered. He pulled a red kerchief from his pocket releasing a strong odor of fish and wiped his hands. He replaced the kerchief and drew a map with his fingers in the palm of his hand, describing landmarks along the route to the address he provided.

Turner thanked him, and decided to take a carriage rather than walk the several blocks to the Cross home. He was astonished by the ease with which he had located Misella's father and dumbfounded to discover that the poor fisherman was now a merchant with his own fishing fleet. The lovely gray, thatch-roofed house in front of him provided evidence of Johnnie Cross' success.

He walked up the stone steps and lifted the knocker, but before he could drop it, the door flung open. "Father, home already?" The young woman looked startled. "Oh, I beg your pardon. I heard your approach and thought Father had come home a day early." She tucked a few stray rust-colored curls under her linen cap, a blush infusing her face. "I'm afraid you will have to return tomorrow if you want to see him. He's taken the catch to St. Michael's."

"You must be Elinor," Turner said. "Misella told me about you and her other sisters."

Elinor blanched and placed her hand on her chest. "Misella? You know her? Oh, please, do you know where she is?" Tears gathered in her gray eyes.

"Yes, I know," Turner answered solemnly. "May I come in and tell you about her?"

"Of course. I cannot believe we may find her after all of these years." She swung the door wide and ushered him into a small foyer. "Father will be overjoyed." She led him into the dim parlor. The shades drawn against the brightness of the sun left the room cool and inviting. "Please sit down," she said breathlessly, taking his cane and placing it next to a wing-back chair. "I'll bring a glass of lemonade. Would you like something to eat?" She hovered over him, a look of pure bliss lighting up her plain, freckled face. "If only Annabelle were here, too. She would be so excited."

She paused for a moment and took a deep breath. "You probably have heard of Annabelle. Misella will be happy to know that she has married a sea captain and returned to England. I am the only daughter left to care for father. But I don't mind. He needs me, and he is grateful for my help with the household and his business." She laced her fingers together and swung them back and forth. "Oh, I can't wait to tell Father that you know Misella," she said, gliding from the room, her feet barely touching the floor.

Turner bowed his head and uttered a quick prayer, seeking the strength and the right words to tell this sweet sister that she would not see Misella again. Perhaps, it would be better to tell Elinor and allow her to break the dreadful news to her father in her own way. He looked up as Elinor swept into the parlor, a loaded tray in her hands. She placed it on a wheeled side table and steered it over to him.

"Here we are," she said, with a lilt in her voice. She pulled a matching chintz-covered chair close, sat down across from him and poured two glasses of lemonade. She placed one before him along with a plate of cut scones spread with strawberry jam. "You didn't say that you were hungry," she said looking at him with a smile, "but in case you are."

Her thoughtfulness and attention warmed Turner's heart. He hated to destroy the lovely mood she had created in this homey setting. "Thank you kindly," he said and picked up the glass taking a long drink to ease his dry throat. He could not eat. He feared he might choke on a scone. "First allow me to properly introduce myself." He bowed slightly. "Benjamin Turner, Attorney at Law, until recently of the King's Court in London."

She registered a look of surprise and then put out her hand. "I am so pleased to meet you," she said. "I have never had the pleasure of meeting a barrister before." He enclosed her small, callused hand in his, remembering to lighten his grasp from his usual hard clench, although her fingers felt strong and capable of surviving such pressure. "How did you meet Misella?" she asked, her face aglow, her bright smile erasing the distraction of all the freckles.Turner was intrigued by her; he had never seen any other woman display her freckles so openly, not bothering to cover them up with powder or paint.

"It is a long story," he said. "I hope you have time to listen to it now or would you prefer that I return tomorrow after your father …."

"Oh, please," she interrupted, "I cannot wait that long." She leaned forward in her chair. "I'll die of suspense. I have prayed since Misella left us that I would have a chance to tell her how sorry I am for the way I treated her." She hung her head, a deep blush rising to her cheeks, and wrung her hands together. When she looked up, tears once again shone in her eyes. "I wouldn't even say goodbye to her when she left us. I pushed her away, not letting her hug me. And… and I called her Mother's pet, and…" She squeezed her eyes shut forcing the tears onto her reddened cheeks. "I called her a trollop," she murmured.

Turner withdrew his handkerchief from his pocket and gently blotted her tears. "I'm sure Misella forgave you long ago. She told me how much she missed all of you.

She did not blame you for resenting her or her seeming good fortune. In fact, she told me she came to regret her vanity and to realize how her own actions and arrogance had contributed to the breach between the two of you."

Elinor clasped her hands together, a look of joy returning to her face. "You have made me so very happy, Sir. Thank you for finding us here. How did you know where we lived?"

"Misella told me that in his last letter to her, your father mentioned moving to Boston with you and your sister Annabelle." Turner glanced down, unable to continue for a moment. He had to force himself to look at her, willing himself to keep going. "Your father is well-known here."

"Yes, he has created a good life for us here. It will be so much better when Misella is able to join us. Please, can you tell me where she is and when that might be?"

Turner cleared his throat and nodded. "Unfortunately, hers is not a happy story nor does it have a happy ending." He sat forward in his chair and took one of her small hands in his own. "My dear girl," he began, "this will not be easy for either of us. But I will start from the beginning and tell you all that I know."

Chapter 30

Jack Finn slumped over the bar at Reynolds Tavern, lifting his head to stare at the empty glass tipped over in front of him. He righted the glass, sat up, and called to Harry, the burly bartender who was busy sweeping up. "Hey, lad, pitch the broom and let's have another. Come on."

Harry put the broom down and locked the entrance door. "No more tonight, Old Sod. We're closed. Up to bed with you now. I'll help you up the stairs as usual."

Finn shook his head back and forth. "Can't," he muttered. "Can't quit, can't find the chap, can't sleep." He shoved the glass, and it rolled off of the bar bouncing along the wooden floor. Resting both elbows on the bar, Finn dropped his head onto his arms and closed his eyes.

Harry grabbed the broom, picked up the glass and moved behind the bar. He poked Finn's shoulder with the top of the broom. "Let's go. Wake up. I don't want to have to carry you up those stairs like I did last night."

Finn lifted one hand and slapped the broom handle away. "Leave me alone. Go away, unless you can give me a drink or help me find James Logan."

Harry came around the bar and slapped Finn on the shoulder. "Wake up! Enough of the wallowing in your cups. If this woman was your heaven and earth, as you've claimed, and you can't accept what happened to her, then do something about it. Prowl the streets; keep looking for him. I told you yesterday, get away from the harbor; explore the hovels across town. A deserter wouldn't hang around this part of town." He stripped off his leather apron and laid it across the bar. "Or give it up and move on."

Raising his head and opening one bleary eye, Finn muttered, "My heaven has fallen and shattered on this blasted, dirty earth. I told her once that whenever she was frightened to use my Irish motto, and it would help. 'Chin up; eyes to Heaven.'" Finn threw back his head, lifting up his chin and his eyes, and laughed. "There's nothing there. Nothing left for me."

He swayed on his bar stool and would have fallen to the floor if Harry hadn't grabbed him under his arms and lifted him up. Struggling with the weight of him, Harry managed to hoist him over one shoulder, Finn's head bobbing, black curls falling across his eyes. He huffed up the stairs to Finn's room and dropped him on the narrow bed. Covering him with a quilt, Harry said, though he knew Finn couldn't hear him, "It's not the end of the world."

He noticed a notebook laying on the table next to the bed and picked it up. Riffling through it, he was struck by the crossed-off list of taverns Finn had visited in his crazed quest to find Logan. If the Irishman had had a few pints at each of these places, it explained why he showed up drunk and discouraged back at the Reynolds every night. Harry ripped a page from the book, picked up the quill, uncorked the pot of ink, and scratched out a new list—every cheap joint he could think of, hidden in the bowels of town, with directions. He placed the list on top of the notebook and left the room.

The next morning, the sun streaming through the tiny window across from Finn's bed heated his face, shone in his half-opened eyes, made his head pound. He turned over and kicked off the quilt. His throat felt as if it had been raked with a comb, his mouth ash dry. His feet ached, still clad in the heavy workman's boots he had borrowed from Harry. His skin itched from the rough muslin britches and shirt he still wore, his bar-hopping costume that reminded him of his boyhood days working the farm in Ireland. He missed those simple, uneventful days. He'd had enough of adventure, of derring-do that had rendered him a fugitive and prevented him from ever returning home. Now, without Misella, what did he have left to live for? To fight for?

He sat up to take off the boots that plagued him and reached for the jug of water on the bedside table. The paper sitting on top of his notebook fluttered onto the bed as he picked up the water. Confused by the unfamiliar handwriting, he studied the paper, crumpled it into a ball, and tossed it across the room. He resented Harry's nosy interference—he hadn't asked for his help, and he didn't want it. He was done. After guzzling the water, he dropped the jug back on the table, curled up on the bed and closed his eyes.

Misella's face sprang forth, the portrait Turner had shared with him, her mature image unlike the girlhood vision of her that he remembered best from their early days together. She had been a poor, insecure twelve-year old newly arrived at Hawthorn Manor, Sir Richard's protégé, and he the family coachman, rescued from a highwayman's life by Sir Richard. As she grew into a lovely young woman, he had tried to warn her, to protect her from the lascivious Lord Richard Maltby. But Sir Richard, aware of Finn's betrayal and his love for Misella, had turned him over to the authorities and had him sent to Newgate prison. He had not seen her again until she herself ended up in Newgate, abandoned by Sir Richard and accused of murder.

As he lay in his bed, the unforgiving sun beating down on his head, he thought about Ben Turner and all he had done to help Misella. Throughout her trial, he had never given up. His single-minded goal was to save her from the gallows. And he had succeeded.

With a groan, Finn dragged himself out of bed and retrieved the balled-up list from the far corner of his room. He studied the wrinkled sheet Harry had left for him. He would start with the last one on the list, the *Duke of Perth*, furthest from the Harbor, and work his way up the list, no matter how long it would take him. And he would stick with sarsaparilla. No more alcohol, he vowed to himself, until he found Logan.

Chapter 31

Finn sauntered into the *Duke of Perth* pub as if he belonged there, though clearly he didn't, and the seedy clientele slouched over the bar at 10:00 o'clock in the morning didn't think so either. Even with his wrinkled muslin shirt, uncombed hair and muddy boots, he stood out—an unwelcome stranger among the bruised, bearded group of regulars eying him with dark suspicion. Nevertheless, he squeezed himself into the only vacant spot at the stand-up bar, dropped a handful of coins onto the scratched wooden surface, and called out to the hefty bartender. "A shot of whiskey, if you please, my good man. Rough night last night."

The bartender smirked, crossed his arms over the bulk of his chest and remained where he was.

Finn nudged the troll-like creature stooped barely upright next to him, a messy gray braid entwined with beads and feathers trailing down the curve of his back. "I say old chief, the big Gallopus must be deaf or daft if he doesn't want my money. Which is it?" He shoved the pile of coins in front of the old man. "Maybe he'll open his ears for you. Order what you want and tell him to give everybody a drink. Including me."

The old man stared at the money for a few seconds, raised his head and squinted at Finn. "Do I know you?" he mumbled. He shook his head back and forth, the braid flipping from side to side. "Never seen you before. You're not from around here." He pushed the coins back with the stump of his wrist and then thrust the scarred end of it in Finn's face. "See how they treat outsiders?"

Finn grabbed hold of the filthy wrist and shook it up and down as if the hand was still attached. "I'm pleased to meet another outsider. I've been one all of my highwayman days in bloody old England. And in Newgate before I escaped and ended up here, thanks to the pirates who couldn't wait to dump me off their ship."

The bartender wandered over. "In Newgate you say? I know the place well." He held out the fat thumb on his right hand, the letter "F" plainly visible beneath a thin layer of dirt, identifying him as a felon branded for a first offense and soon hanged if caught in Britain for committing another crime.

Finn laughed and held up his own marked thumb which he usually kept gloved or hidden under his shirt sleeve. "We're brothers, my friend, in that fine British tradition of "benefit of clergy." With that, Finn began to recite the passage from scripture that had kept him from the gallows early in his Robin Hood days. The bartender joined him in a loud, boisterous voice:

Have mercy upon me, O God, according to thy loving kindness: according unto the multitude of thy tender mercies blot out my transgressions. Wash me thoroughly from mine iniquity, and cleanse me from my sin. For I acknowledge my transgressions: and my sin is ever before me.

"You'll be having a bumper on me," the bartender said, "Put your money away." Grabbing a bottle and shot glass from under the bar, he poured a generous splash of whiskey and placed it in front of Finn. "Where are ye from, lad? I'd wager from the mouth and the brashness of ye, must be Connemara."

Finn smiled and nodded. "That's right, I'm a Connemara lad." He guessed he would have to drink the whiskey after all despite his earlier determination to remain sober until he found Logan. It wouldn't do to offend his newfound friend. He tossed back the shot. "Up the Irish," he said, slamming the glass onto the bar.

With a nod of approval, the bartender refilled the glass and helped himself to a shot. "I'm a Cork man, me self," he said, downing the whiskey. "A long way from home, but the heart never leaves."

Finn nodded in agreement. He poured another round, filling the old Indian's glass as well. "Indentured I was for ten of my fourteen years' sentence to the Scots bastard who owned this place," the bartender scoffed. "Drank himself to death when he wasn't pounding the devil out of me. Nobody cared. I took the place over after he died. I'd done all of the work anyway." He shrugged his beefy shoulders.

Finn wanted to keep him talking. "You deserved the place then. There's none can argue with that. I'm looking to find some decent work here beyond the few odd jobs I found after I arrived two weeks ago." He tossed back his second shot of whiskey. "Hoping to find an old friend of mine who might help me. He told me if I ever ended up in Annapolis to look him up. This is where he intended to stay if he ever managed to get here."

The bartender frowned. "What's his name? Maybe I know him."

"Logan," Finn answered. "James Logan—a giant of a man. Can't miss him in a crowd."

The old Indian's head bolted up. "The woodsman," he muttered. "I know him. You'll not find him. He doesn't want to be found."

In his excitement, Finn grabbed the Indian's arm too hard causing him to flinch and pull away. "Please, can you take me to him right now? I'll pay you."

The Indian shook his head, rubbing the spot on his arm where Finn had held him. Flipping the loose braid back over his shoulder, he mumbled, "Moves around a lot. He finds me, when he needs supplies. I don't find him."

"When will you see him again? How soon before he'll need supplies?" When he noticed a look of concern cross the bartender's ruddy face, Finn took a deep breath and tried to control himself. He sensed that his eagerness was creating suspicion in the Indian as well who studied him with his piercing, inscrutable eyes before he answered.

"Can't say. Maybe a few settings of the sun. Or many."

Finn tried to hide his growing frustration. "If I give you a note to deliver to him, could you do that for me? I'll pay you well for your trouble."

The bartender chimed in. "Can the lad read? Cause old Gray Feathers here can't, so he can't help him if he's ill--iterate."

"He's schooled," Finn asserted, praying that this might be true. "That's where we first met as youngsters." He pulled his notebook and the stub of a wood pencil from his pocket. Flipping the book open to a blank sheet, he wrote:

James Logan,

My name is Jack Finn, a very close friend of one Misella Cross, an indentured convict aboard the Seaflower that recently landed here. I followed her here at great peril. I know that you worked that ship and were there when Misella Cross died and was buried at sea. I need to know how and why she died. Can you meet me at your convenience? I'll come to any meeting place you choose.

Yours in desperation,
Jack Finn

He tore the sheet from the book, withdrew a five-pound note from his pocket and added it with the note before he folded it in half and then in quarters. He wrote Logan's name in bold letters on the outside and handed it solemnly to the old Indian.

"Please," he begged. "Get this into his hands as soon as you can. I'll return every morning to await his response. And I will go wherever he wants to meet me. I pray this will reach him soon. Thank you for your kind help."

The Indian snatched the note with his good hand and tucked it into the soiled leather pouch he wore around his scrawny neck. He pointed a crooked finger at his empty glass.

Finn signaled the bartender to fill it and pushed the pile of coins over to the Indian. "I'll see you tomorrow," he said to the two men as he turned away from the bar and walked out the door.

When word finally came after a week of mornings spent reliving his Newgate days with Declan Ryan, the bartender who now considered him a long-lost friend, Finn managed to keep his elation in check. The Indian waited for him in his usual place at the bar, but he stood straighter, his gaze more alert. "You come with me now," he told Finn. "For two moons."

"Now? Do you mean that we'll be gone two days? Shouldn't I bring food or weapons?"

The Indian grunted. "Now. We go deep in the woods. You help me bring supplies." With that, he pushed away from the bar and glided to the door, his moccasins barely skimming the floor. He turned and waited for Finn to follow him, which he did—hope fueling his heart and bringing him back to life.

Chapter 32

Though he tried to keep pace with the old, wordless Indian, Finn trailed behind him as he wound his way out of town. When he reached the edge of the forest, the Indian stopped and waited for him to catch up. Finn decided that maybe this was his punishment for making fun of Turner and his insufferable cane whenever on their travels Turner had struggled to keep up. The old, bent Gray Feathers was teaching him a lesson in humility.

They moved further into the trees; the cool interior offered shaded relief from the intense summer sun. The Indian hesitated at a small opening in a thick clutch of elderberry vines and pushed his way further in. Finn followed, batting at a swarm of mosquitos that surrounded his head. Resting on a flat stone in the middle of the small clearing sat a fat burlap sack, its top wound and knotted with a thick rope of twine. On the ground next to the stone lay a pair of shabby beaded moccasins, larger than the ones the Indian wore. The Indian pointed to them. "Put them on; leave your boots."

Finn did as he was told though he wondered if the leather moccasins could protect his feet as well as his heavy boots. At least, they fit and they felt comfortable, which made him wonder how the Indian knew they would. He watched as the old man hoisted the bag over his shoulder, pulling the braid free and flipping it over his other shoulder. He grunted once with the weight of the bag, but stepped out of the clearing ready to continue their journey. "I can carry that for you," Finn offered, but the Indian shook his head. "Later," he said, and proceeded with the same lightness of foot as before.

They walked for hours along a narrow, light-dappled path, not really a path so much as a meandering row of wild grass bent over, no doubt, by the touch of many other tribal footsteps. Finn dared not complain, but he was hungry and panting and parched. How out of shape he had grown in the days spent "wallowing in his cups," as Harry would say. But he had to admit that his feet felt great.

They came upon a small lake surrounded by tufts of wild grasses dotted here and there with clumps of wildflowers. The Indian stopped and dropped the bag under a mighty oak tree, its trunk thick with lichen. "We camp here till sunrise." He unknotted the twine, opened the bag, and retrieved two clay bowls and a thin leather pouch. He laid the pouch on a cloth-like woven strip and opened it to reveal chunks of corn pone and generous slivers of dried meat. Finn could have cried with gratitude. He grabbed a bowl and followed the Indian into the water, clear and sweet enough to drink his fill.

The Indian plucked a handful of wild blossoms, dunked them in the water and carried them to shore where he laid them atop the corn pone. He gathered great handfuls of twigs which he piled up and lit with a flint drawn from the bag. He filled his bowl with some of the flower-decorated corn pone and a few strips of meat, crouched with legs crossed next to the fire, and began to eat with an air of quiet dignity.

Finn copied the Indian, slipping off his moccasins and setting them next to the fire to dry before crouching and tackling his meal. After the Indian had packed his clay pipe with tobacco leaves, lit it with a twig dipped in the fire, and sat puffing contentedly, Finn asked, "When do I meet Logan?"

"First sunlight; we wait." He piled more wood on the fire. "You sleep, I watch." He drew a thin woven mat, rolled tight and tied with twine, from the bag and tossed it to Finn. After Finn untied it and opened it flat, the Indian gestured for him to lay it close to the fire. Finn stretched out on the grass mat as dark began to close in, and the sounds of night animals filled the forest.

"Wake me in a few hours," he said, "and I'll take over the watch." The Indian chuckled in the darkness but said nothing.

Finn stared at the night sky, his mind churning with thoughts of Misella. She had survived so many challenges in her young life, had stood at the threshold of death before and always managed to step back. He could not believe that this time she was gone. He still felt her presence as he had during the years he was separated from her.

He remembered the first near fatal time—when she had almost drowned, unable to swim, pushed into the sea by Isobel. He reached the twelve-year-old Misella just in time, dragged her to shore, and throttled her until she coughed up half the ocean, it seemed. He couldn't save her from the clutches of Sir Richard, though. Nor could he have saved her from the gallows as Ben Turner did. Or from the ravages of her voyage to the New World. Turner had tried.

What had gone wrong this time? He had to find out what happened to her on that ship. He could not accept the cruel irony that she was the only one to die—maybe through Logan he could finally face the truth and admit to himself that he would never see her again. He swallowed his sobs, but he could not suppress the silent tears that dripped soundlessly into the grass.

He awoke in the gray dawn to the murmuring of voices and the crackling of the rejuvenated fire. He sat up, somewhat disoriented, and saw the Indian crouching by the fire with a Goliath of a young man towering next to him on the ground though he leaned forward with his arms resting on his bent knees. They both looked up, the Indian grinning, the young man's face hidden by a mane of dirty-looking blond hair.

He pushed the hair aside and stood, like a behemoth rising out of the ground, his face obscured by a thick, curly beard and mustache the same color as the hair. "Hello," he mumbled, coming around the fire with his large paw of a hand held out toward Finn in greeting. "You are Misella's friend."

Finn jumped up and grabbed his hand, shaking it with heartfelt warmth. "Yes, Jack Finn. So glad to meet you. Thank you for coming to see me. So you do remember Misella?"

"Of course. I owe her my life," he said with a shy dip of his head. "I wouldn't be here if not for her help."

Jack was startled and a little jealous. "How did she help you?" he demanded in a harsher tone than he intended. As Logan dropped his hand and stepped back, Jack realized that this timid-seeming young man resented the apparent insinuation in his tone. "I'm sorry," he said. "I don't mean to be rude. Please tell me, if you don't mind."

Logan nodded with another shy dip of his head, his blue eyes lighting up. "I had made up my mind to desert the ship when we docked at Annapolis. I waited until the convicts had been sold off and the whole crew, including the Captain, went ashore to celebrate. Misella took my night duty and rang the bell every hour giving me a five-hour head start before the Captain returned."

"Annapolis?" Jack said, shaking his head in confusion. "But she was dead before then—and buried at sea."

"No, no," Logan blurted out. "Not her. She's not dead. She's not the one that died."

Jack stumbled backwards, his bare feet tripping over the grass mat, and sat down hard. He scrambled back up, reaching out and grabbing on to Logan's arm with both hands. "What are you saying? What do you mean, she's not the one?" he asked, his voice rising. "Where is she?"

Logan freed his arm from Jack's vise-like grip, flexing the muscles and swinging the arm back and forth to restore the circulation. "She must be in Boston. That's where the Captain was taking her. It was another young girl who died, Margaret MacDonald. No, not died. Murdered by Amos Bristol, the First Mate." Logan's eyes blazed as if sparked by the fire behind him. "If I ever get my hands on that vermin, I swear I will crush the life out of him as he did to her."

"But Misella is listed on the transportation contract as dead and buried at sea." Jack still could not grasp that Misella had somehow returned to life. "How did that happen?"

The younger man shrugged his massive shoulders. "I don't know why Misella's name was listed in place of Margaret's, but Bristol and the Captain would know. Probably to cover up what he did to Margaret. As innocent as an angel, she was."

Jack was surprised to see tears gathering in Logan's eyes before he turned away and swiped his sleeve across his face. "What did she look like?" he asked, more out of sympathy for Logan than any curiosity about the girl.

"If you know Misella," Logan answered with a sniff and another swipe across his eyes, "you'll know how Margaret looked. Like she could have been Misella's sister, or her twin, the Captain said, before she was trussed up and tossed like rubbish into the sea."

The light flashed on in Jack's brain. *Of course,* he thought to himself, *they changed Misella's identity so that the Captain could protect his investment, his payment due on delivery from Ben Turner.* He had to reach Boston right away before Ben Turner departed for England—to tell him the amazing news about Misella's rebirth and to find the new Margaret MacDonald.

Chapter 33

Ben Turner held tight to Elinor's hand as they sat across from one another in her parlor. Without flinching, he began the story of Misella's arrival at Hawthorn Manor, her cruel reception by Isobel, the daughter, and Sir Richard's wife, her life as a scullery maid confined to the garret. Elinor listened without saying a word, only releasing an occasional gasp of shock as Ben described how Sir Richard had seemed to mentor Misella, isolated her, removed her only friend, Jack Finn, and had him confined in Newgate prison, and finally had seduced and impregnated her.

Elinor cried when she learned that Misella had given birth alone and penniless in London, abandoned by Sir Richard and consigned to a life of prostitution. When he told of the baby Lily's death under the wheels of a carriage, she jumped up, her apron clutched to her mouth to contain her sobs. "Oh, Sir, please," she moaned, "I can bear no more. I don't know how poor Misella could either. Give me a moment, please. I will return." She rushed from the room.

Turner struggled to control the black despair that threatened to overwhelm him.

For Elinor's sake he needed to remain calm, for the worse part was yet to come. Perhaps he should wait, he decided, until the next day to tell her of Misella's death, when her father would be there. He sensed that each of them would try to remain strong and thus support one another.

Elinor returned with her face composed, her bearing stoic, though her watery reddened eyes bespoke her misery. "I am so sorry, Sir. It won't happen again. Please continue with Misella's story."

Turner stood and buried her hand in both of his. "My dear, I wish I did not have to tell you all of this. It is painful, I know. I would like to return tomorrow when your Father is here and tell you both the rest of her story. Would you find that agreeable? I would like him to know all I have told you before I continue."

He knew that Elinor suspected the worst and had needed to steel herself in private to prepare for the ending of the story. She was not an obtuse young woman. In fact, he admired her gentle compassion, her fortitude. He had to admit that he found her plainness and simplicity genuine and appealing, a welcome relief from the turmoil he had always experienced with Misella.

She offered the ghost of a smile. "Yes, of course," she murmured. "I agree that would be best. I will prepare Father so that when you return tomorrow, we will both be ready to receive you. Late afternoon, if you can. That would allow enough time for Father to settle in." She felt drawn to this kind, compassionate gentleman. Yearning to spend more time in his wise presence, though she dreaded hearing the tragic end of Misella's story, she added, "And please, Sir, do plan to have supper with us."

Turner felt a sudden jolt of happiness that pierced the cloud of gloom hanging over him since Annapolis. "Thank you, my dear. I am delighted to accept."

Chapter 34

Mr. Briar huffed through the door of his bedroom, hat in his hand, his gray hair standing up above his creased brow as if he had been overtaken by a brisk wind. Misella was surprised to see him back so soon; she had waited to clean his room until she saw him duck out the front door not wanting to risk being alone with him after the previous night's work session. "Hurry, Miss, Mrs. Dobbs needs you in the parlor immediately."

Misella supposed this had something to do with her morning confession to Mrs. Dobbs about Mr. Briar's unhappiness with her work. She feared Mrs. Dobbs may have talked to him about it and found out from him that she had lied. If so, she faced another attack from Mrs. Dobbs just when she seemed to have warmed up a tiny bit.

Leaving her bucket and rags in the room, she rushed down the stairs and into the parlor, stopping dead just inside the door. Across the room, sitting stiff-backed as a Lord in the only upholstered chair sat Amos Bristol, the *Seaflower's* notorious First Mate in full uniform.

Misella's throat constricted, stopping her breath and stealing her voice. A chill tingled in her legs and traveled up her spine. She leaned against the door jamb and fought to keep her balance.

He stood, tucked his tri-cornered hat under his arm, and with the shadow of a smile on his pale, pock-marked face said, "Well, hello there. . . Margaret. I was just telling Mrs. Dobbs how the Captain left me here in Boston to line up some new crew members before his next arrival—and to help Mrs. Dobbs keep an eye on you."

Misella knew that he was lying. The Captain would not set sail without his First Mate unless he chose to do so. More likely, the Captain had relieved him of his position, leaving him behind when the *Seaflower* sailed out of the Harbor.

With his hand holding his sheathed sword in place against his leg, he turned toward Mrs. Dobbs and bowed, then faced Misella with an ugly grin. "I have offered to accompany you to purchase kitchen supplies for her the day after tomorrow. So I will return on Wednesday with a carriage, and we can commence with our little shopping trip. Is that satisfactory with you, Mrs. Dobbs?" He asked the question while keeping his menacing gaze trained on Misella.

"Why, that would be much appreciated, Mr. Bristol," crooned Mrs. Dobbs. "I know you must have far better things to do than to run errands for me, but rest assured that I will let Ebenezer, excuse me, Captain Barclay know how much I appreciated the help from such a fine, young man as yourself."

Bristol bowed again in her direction and grabbed Misella's hand as he exited the room. Squeezing it hard, he said in a loud voice, "Until Wednesday then, Margaret. Good bye."

Misella scrubbed her hand across her apron, revolted by his touch, fear weakening her knees. She was trapped, she well knew, in Bristol's web of lies. She could not extricate herself, could not reveal the truth about Bristol without implicating herself and the Captain and subsequently, Ben Turner.

"Return to your chores, Miss," Mrs. Dobbs ordered in her usual harsh voice. "I'll draw up a list of necessary items by Wednesday." Looking past Misella, she noticed Mr. Briar darting toward the front door again as Amos Bristol left. He would have escaped earlier had he not encountered him coming up the walkway and shown him inside.

Mrs. Dobbs called out, "Mr. Briar, may I have a moment with you, please?" He stopped, removed his black hat, and turned to enter the parlor. Mrs. Dobbs flicked her hand at Misella, dismissing her as if she were a bothersome fly.

Misella hurried from the room, heartened by an idea that occurred to her as Mr. Briar brushed past her and dutifully joined Mrs. Dobbs. Perhaps she could solicit Mr. Briar's help with Bristol. She returned to the cleaning of his room, but moved her bucket aside and sat down at his desk. She drew a sheet of parchment from the stack on the desk and with careful thought, wrote him a note:

Dear Mr. Briar,

As you are one of God's most devout servants here on earth, I am appealing to you for your holy guidance on a matter that causes me great concern. The Seaflower's First Mate, Amos Bristol, pursued me relentlessly throughout that journey in an effort to violate my purity, a goal he never achieved under Captain Barclay's watchful eyes. Mr. Bristol has remained in Boston to fulfill some requirements for the Captain until he returns. Today, as you know, he visited Mrs. Dobbs, and, with her permission, will return on Wednesday to pick me up and take me shopping with him, unchaperoned, for whatever Mrs. Dobbs needs. I am afraid to be alone with him. Can you help me?

Your most humble, grateful, and lowly servant,
Margaret MacDonald

P.S. "*Let us consider the duty that God's law doth require of us.*"

Misella was well aware of the irony of her appeal to Mr. Briar, whose erotic desire, she had sensed the night before, presented a possible threat to her future safety. But the threat from Bristol was far more immediate and dire. She hoped with her note to ignite Mr. Briar's sense of holy outrage, and if, underneath, Bristol's intention sparked in him a hidden touch of jealousy—that could help her as well. She prayed that Mr. Briar would not show the note to Mrs. Dobbs.

Chapter 35

Mrs. Dobbs had acted all day as if nothing had changed. She did not mention Amos Bristol and, in fact, rarely spoke throughout dinner. Grim-faced at evening prayers, she ignored both Mr. Briar and Misella, focusing her attention on the readings. She turned away when Mr. Briar approached her afterwards and refused to speak to him, addressing Misella in his presence. "See that Mr. Briar's tea is delivered promptly."

She swept out of the room ahead of Mr. Briar, who trailed self-consciously after her. Both of them had disappeared when Misella left the parlor. The kitchen was silent and deserted. Hands shaking, she spilled some of the tea leaves on the floor as she added them to the tea pot. Grabbing the straw hand broom from the pantry, she hurried to sweep up the dry leaves before Mrs. Dobbs arrived to check on her. But Mrs. Dobbs never appeared.

With trepidation, Misella approached Mr. Briar's room that evening with his tea service. He sat hunched over his desk as before but glanced up at her as she set the tea tray down. A frown clinched his frowzy eyebrows together so that they stretched like a gray caterpillar across his wrinkled brow. He waited for her to pour his tea before he said in his gravelly voice, "Mrs. Dobbs says you are a whiner who likes to make up stories."

Misella remained standing, her hands clenched, fear coursing through her that Mr. Briar not only disbelieved her cry for help, but had also betrayed her to Mrs. Dobbs.

"No, Sir, I am not a dissembler," she said, her voice unsteady. "My Father taught me the value of an honest tongue from the time I was small, along with many lessons from his Book of Psalms. I have tried to live by those examples."

Mr. Briar's frown remained intact. "Hmmm. If that is so, then why are you here as a convicted criminal?"

Misella struggled to remember the details Margaret had told her about her incarceration for theft. "I…I was caught taking some lace from my mother's employer…but only what she had coming to her to cover her missing wages. She couldn't work any longer because she was ill so he…her employer dismissed her without paying her for work she had completed."

Mr. Briar took a long sip of tea, placing the cup with care back in its saucer before he continued. "That sounds rather dubious to me, as I'm sure it did to the constable and the judge who sentenced you. Nevertheless, I shall give you the benefit of clergy"—his grimace intended as a smile—"or rather, the benefit of the doubt this time. I do find it egregious for Mrs. Dobbs to allow Mr. Bristol to accompany you without a proper chaperone. She is too trusting, perhaps, and oblivious to the dangers of concupiscence. Therefore, I will join you for the outing to the market."

Weak with relief and gratitude, Misella sat down on the extra chair next to him. "Thank you, Sir," she murmured. She jumped up when she noticed his empty cup and poured him more tea.

He nodded with approval. "Mrs. Dobbs has agreed to this arrangement with the caveat that she return to her position as my amanuensis.Therefore, I will no longer need your services; however, I am sure she will find some evening chores for you to do instead."

Misella bit her lip to keep from emitting a cry of joy. She could not believe that all of her recent worry about both men had been solved. "God bless you, Sir," she murmured, bowing her head. "I am grateful for your assistance." She picked up the candle holder from the tray, moved to the door and opened it to find Mrs. Dobbs lurking outside, her Bible pressed against her flat chest.

She glared at Misella, her eyes aflame in their bony sockets. Leaning forward, she whispered in Misella's ear as she brushed past. "You will pay for your duplicity, Miss. I intend to find out more about you from Amos Bristol. I knew you could not be trusted."

How foolish I am, Misella thought as she descended the stairs, her heart thumping once again with fear, *to think that I could outwit Mrs. Dobbs or Amos Bristol.* Despondent, she returned to the dark kitchen and placed the candle on the table. She hesitated for a moment, and then, despite Mrs. Dobbs' orders, she refused to extinguish the flame. Its soft glow lit her way into the pantry again. She refused to scurry around in the dark like a rat as she prepared for bed.

Chapter 36

On Wednesday morning, as Misella waited in the kitchen for Amos Bristol to arrive, Mrs. Dobbs handed her a list of items to pick up at the market. "Mr. Briar will handle the money to pay for these," she said with a sneer, folding her arms across her bony chest. "I certainly cannot entrust you with anything of value." She eyed the candle, reduced to a stub, sitting on the table. "And since you have been wasteful with my candles, you will replace them at your own expense. I know you have money. I saw Captain Barclay slip you a few coins before he left. I cannot imagine why." A look of disgust tightened her dry lips and reddened her cheeks. "Or perhaps I can," she snarled.

Mr. Briar's head peeked around the doorway, his face beneath his round black hat flushed, one hand holding his eyeglasses in place. "Ahem, pardon me, Mrs. Dobbs, Mr. Bristol has arrived and awaits us in the hallway. Shall I tell him that Margaret will be ready soon? He is anxious to leave, he said, as the carriage driver charges by the hour."

Mrs. Dobbs seemed annoyed by the interruption. "He's a bit early," she grumbled. "How long have you been standing there?"

Mr. Briar coughed and muttered what sounded like "just a few seconds." He pulled a small handkerchief from his vest pocket, removed his glasses, and patted his face. "We'd best hurry," he mumbled, "and not keep the gentleman waiting any longer."

Stepping aside so that Misella could pass, Mrs. Dobbs addressed Mr. Briar as he hovered in the doorway. "Keep a close eye on this one. See that she doesn't filch any items. And make sure she pays for the candles."

"Yes, ma'am, I will," he responded, with a grimace. "You can rely on me. My only aim is to please you."

Amos Bristol leaned against the front door in his full dress uniform, a pained expression on his face. He straightened up as the three entered the hallway and smiled. "Good. All ready for our little excursion? Off to market we go." He pulled the door open and bowed as Misella and Mr. Briar stepped onto the porch. "We'll be back in a heartbeat," he said to Mrs. Dobbs with a deeper bow. "I wish you could join us."

She patted his arm. "Unfortunately, I'm much too busy, and I detest crowds," she simpered, closing the door gently after him.

A lop-sided carriage waited for them in the road, one front wheel smaller than the other three. A scrawny-looking horse tethered to the carriage munched on the weeds springing up around Mrs. Dobbs' walkway. As they approached the carriage, the rumpled-looking driver pulled a small step stool from under his seat and tossed it on the ground. "There you go, folks," he drawled. "Step right in and we'll be on our way."

Amos Bristol set the stool down in front of the coach door. "Not exactly an elegant conveyance," he said with a smirk, "but the only one I could find on short notice. Better than walking all of the way to Faneuil Hall, wouldn't you agree?" He whipped open the door and stepped in first. Mr. Briar followed him, taking the seat opposite Bristol.

Misella climbed in, closed the door behind her, and sat next to Mr. Briar on the torn leather seat. *Let the driver retrieve his own step stool,* she thought. But the carriage began to move, abandoning the stool on the side of the road. Looking out of the clouded window, she said, "The driver has forgotten to pick up his step stool."

Bristol shrugged his shoulders. "He'll leave it there until we return. That's the problem with sharpers and laggards like him—and you, Margaret. You have to be trained, told what to do—and disciplined when you fail to do it right. Don't you agree, Mr. Briar?"

Mr. Briar cleared his throat, fiddling with his hat that reposed like a large-winged dead bat in the middle of his lap. "Yes, certainly," he mumbled. "We must be trained to follow God's commandments and learn to discipline ourselves."

Misella clenched her fists and bit her lip but remained silent, staring out the window. She devoted her attention to the scenes of Boston as the carriage bumped toward the market near the harbor. The rows of brick homes with church steeples rising in the distance reminded her of Portsmouth when she was a child. She remembered walking for miles with her family to the market there: her father pushing the wheelbarrow loaded with fish; laying out the fish on wooden boards in his assigned stall; watching the sailboats depart from the bay; playing hide and seek with her sisters; darting through the market stalls. The memories brought unwelcome tears to her eyes. She brushed them away not wanting Bristol or Mr. Briar to see them as a sign of her weakness.

When the carriage arrived in front of the building, she noticed that Faneuil Hall resembled the country market in Portsmouth with brick walls enclosing the open ground floor of the market house. A second floor above provided cover from the elements and protected the stalls underneath, although a number of stalls selling dry goods stretched out beyond the walls. Hanging from pegs, scarves and aprons flapped in the wind; wind chimes jingled; hand-carved bird houses swung back and forth. The entrance to the Hall teemed with people pushing their way in and bumping into those on their way out carrying boxes and bulky canvas bags.

Their carriage driver jumped down from his perch and approached the empty coach standing next to his, its door facing away from the entrance. Leaning casually against the side of the coach, he bent over and snatched up the fringed step stool from the ground beneath the coach door. Setting it down next to his carriage door, he flung open the door and said, "All ready for you, folks. Welcome to the Hall. I'll wait right here but hurry it up, won't you? I have another appointment this afternoon."

Bristol stepped down and confronted the driver, bumping him with his shoulder. "You'll finish with my time first, however long it takes—and not before. Understand?"

The driver backed up and removed his soiled cap, unleashing a mop of greasy hair. Bowing low with a flourish, hat in hand, he said, "Absolutely. At your service, Sir."

Bristol pushed him out of the way as Mr. Briar exited the carriage. As Misella was about to step down, Bristol kicked the stool aside. "Put the stool back where it was," he ordered the driver. Misella had to jump down from the carriage, her skirt flipping up around her knees. "Nice pair of legs," he muttered so that only she could hear him. "I can't wait to see more of them, Margaret."

Misella quivered with fury but held her tongue, determined to ignore him. She joined Mr. Briar who waited for her in front of the carriage. Pulling the shopping list from her pocket, she said, "We will need to stay together, Mr. Briar. Please don't lose me."

Mr. Briar nodded. "Come along then," he said taking her elbow and directing her through the crowd. "Not to worry. I'll stay with you."

Misella could have hugged him. She hurried with him along the stalls, familiar with the layout of goods from her Portsmouth days. She knew that the staples on her list such as flour, sugar, corn meal and tea would be located in the center of the building away from gusts of wind or rain. They stocked up on these; Mr. Briar paid, and Misella carried the heavy, packed box.

Mrs. Dobbs grew many of her own vegetables and fruits, but they had to stop for lemons at these busy stalls and then headed straight for the fish stalls; the cheapest fish, Misella recalled, would be those at the far end of the building. She struggled to keep up with Mr. Briar, stopping occasionally to catch her breath and shift the box from one hip to the other. They purchased several scrap pieces of cod and sheepshead, as the list directed, and added the oiled paper-wrapped fish to the box. Misella stopped at the meat stall to pick up a tub of lard.

She had noticed the candle stalls close to the entrance when they entered the Hall and had suggested to Mr. Briar that they purchase the candles at the end of their shopping trip on their way out. He agreed. She stopped there, balancing the box on her hip while Mr. Briar held his hat with both hands and gazed at the crowded surroundings. She managed to pull her coin bag out of her pocket, loosen the strings with her teeth, tip the bag, and pour two coins into her hand. She bought four tall candles for the two shillings and added the package to the box. "We're done, Mr. Briar," she huffed. "Thank you for accompanying me."

He nodded, scurried around a group of older women selecting aprons and headed for the carriage. Misella trailed after him, her arms aching, her chin holding the packaged candles in place atop the loaded box. Mr. Briar had already entered the carriage when she reached the doorway. Bristol leaned out of the open doorway from his seat across from Mr. Briar and said, "Put the box next to Mr. Briar, not under the driver's seat. We don't want that sharper pawing through it and taking whatever catches his eye." Mr. Briar scooted over leaving room for the box.

Misella hoisted the box onto the seat. Bristol patted the empty space beside him. "Hop in, Margaret. You can sit next to me." He turned toward her, away from Mr. Briar's line of vision, and smiled, his right hand gliding up and down his leg.

Misella backed away, picked up the step stool and handed it to their driver. "I'd like to sit up on the seat with you," she told him, "where I can have a better view of the city my first time out. Is that alright with you?"

"Why certainly, little lady," the driver drawled, "I do get lonely up there all by myself." He plopped the stool down, and she scrambled up to the seat, not giving the two inside the carriage time to object. She would rather take her chances with this unsightly imp than allow the monster Bristol anywhere near her. The driver tossed the stool next to the coach in front of his carriage, climbed up and grinned at her, exposing his brown-stained teeth. "Hang on," he said picking up a switch in one hand and the reins in the other. "Here we go." He flicked the switch at the skinny rump of the horse who clopped out into the road and ambled down the street.

When they returned without incident to Mrs. Dobbs' house, the carriage driver jumped down, picked up his stool and placed it so that Misella could climb down easily before he moved it to the doorway and opened it. "Here we are gentlemen, back safe and sound."

Misella leaned in and winched the box into her arms before Bristol and Mr. Briar exited the carriage. The driver waited for Bristol to pay him, counted the coins, and shoved the step stool under his seat. He called after Bristol as he strode up the walkway, "I'm available anytime, Sir. You know where to find me."

Bristol waved a hand in his direction and stopped to wait for Misella as she struggled with the box, allowing Mr. Briar to go ahead. Walking beside her, he whispered in her ear, "Don't think for one sweet moment that you are safe. You're going to pay for your betrayal of me to the Captain. I'll find a way to get you alone."

Misella continued on as if she had not heard him, but her heart pounded in her chest as she wrestled the heavy box through the open doorway where Mrs. Dobbs waited, greeting Bristol with a sunny smile. "I cannot thank you enough, Mr. Bristol, for your help today. You can be sure I will let Ebenezer know how much you have done."

"Oh, it was no trouble at all, Ma'am, he said, in his most obsequious voice, dress hat in hand. "I enjoyed the opportunity, and I'm happy to do it again next Wednesday." He said good-by, about to leave, but hesitated at the open door. "By the way," he added, facing her again, "Mr. Briar needn't bother coming along next time. My aunt will be happy to accompany me when we pick up Margaret. She has some shopping to do then as well."

"Wonderful," said Mrs. Dobbs. "I will look forward to meeting her and telling her what a charming young nephew she has. But I'm sure she knows that."

Bristol smiled. "Good-by, Margaret. See you next week."

Mrs. Dobbs turned toward Misella as if she had forgotten her presence. With a frown drawing her sparse eyebrows together, she grumbled, "Why are you standing there like a dumb scarecrow? Take the box into the kitchen and put everything away."

Misella stumbled into the kitchen, dropping the box with a thud onto the table. She wanted to sit down, rest her head on her arms, and cry with exhaustion and defeat. She had run out of ideas for escaping Bristol's relentless pursuit. She could think of nowhere else to turn.

Chapter 37

Elinor opened the door slowly in answer to Ben Turner's light knock. "Good Evening, Mr. Turner," she said, her eyes downcast, her free hand fumbling with the wide collar of her brown muslin gown. "Please come in." She led him into the dim parlor. "Please sit, Mr. Turner. Father will be down soon. He wanted to change into clean clothes before meeting you. He didn't want to greet you smelling like Boston cod."

"I wouldn't mind the smell," Ben responded. "Not after years of inhaling the odorous air of London. Nor will I mind if you simply address me as Ben. That is, if I may call you Elinor?"

Elinor blushed, her freckles obscured under a layer of deep crimson. Ben feared he had offended her, had become familiar too quickly. He hardly knew her, but he had felt such a strong connection to her the day before. "I'm sorry for upsetting you" he said. "I must learn to mind my manners."

"No need to apologize…Ben," she responded. She lowered her eyes and stared at her hands clasped together against her breasts. "Please do call me Elinor. Your manners are not a problem. It is I who must learn better control of my emotions. Strong feelings, I'm afraid, always send a flush to my face."

Ben placed his hand under her chin and raised it gently. "No, my dear," he said. "I am charmed by your genuineness and honesty. I would not want you to change anything."

She reached up and took his hand. "Thank you," she murmured, holding on to it until she heard her father's footsteps on the stairs. She stepped back, withdrew her hand and turned to her father as he entered the parlor. "Here you are, Father," she said brightly. "Come meet Misella's friend and counselor, the Honorable Benjamin Turner."

Dressed as if ready for Church, Johnnie Cross bowed slightly, his linen waistcoat buttoned, his starched white collar luminous against the bronze of his neck. His face, leathered and lined with fine wrinkles, gave testament to his many years on the water, as did the curve of his shoulders. His blue eyes tense, he seemed anxious as he shook the hand Ben held out in greeting. "It is my pleasure to meet you, Sir, to welcome you to our home, and, above all, to thank you for what you have done for our Misella."

Elinor took his other hand. "Let us sit down together, Father, and Mr. Turner can finish telling us about our dear Misella." She led him to the three chairs she had arranged in front of the marble fireplace, its stacked logs unlit on such a warm July afternoon. "Please sit down, Mr. Turner," she said quietly. Both she and her father waited for Ben to ease himself into a chair before they sat down.

Johnnie Cross leaned forward, his hands clutching the wooden arms of his chair, and addressed Ben, his voice subdued. "Elinor has told me everything you shared with her yesterday Sir. We both realize that the rest of what you have to tell us now may be painful for us to hear. But we are ready."

Ben removed his handkerchief from his pocket and wiped his brow, then laid it, folded in his lap in case he needed it again. "I want you both to know," he began, "how much I grew to love and admire your Misella—for her courage and for her faith in God which she told me, Sir, she learned from you."

Johnnie Cross grimaced, shaking his head back and forth, a shock of silver-streaked black hair flipping across his brow like a Sheepshead caught on a hook. "No. I failed her. It is my fault that she ended up as she did. I knew—I knew that sharper, Sir Richard Maltby, was not trustworthy, and yet I allowed him to take my precious daughter from us for his nefarious entertainment. I will never forgive myself. My poor Misella," he said, his voice choked with emotion, but he looked Ben squarely in the eye as he confessed. "She trusted me, and I betrayed her."

"No, Sir." Ben sat forward, his own discomfort and grief forgotten. He reached out to touch Johnnie Cross' hand. "She forgave you long ago. She found strength throughout her ordeal by consulting the psalms you had trained her in—you helped her more than you know. She loved you; she told me many times how much she missed you." He glanced with tenderness at Elinor. "And you, as well. On her darkest days during her trial, she thought about her childhood, the times she sat with her father, she told me, by the fire and listened to you reading the psalms and telling her stories. Those memories kept her strong."

Head down, Johnnie Cross sighed. Unable to look at Ben or Elinor, he stared at the floor. "Please. Tell my daughter and me the rest."

Leaning back in his chair, Ben noticed through the lace curtains of the parlor's darkening windows that the sun had already set, and the gloom of twilight would soon take over. Elinor noticed, too, for she arose and quietly retrieved flint and a wood match from a side table drawer, struck them together, and lit the two large candles on the mantel. When she resumed her seat, Ben continued with Misella's story.

"I knew well that in being transported, Misella would have to endure not only a horrific journey across the Seas, but also a ghastly future when she arrived in America. To spare her, I promised the ship's captain a large sum of money to keep her safe and to arrange for her freedom, if he could, after she arrived."

Johnnie Cross stood up, determination overshadowing the pain on his face. He pulled a flat leather purse from the pocket of his waistcoat. "I must pay you back, Sir, every pound. I may not have all of it here at the moment, but I will get the rest soon. Please," he pleaded, "tell me what you paid. I am indebted enough to you already."

Struggling to maintain his composure and prevent his voice from quavering, Ben said with strained vigor, "The payment is no longer needed because…" His voice faltered, "Because Misella did not survive the crossing."

Johnnie Cross slumped back down into the chair, his face pale, his eyes squeezed shut. "God help me," he uttered.

Elinor cried out, "Oh, no." She clutched her hand over her mouth, and closed her eyes for a moment. When she opened them, her face wet with tears, she reached for her father's hand, encasing it in both of her own. "You gave Misella all of the love you could give her while she was with you, Father, and that was more than enough to last her for all the years you were apart. You hoped only to improve her life. You are not to blame for Sir Richard's actions or his character.

"I am the one who needed Misella's forgiveness," she continued, removing her hands from her father's and retrieving the damp, twisted handkerchief from her lap. "For my hatefulness toward her. I hated her from the day she was born, and she knew it, because I made sure that she did." Elinor blotted her face with the limp handkerchief. "And now I can never tell her how sorry I am." She covered her face and could say no more.

Johnnie Cross stood up, put his arm around Elinor's quivering shoulders and hugged her to his chest, his face distorted with grief. "Oh, my dear," he said with quiet tenderness, "we both regret the past, but we cannot erase it. We learn from it, and you were just a child yourself. So much changed for both of us after your mother died. You grew up, Elinor, and became the rock your sister Annabelle and I relied upon. You alone were the source of our hope and our joy." Elinor raised her head and kissed his cheek.

"I cannot express to you both how sorry I am," Ben rasped, his voice sounding harsh in his effort to control his own fear of weeping, for he did not want to make this moment more difficult for Elinor.

Johnnie shook his head again, and looked at Elinor. "We suspected this, didn't we, Ellie." He turned to Ben. "We knew in our hearts that if Misella was alive, you would have told Elinor yesterday." His voice broke when he asked, "How did she die? Why?"

Ben wished he had more to tell them, could do more to comfort them both. "I don't have that information, but I will find out. Jack Finn, a young friend of Misella's in England, accompanied me to Annapolis—to make sure that she had arrived safely. He remained in Annapolis to see if he could find out more information."

Johnnie Cross looked puzzled. "I don't understand, Sir, why you, a respected barrister in London, would pay all that you did to secure my daughter's safety and then travel all this way just to validate her arrival."

Ben blushed, aware that Elinor was staring at him, perplexed herself by the question she had been too polite to ask the day before. He cleared his throat, wiped his forehead again, and decided to tell them the truth about his feelings for Misella. "In the process of defending your daughter…your sister," he said turning to Elinor, "I fell in love with her."

Elinor bowed her head, her hands twisting the handkerchief she held in her lap. She raised her head, her eyes searching his face. "I understand," she murmured. "Everyone loved Misella. She was innocent and not to blame for what happened to her. You sacrificed everything to save her life. And Father and I are grateful."

Ben sat forward in his chair, tempted to still her hands with his and suspend his confession. But he continued, determined to hold nothing back. She, even more than her father, deserved a full explanation. "I asked her after her conviction to marry me, told her I could arrange a "benefit of clergy" for her. With a simple branding on her thumb, she would have been freed, and I would have taken care of her as my wife."

He sighed and shook his head. "I was foolish—a lonely old man thinking only of myself, what I needed. Misella courageously refused my offer of marriage." He wiped his brow again and gazed at Elinor. "She didn't love me. How could she? A man some thirty years older than she? She chose her own path despite how difficult she knew it would be." Reaching into the inside pocket of his bunched-up, wrinkled waistcoat, he withdrew the little portrait of Misella. "I admired her so. I could not let her suffer without trying to help her."

He handed the portrait to Johnnie Cross who accepted it, Ben thought, with reverence. "I resigned from my law position and decided to come to America to help not just Misella, if she needed it, but other indentured women like her. Most, through no fault of their own except poverty and exploitation, suffer here as they did in England with no advocate to help them."

Wordlessly, Johnnie Cross passed the portrait of Misella to Elinor who touched her handkerchief to her eyes as she studied it. "So beautiful," she whispered. "She always was. I was the plain one." She glanced up from the portrait with a weak smile. "Misella used to tease me about my looks. 'Torchy,' she'd tell me, 'you are destined to be the spinster of the family.' That was her nickname for me because of my red hair and the way I blushed all the time." With tears still shimmering in her eyes, Elinor attempted to return the portrait to Ben, but he nudged it back into her palm and wrapped his own large hand around hers.

"No," he said gently, "this belongs to you and your Father. I no longer need it."

"Thank you, Ben," she said, with a catch in her voice. "We are grateful that you came here intending to aid Misella and have ended by helping us." As she studied his face, an aura of melancholy overwhelmed her. "You will return to London I presume now that your purpose in coming here—for Misella—has concluded. When do you leave?"

Though he suspected that her father was surprised by Elinor's interest in him and her questions about his departure, Ben held onto her hand. "I am not leaving, Elinor," he said with the ghost of a smile. "I have decided to stay on in Boston and continue with my plan to start a practice here to counsel indentured slaves, for that is what they are. Lord knows they need someone to advocate for them."

Ben's words brought a look of pure joy to Elinor's face, along with a deep flush, and infused her voice with excitement. "Oh, Sir, I could assist you with your work, if you will allow me to. I would feel as though I were helping Misella." She turned toward her father. "Don't you agree, Father?"

Johnnie Cross bolted up, seemingly sparked by a renewed sense of energy that straightened his shoulders and lifted his chin. "Yes, that is an excellent idea, Ellie." He addressed Ben with an urgency and a sincerity that confirmed for Ben the inherent decency of the man. "I, too, want to be of service, Sir," he said, "if you will let me—in Misella's memory and to amend my past failure. I betrayed her then. Please let me make up for that now by assisting you in any way I can."

Ben pushed himself out of the chair and stood, the tightness in his chest that had plagued him since the discovery of Misella's death had disappeared. Finding Elinor, his growing affection for her, and her sincere interest in him had renewed his faith and his hope for the future. "Of course, my friends, I would be honored to accept your help. I will need it. Justice, any shred of humane treatment for these poor discarded dregs of British society, will not be easy to achieve. I welcome you both to the fight."

He took a deep breath, noticing for the first time the tantalizing aromas coming from Elinor's kitchen. "I believe," he said, looking fondly at her, "that you invited me to stay for dinner. I hope the invitation still holds, for I am famished."

Chapter 38

Over the next month, Ben spent almost every evening at the Cross home while Johnnie Cross helped him review the procedures for securing his law license. "You have one advantage anyway," Johnnie told him, as the two sat in the parlor sipping their brandy. "Your law education at the Inns of Court in London should automatically admit you to practice here once the examining committee approves your credentials and your character. Many of the lawyers practicing here have come from London with similar training."

Ben scowled. "Oh, oh. My reputation as a gadfly who often attacked the *status quo* of the law might disqualify me. Some of those lawyers probably know that I was not admired by the King's Court. Misella's case and my defense of her became cheap fodder for the papers all over England."

Johnnie shook his head with a faint smile. "No, Ben. Your brilliant defense saved her. Ellie and I will never forget that or your compassion and kindness. If necessary, I'll appear before the committee as a character witness for you. So will Ellie. I know some of the men on that committee; in fact, one of them, John Holloway, is my lawyer." He hesitated for a moment and then said with determination, "Of course, I'll switch over to you once you have your license."

He stood up and set down his drink. "Let's ask Ellie what she thinks. As my bookkeeper, she often meets with John if he has any questions about my accounts. She has a way of sorting through the flimflam to get to the heart of things." He called out for Elinor.

She swept in from the kitchen wiping her hands on her apron, a spring in her step and a smile lighting up her face. "What are you two up to? I suppose you want me to hurry up with your dinner." She rested her hand on Ben's shoulder, and he covered it with his. "You both look so serious."

Johnnie took his seat again. "Ben's worried," he said, "that he won't qualify for a law license here because of his 'bad boy' reputation in the London courts—for defending poor and discarded souls like Misella, and winning! Ease his mind, can you?"

Elinor sat down in the chair next to Ben and took his hand in both her own. "That's just plain silly, Ben. You think the committee will punish you for your success? That doesn't make sense. I'm aware of the enmity often directed at professional lawyers in this town. But that's because of the imposters and pettifoggers who have tarnished the profession with their greed and lack of principles. You, dear one, are so far beyond and above those sharpers.

Ben squeezed her hand. "You always make me feel better, Elinor. Thank you for that—and for defending an old, run-down lawyer and allowing him to spend time with you. And offering him a place at your table."

"Oh, Ben," she said, lowering her voice and clinging to his hand as if she couldn't let go. "You know I want you at my table—and I always will."

"Ahem." Johnnie cleared his throat. "We had better get back to business."

Elinor released Ben's hand and stood up, her face flushed. "And I had better get back to the kitchen." Before she left, she told her father, "Tomorrow Ben and I will start investigating the system for employing indentured servants. We know nothing about how those contracts are designed to work. Mr. Holloway has agreed to meet with us and explain the process."

Johnnie agreed. "A good idea, and while you're at it, you might start looking for rental space for a law office." He turned to Ben. "Don't you think it's time?"

Ben responded, "Yes, to the research about indentures. We'll do that, Elinor. Do you object, Johnnie, if your daughter is out all day with me minus a chaperone? Although I am old enough to be her father. The looks of me ought to squelch any gossip."

"Stop that kind of talk, Ben." Elinor stamped her foot. "I've told you before that age means nothing to a relationship unless you allow it to. Don't disrespect me and my affection for you by cheapening it like that."

Distressed, Ben bowed his head. "I'm sorry, my dear," he murmured, "you are right to chastise me. I guess I still need time to absorb the amazing idea that you wish to keep company with me—that you care for me." He looked at her, his eyes watering.

"Well, I do," she whispered. "I do." Before she turned to leave the room, she said with a half-smile, "Dinner will be ready soon, you two. I'll call you to the table."

Johnnie didn't say a word, allowing Ben a moment to recover. When Ben picked up his glass and took a drink, Johnnie resumed the conversation where he had left it, "So about that law office space."

Ben shook his head. "Too premature to look for an office before I even have my license. I appreciate your confidence, but the prudent side of me says I had better wait."

"Don't worry. I can guarantee you will receive your license." Johnnie reached inside the folder he held in his lap and pulled out a piece of parchment. "Once you have taken this oath, you'll be entitled to practice law here."

Ben took the paper and stood up. Holding it close to a candle on the mantel, his good eye squinting to decipher the script, he read:

> *You shall do no falsehood, nor consent to any to be done in the court; and if you know of any to be done you shall give notice thereof to the Justices of the court that it may be reformed:*
>
> *You shall delay no man for lucre or malice or take any unreasonable fees: You shall not wittingly or willingly sue or procure to be sued any false suit, nor give any aid nor consent to the same, upon pain of being disabled to practice as an attorney*

for ever. And furthermore, you shall use yourself in the office of an attorney within the court, according to your learning and discretion.

Ben handed the paper back to Johnnie. "I know these rules well. I could recite them in my sleep. They're very similar to the oath I took in England. Swearing to this does not bother me." He sat down and lifted his glass to his lips, but set it down again before taking a drink. "The question is," he continued, "will the courts here interpret these rules the same way I do and allow suits to proceed fairly for everyone? Or will they obstruct and deny fair counsel for the poor as the courts did in England? I had to fight like Hades and launch a public campaign in order to get the court to let me defend Misella against a murder charge. Will that happen here when I attempt to defend poor indentured servants or will the court simply declare these false suits?"

Johnnie looked troubled. "That I can't guarantee. But it seems to me you are the very person to test that in our courts."

"I pray you are right, Sir." When Elinor appeared in the doorway announcing that dinner was ready, Ben hauled himself up out of his chair. "Just in time, my dear," he called to her. "As usual, I am famished—for your company and for your delicious cooking." He winked at her as he passed into the kitchen.

Chapter 39

Savoring the excellent dinner Elinor had prepared and cherishing his growing affection for her, a jaunty Ben Turner arrived long after dark at the boarding house where he had secured lodging. He bounded up the steps to the front door, not needing his cane. In fact, he felt twenty-five again, as if thirty years had magically disappeared. *Spry as Jack Finn,* he thought. Inserting his key into the door, he whistled a few bars of *Black-Eyed Susan.* A candle burning on the table in the hallway revealed a folded note with his name on it. He picked up the note and the candle holder before heading up the stairs to his room.

He closed his door and set the candle on his bedside table. Leaning his cane against the wall next to the bed, he opened the note:

Ben,

I found Logan. He is with me now. We rode as fast as we could, praying you were still here. We have astonishing news. We are waiting for you down the hall in Room 4. Come as soon as you can.

Jack

Ben grabbed the candle holder and left the room. He knocked softly on the door of Room 4. The door flew open, and Jack pulled him inside, a wide grin stretching across his unshaved face. Damp curls matted his forehead as if still under the control of his tri-cornered hat. The hat sat on the single bed next to a hulk of a young man grinning under a wild heap of whitish blond hair that drifted across his massive shoulders.

Not wanting to disturb the other boarders on the floor, Ben closed the door quietly behind him, and asked in a loud whisper, "How in the name of King George did you find me at this place?"

Jack laughed out loud, covering his mouth when he noticed Ben's alarmed expression, and lowered his voice. "We rode as fast as we could—on horses borrowed from an old Indian friend. We split up as soon as we arrived, intending to canvass every lodging establishment in Boston asking for you. Logan found this one right away. Smart man. He figured you would stay close to the harbor when I told him you planned to find Misella's father before you sailed for England. I thought you'd opt for a cheaper room further away from the dock—knowing what a skinflint you are." Finn chuckled. "Logan secured lodging for both of us when he found out you were here." He turned to the younger man who sat beaming on the rope bed.

Jack grabbed the candle holder from Ben's hand and held it up so that the light shone on Logan's bearded face. "Stand up, James Logan," Jack said, "and meet the Honorable Ben Turner, Misella's counselor and good friend."

Logan lurched up and bowed, a serious expression erasing his grin. "Happy to make your acquaintance, Sir," he mumbled, staring down at the top of Ben's graying head. "Misella told me about you once—when we were together on the ship--what you did for her." He remained standing, shifting from one booted foot to the other as if unsure about what he should do next.

To put him at ease, Ben reached out and grabbed one of Logan's hands hanging ham-like by his side and hoisted it into a handshake. "If you were a friend to Misella," he said, "then you are a friend of mine. Thank you for that and for your efforts to help Finn get here. Though I don't understand the hurry. Unless Finn missed me so much he couldn't bear being apart from me any longer."

"Ho, ho, my friend," Jack chortled. "We needed to reach you before you left for England. And I'm glad we did. You'll want to stay now when you hear the news." Jack abandoned the jocular tone. "Misella is alive," he declared, his voice husky with emotion, "indentured here in Boston."

Ben stumbled backwards, falling with a thump against the door. "You've gone mad," he yelled, forgetting the rule of quiet after the ten o'clock hour. "Your grief and rage have destroyed your brain."

"No, Ben," Jack murmured. "It is true. Logan knows that Misella was alive when the ship docked at Annapolis, before he deserted. We have figured out together what happened to her after he left. Logan says a different young girl died at sea—Margaret MacDonald. We believe Captain Barclay switched their identities in order to protect Misella and maintain his bargain with you. Apparently, the two young women looked very much alike."

Pulling himself upright, Ben struggled to gain his equilibrium and to comprehend the news that Misella was alive. "I am afraid to believe it, Finny," he muttered. "I can't until I see her with my own eyes."

"I know, Ben," Jack said, clutching Ben's shoulders in his hands and giving them a shake. "Nor can I. We cannot believe it until we can find her, see her in the flesh, touch her, verify for ourselves that she is not a fantasy of Logan's imagination."

Logan took a menacing step toward Jack. "She's not," he sputtered. "That's a dirty insult. I swear I saw her alive before I left the ship—with my own eyes. Are you doubting my word and my honor after all I've done to help you?"

"No, no, I believe you," Jack said, "and I'm grateful. I have had time to absorb this news, but Ben hasn't, and he tends to be a doubting Thomas anyway. You know how lawyers are—they need proof. Eyewitness accounts are never enough, always suspect. Hard evidence is the only kind they'll accept."

A look of consternation shadowed Ben's face, and Jack expected an explosive response, but Ben, deep in thought, ignored the bait.

"I located Misella's father and sister weeks ago," he said slowly, "and have informed them of Misella's death." He rubbed a hand across his eyes and shook his head as if trying to imagine telling them to change the ending they had just begun to accept. "We must find Misella first, and confirm that she survived, before I can share the news with her family. We must be certain before I raise their hopes again."

Jack heartily agreed. "If this is true that Misella has become Margaret MacDonald, then we can be certain that she is here in Boston. I checked the list of sales at the Court House in Annapolis for the convicts aboard the *Seaflower*." He clapped Ben on the shoulder. "Used one of your tactics, Ben. Pretended I was an agent for the merchant Andrew Dunning. Margaret MacDonald's indenture was purchased by a Mr. Briar, servitor for Mrs. Gretchen Dobbs of Boston. Our search for Mrs. Dobbs begins tomorrow."

Chapter 40

On a steaming Tuesday morning after an exhausting first month of service to Mrs. Dobbs, Misella hid in the garden to catch her breath for a few minutes. She crouched behind the weeded row of tomato plants in her stained muslin gown and fanned her heated face with a rhubarb leaf plucked from the stalks piled in her basket.

"You'll cook a rhubarb torte for dinner tonight," Mrs. Dobbs had ordered. Misella answered with a mealy-mouthed, "Yes, ma'am," though she knew this was intended to punish her for soliciting Mr. Briar's help with Amos Bristol. Lighting the stove in the tiny kitchen meant sweltering heat as she prepared dinner, and would render her windowless pantry uninhabitable for sleeping.

"I thought she'd thank me for returning Mr. Briar to her," Misella grumbled to herself. She dropped the leaf into the basket and rubbed her bruised arms, swatted repeatedly with the broomstick, Mrs. Dobbs favorite weapon. "Instead, she treats me worse than ever."

"Missy!" Mrs. Dobbs screamed from the opened back door, her voice sending shivers down Misella's wet back. "Where are you? I don't see you working."

Misella stood up, brushing dirt from her lap. "I'm here Mrs. Dobbs, just finished picking the rhubarb."

"Get in here to the parlor. Don't bother to clean up. I'm sure your brother won't mind seeing you like this after all of these years."

"But I don't have a brother," Misella blurted out, forgetting her new identity. "I mean, not anymore." Fear gripped her heart and set the blood pounding in her ears. *This is Amos Bristol's doing*, she thought to herself. He had warned her after the shopping trip that he would get even. "Don't think for one sweet moment that you are safe," he had whispered in her ear when he walked her and Mr. Briar to Mrs. Dobbs' door. "I'll find a way to get you alone."

Now, as Misella stumbled to the back door at Mrs. Dobbs command, the basket of rhubarb clutched to her aching chest, she felt in her bones that Bristol was setting up another trap for her. He knew about Margaret's family. How could she refuse to see her long-lost brother and accompany him wherever he wanted to take her?

When she hesitated on the steps, afraid to face what lay ahead, Mrs. Dobbs grabbed the basket from her. "Stop dawdling. You're a strange creature. I'd think you would be anxious to see your brother after all of these years. He has an older man with him, a shabby-looking fellow that he neglected to introduce to me. I agreed that you could walk outside with them for an hour as your brother requested. So you had better get moving before I change my mind." She pushed her from the kitchen.

Her back bent with fatigue and worry, shoulders sagging, Misella shuffled into the parlor. The young man stopped pacing and turned to her, his face flushed beneath a wayward crop of dark curls, his blue eyes filmed with tears, a woolen cap crushed in his hands. "Hello, Margaret," he said, his voice trembling. Dropping the cap, he held his arms out, cross-like, and waited for her to come to him.

"Jack," she cried, her fear changing to disbelief. She ran to him, her exhaustion forgotten, and held on tight as he wrapped his arms around her. "Oh, Jack, I thought I would never see you again," she choked, tears clogging her throat. "How did you find me?"

"We never stopped looking," he murmured into her hair. He kissed her ear and her cheek before he released his arms. "Ben and I—we are indestructible," he said, a lilt returning to his voice. With a grin, he twirled her so that she faced the chair in front of the empty fireplace where Ben Turner sat, a large handkerchief pressed to his lips. He mopped his face, and then raised himself slowly from the chair.

"Hello, Misella," he whispered. "How lovely to see you again."

She unlocked Jack's arms from around her waist and reached for Ben's hand. Ignoring the handkerchief trailing from his fingers, she lifted his hand to her lips."You have helped to save me once again, Ben Turner," she said with a catch in her throat that softened the words. "But why are you here and not in England where you truly belong?"

"Not any longer, my dear," he said in a quiet voice without his usual gruffness. When he noticed Mrs. Dobbs hovering in the doorway, he raised his voice. "I am here as the King's advocate," he blustered, "sent to oversee the treatment of our indentured servants. His Majesty wants to ensure that they are treated fairly. We have received some disturbing accounts of malfeasance by public officials and some contractors."

Mrs. Dobbs' head jolted back as if she had sustained a punch to the jaw. She clutched the cross hanging around her neck with both hands. The blood drained from her face, rendering it more colorless than usual.

Ben nodded in Mrs. Dobbs' direction and softened his tone. "Although not a problem with this establishment, I am sure." He bowed stiffly toward her and smiled.

She let go of the cross and fluttered into the room. "Oh, I agree, Sir, I have heard such stories myself. But now, Margaret, you and your brother need some time alone to get reacquainted. Why don't you take a walk to the park—such a beautiful day. You needn't return for a few hours."

Jack grabbed Misella's arm and steered her to the doorway. "Yes, let's take that walk, Margaret, as we used to do in London years ago. Thank you, Mrs. Dobbs." He turned with a formal bow to Ben. "Won't you join us, Mr. Turner? Unless you have business to conduct elsewhere."

Turner hesitated for a moment and then thumped his cane on the floor. "I believe I will join you for a walk. I do have a call to make, but that can wait for a few hours. The mayor should be available later. I have a few names to check with him."

Mrs. Dobbs stepped aside to allow him to join Jack and Misella, trailing the group to the front door. "Margaret knows the way to the park, don't you dear?" she called after them as they made their exit. "Please take your time. No need to hurry back on my account."

"Yes, ma'am," Misella yelled back as Jack looped her arm in his and hurried her down the stairs. He put his other arm around her and pulled her close. She leaned into him, holding his arm tight with both her hands as if she feared he might disappear if she let go.

"Oh, Jack," she almost babbled, "Jack, you always manage to show up when I least expect to see you. And when I need you most. I was so worried today. I expected to see one of Amos Bristol's thugs waiting for me in the parlor, pretending to be my long-lost brother with some devious plan to deliver me to Bristol."

Jack stopped short causing Turner to bump into him from behind as he struggled to keep up with the two lovebirds. "Amos Bristol? The First Mate from the *Seaflower*?

He's here, in Boston?" Jack grabbed her forearms and turned her to face him.

Misella looked puzzled. "Yes. Ever since the Captain released him from his position. How do you know him?"

"Logan," he said. "Remember him? He's here with us. That's how we learned you were alive as Margaret MacDonald."

"Logan! Yes, of course, I remember him. He helped me survive on the ship, but he deserted in Annapolis."

Fear shadowed her face and elevated her voice. She grabbed Jack's hand. "You have to warn Logan. He's in danger. Bristol is obsessed with finding him and making him pay for betraying him. He blames both of us for the loss of his job. He has threatened me already with violence."

She became more agitated, her face filmed with sweat, her hands clutching at Jack's. "He is coming tomorrow with Mrs. Dobbs' permission to take me shopping for her. He is supposedly bringing his Aunt with him as a chaperone. But I know that is a ruse. I fear he will find a way to rape me as he did Margaret." Her voice cracked as tears coursed down her cheeks.

Jack gathered her to him. "Please don't cry, my darling. Don't worry. We found you, didn't we? We will find Bristol today, Logan and I."

"And I," Turner barked, stepping forward. "The scoundrel will pay for what he has done. We will see to it." He handed his handkerchief to Misella. "Dry your eyes, my dear, and remember who you are. You must have faith."

Chapter 41

Jack, Ben and Logan, the three unlikely musketeers, huddled in darkness against the clapboard side of one of the seedier boarding houses in Boston still squabbling about their plan. After they had spent hours in the afternoon heat locating Amos Bristol's lodging, Ben Turner had insisted that he should confront Bristol first when the scoundrel returned from dinner, "around nine or ten o'clock," the slatternly boarding house proprietor had told them.

"I can convince him," he assured the other two men as they waited for Bristol, "that I represent the Royal Navy about a reassignment and ask him to accompany me to the pub down the street for a drink. You two can meet us there."

"No," Jack grunted. "I'll approach him first, say that I've heard he is looking for an assignment, and offer to introduce him to a contractor waiting at the pub."

"Bollocks," barked Logan, towering over the other two. "I'll grab him as soon as he walks up and drag him to the back of the house, knock him about a bit. After he writes the note to Mrs. Dobbs cancelling tomorrow's shopping trip, you two can take the note and leave. Then I'll kill him. That's the only way to deal with a cockroach like him. Strike fast and first before he knows what hit him. He'll fold like the powder puff he is, and the world will be rid of the likes of him."

"I don't like this idea," Turner mumbled. "Too risky for you. We should share the job equally, and I cannot condone killing him, much as he deserves it. We can put the fear of God and the King into him so that he disappears like the coward you say he is."

Logan laughed out loud, the sound cutting through the close night air. "Crawl away and disappear? Never. Does a cockroach ever give up? I know him, you don't. After he writes the note, your help will no longer be needed. Debate is over. Understand?"

"Okay," Jack agreed. "You win. No more discussion. We'll wait in silence." Turner snorted, but he held his tongue.

They didn't have to wait long before Amos Bristol sauntered along the boarded pathway leading from the Bluegill pub to the backstreet boarding house. He stumbled over the twine the three had tacked down low between the staircase posts, falling onto the porch. Jack and Turner hurried toward him, stepping over the twine, each grabbing an arm and hoisting him upright. "Oopsy daisy there. Let us help you, Sir," Jack crooned. Before the stunned Bristol could utter a word, they dragged him to the side of the house and delivered him to Logan.

Clapping one huge hand over Bristol's mouth, the other clamped on the scruff of his neck, Logan lifted him off of the ground. "Hello, Bristol," he muttered into his ear. "I hear you have been looking for me. Let's get reacquainted, shall we?" Logan moved quickly to the backyard, his prey dangling several inches off of the ground, his feet jumping as if he were dancing an Irish jig.

Logan dropped Bristol on the patchy grass, shoved Turner's handkerchief into his mouth far enough to make him gag, and wrenched an arm behind his back. "Listen closely, you little cockroach," he ordered in a loud whisper. "You are going to write to Mrs. Dobbs. We will tell you what to say. Understand?" Bristol nodded, his feet pummeling the ground in fear or pain.

Jack struck a piece of flint against a nearby stone and lit the candle he had brought with him. He held the light up to Logan's glowering face so that Bristol could see he didn't stand a chance of refusing to do what they asked. He shielded the candle so that the light could not be seen from the house or the empty street. "Let's move," he urged the other two. "Everything's ready."

He led them into a circle of untrimmed bushes behind the boarding house to a makeshift table he had set up earlier—a board laid across a couple low stumps. He pulled a piece of parchment from inside his jacket and retrieved a small vial of ink and a quill from his pocket. He laid them on the board.

Logan wrapped a beefy arm around Bristol's narrow chest, with his hand driving the poor sod's twisted arm further up behind his back. He half-carried the First Mate to the makeshift table and dropped him on the ground. "Sit up, you sniveling coward," he snarled, "this is for Misella—and for Margaret. Pick up the quill."

Bristol's pocked face, contorted now with fear and pain, dripped with sweat. Mucus leaked unhindered from his nose into the folds of the handkerchief that extended from his gagged mouth. He emitted the ghost of a whimper as he tried to move his released arm back in place. But he picked up the quill with his other shaking hand, dipped it into the open vial, and waited for the dictation.

Jack leaned down and held the candle close to the paper. "You write exactly what I tell you," he said. Bristol nodded.

> Dear Mrs. Dobbs,
>
> I regret to inform you that I must cancel our scheduled shopping trip for tomorrow. I will be leaving early in the morning on a ship bound for London so that I can reunite with Captain Barclay and resume my previous position.
>
> Hoping to see you again upon my return.
>
> Your most obedient and grateful friend,
> Amos Bristol

Jack snatched up the parchment, waved it back and forth a few times to dry the ink, folded it and inserted it carefully into the inner pocket of his jacket. He extinguished the candle and grabbed the vial of ink and the quill. "Let's go," he said to Turner who stood watch a few feet away. "I'll slip this under Mrs. Dobbs' door tonight and meet you back at the house."

Leaning on his cane, his knees and back screaming for rest after the long, arduous day, Turner straightened up. "I'm coming with you," he said. "We are in this together. And don't argue with me."

"Godspeed, gentlemen. Tell Misella good-bye for me," Logan called after them before dragging Bristol further into the bushes. "You won't see me again. I'm taking the horses to Annapolis, and myself back to the woods. I'm a woodsman at heart."

Chapter 42

On the Sunday afternoon after Bristol's sudden departure, Misella, clutching the drawstring bag she always carried with her, stood with Ben Turner staring at the gray house where her remaining family waited for her. Mrs. Dobbs had graciously agreed to give Misella the afternoon off when Ben Turner had requested it. "Oh, certainly," she had gushed when Turner asked, "dear Margaret needs some time to enjoy Boston with you and her brother. Why, she could have this time off every week, Sir."

Although Jack Finn joined Misella and Ben for part of their journey, he did not accompany them all the way. "The driver will drop me off at the park," he told Misella as he sat down next to her. "I'll wait a few weeks before meeting your father and sister. Let them get to know you again before they have to try and accept the likes of me—a wild Irish lad, an ex-highwayman and a pirate who wants to marry you as soon as you are free—if you will have me." He leaned close and brushed her flushed cheek with his lips.

Misella leaned away from him, ignoring the kiss. "I appreciate your decision to wait before you meet them, Jack," she murmured, twisting the strings of her canvas bag around and around her fingers. "I'm not sure they can even accept the likes of me again." She looked at him, doubt clouding her eyes. "So much has changed in my life, Jack."

Jack grasped her hand, unwinding the strings from her fingers, the troubled look in his blue eyes belying the jauntiness in his voice and the dark curls that danced as usual across his tanned forehead. "No worries, Misella. My grandmother Shanny was the soothsayer of our village. Did I ever tell you about her?" When Misella shook her head, he continued, "She proclaimed that after her death, I would inherit her ability to predict the future. And I can," he added with a grin and an audacious twinkle in his eye. "Hereby, I declare that only good things lie ahead for us."

Misella withdrew her hand from Jack's, annoyed by his sunny sense of optimism which she could not share, but she remained silent.

After dropping Jack off at the park, Ben confessed to Misella as they journeyed to her father's house that he had developed strong feelings for Elinor. "She's a lovely, caring woman," he told her. "Though much younger than I, she understands me—she seems to enjoy my company. And I very much enjoy hers," he admitted in a quiet voice and with a blush on his cheeks that startled Misella.

She lurched forward on the seat, her canvas bag slipping from her lap to the floor, the green-eyed monster clawing at her heart. Though she had rejected Ben's love and his marriage proposal, she still craved his flattery and undying devotion. That he had switched his devotion so quickly to her sister violated her trust in him. It felt to Misella that he had joined the opposite side, leaving her to tackle this treacherous reunion on her own. She couldn't help feeling abandoned by her most loyal supporter when she needed him most.

"I must say I am very surprised, Ben," Misella said when she recovered from the shock. "Not that I mind your affection for Elinor—not at all. Why should I care? It's just that I can't believe red-haired, freckled Elinor—the spiteful, jealous Torchy I remember from my childhood—would appeal to a wise, experienced barrister like you."

Ben smiled and patted her hand. "She's changed, Misella. I think you may be surprised by the grown-up Elinor," he said.

Now, at the doorstep of her Father's house, on the brink of reuniting with him and Elinor, Misella lost her courage. Her anxiety at the prospect of seeing them again reappeared, and she trembled. "I cannot do this," she moaned to Turner, stopping his hand as he reached for the door knocker. "I'm not the unsoiled, innocent young girl I was when they last saw me, waving to them from Sir Richard's carriage."

Turner rested his cane gently against the door and took Misella's hands in his. "Listen to me, Misella. You know that I have never lied to you. Your father does not blame you; he blames himself for letting you go. You are not the prodigal daughter, returning in disgrace. Whatever fear or pain or embarrassment you carry about your past can in no way match the depth of his. He needs your forgiveness. He needs you."

Misella bowed her head, swiping away the angry tears that clouded her eyes. "I'm not sure I can forgive him—or want to. He let me go; he never tried to stop it; he never spoke up on my behalf." She faced Turner with defiance. "Or forgive Elinor either. Though you revere her now, you didn't know her as I did. She was hateful to me the day I left." Her voice dropped to a whisper. "She called me a trollop. How prophetic was that?" she asked with a bitter laugh. "Of all the hardships I have had to face, meeting the two of them again is the most difficult," she murmured. "Forgive them? No, I don't think I can."

"I'm here to help if you need me," Turner said. He retrieved his cane but held on to Misella's hand.

An empty promise, Misella thought.

Before he could knock, the door flew open, and Elinor cried out, "Misella! Is it really you?" Tears trickled down Elinor's inflamed cheeks. She stood breathless in a blue-striped gown, her best Sunday gingham. "I cannot believe that you are home at last."

Misella stared with surprise at this grown-up version of the awkward, unkempt sister she remembered—who seemed sincerely happy to see her again. She reached up and touched Elinor's flaming red hair, bound neatly now in a demure bun. "Hello, Torchy," she said, her voice breaking. "May I come in?"

Elinor locked her in an embrace and held on. "How I have missed you," she cried. "Even your insults." She pulled back enough so she could study Misella, seeming not to care that Misella, arms rigid at her sides, had not returned her embrace. "How beautiful you are. You look the same; I knew you would, just a wee bit older. Not wrinkled and spinsterish like me," she joked.

Her arm encircling Misella's thin waist, her other hand clenching her sister's cold fingers entwined around the strings of a canvas bag, Elinor drew her across the threshold and into the hallway. "Please close the door behind you, Ben, when you come in," she called over her shoulder.

In her excitement, the usually sedate Elinor could not seem to stop babbling, a side of her that took Ben Turner by surprise. He liked her this way, and he did not mind that she had at first ignored him completely. He wanted to remain in the background, savoring the sisters' reunion.

Elinor guided Misella to the parlor. "Father," she said softly, "Misella is here."

Earlier, when she and her father had returned home after attending Mass, her father had decided to stay in his room. "I'll come down when Misella arrives," he told Elinor. "And I'll be waiting in the parlor."

Johnnie Cross sat rocking in front of the empty fireplace, in the chair he had brought with him to the New World. He seemed lost in his thoughts, unaware of the previous commotion at the front door.

He stopped rocking and stood up to face them, dressed not in his Sunday best. Surprised, Elinor blurted out, "Father, you changed your clothes." He wore his old Portsmouth fishing outfit—patched muslin britches and a wrinkled, ill-fitting flannel shirt overlaid by a once-brown woolen vest faded to a faint ochre. Elinor dropped Misella's hand and stepped closer to him. "I thought you had thrown these worn-out clothes away years ago," she murmured. "When you no longer needed them."

"I've been saving them for this very day," he said, ignoring Elinor's disapproving frown and addressing Misella. "These are the clothes I wore the day you left us, Misella," he croaked, "I am.... happy to see you. I didn't think it possible..." His voice cracked, and he bowed his head to hide from her the shame in his eyes.

Steely-eyed, Misella confronted him. "You mean the day you sent me away," she said in a harsh voice, refusing to participate in the deception of this staged drama.

Elinor gasped, a dark flush suffusing her face, shocked by Misella's cruel rejection of her father's overture, his sincere attempt to recapture the past, to welcome her back.

Johnnie sighed, breathed deeply, and, difficult as it was for him, he looked Misella squarely in the eyes. "Forgive me. I am…I am so sorry, my dear…for abandoning you." He could say no more but held his hand out to her as if in supplication.

The words she had longed to hear for seven years did not matter to her now. How often she had tried during that time to visualize him in her mind, to remember him like this. She had not forgotten him. Though his hair had silvered and his back bent, his face bore evidence, she thought, that he had paid for losing her, for missing her. She saw guilt in his eyes, heard shame in the timbre of his voice, and she knew that he had missed her, perhaps more than she had imagined or hoped. But a few words wrung from him now could not so quickly mitigate her pain or ease her immense sorrow for all she had lost.

Not wanting to stare at him any longer, she looked down, fumbling with the drawstrings of her bag until she managed to untie them. Reaching into the bag, she retrieved the tattered book of psalms that had traveled with her since she left home. Approaching him, she placed in his outstretched hand the stained book with its broken spine and its loose pages tied together with twine. "I can at least return your book to you now…because I know them all by heart. I have had seven long years to memorize them."

Misery evident in his face, he reached out with his other hand to draw her into an embrace, but she stepped back. "You've done well since I've been gone," she said, looking pointedly around the parlor at the polished mahogany side tables, the chintz-covered chairs, and the gleaming harpsicord standing in the corner. She turned toward her sister. "Elinor, you must have a brighter kitchen to cook in than the shabby one in our old shack. Or do you have a hired cook now in your fancy new life?" she asked, with a sneering half-smile. "An indentured servant, perhaps."

Elinor blushed an angry red but controlled her voice. "I'm still the cook, Misella," she said softly. "And I hope you will soon live here with us. When Captain Barclay returns and releases you from your indenture." She hesitated, glancing for a moment at Ben. "Father offered to buy your indenture, but Ben has explained to us that Mrs. Dobbs controls the contract as a surrogate…for the Captain…" Her voice trailing to a halt, she looked with desperation at Ben who nodded and smiled at her. "If you…want to live here, that is. M-m-maybe we could be a family again."

"Where else would I go?" Misella asked with a cold grin. "One's home is the place where they have to take you in, isn't it? At least, that's what some of the trollops used to say in prison."

Elinor's eyes filled with tears. She wiped them away with her flowered handkerchief and dabbed at her nose. "I'm sorry, Misella," she whispered, "for my hateful words to you the day you left. I wanted to take them back the moment I said them. I have prayed that someday I would find you again and have the chance to redeem myself for my malicious behavior to you. "

Ben moved to Elinor's side and put both of his arms around her. "Don't be callous, Misella," he said. "It doesn't become you. If you can't forgive your sister yet, can you at least give her a chance to redeem herself? Isn't that what we all seek—redemption for our past mistakes?"

Misella sighed with exasperation and closed her eyes for a moment. "What I don't need right now, Ben Turner, is another lecture from you. Or a reminder of how indebted I am to you. What you are asking of me is to forget what I have endured and blithely start over as if I can make seven years disappear like smoke."

"No, my dear, I will simply ask you to help Elinor in the kitchen with dinner," he said quietly. "It's not an order. But I would like to see the two of you get reacquainted."

Elinor clasped her hands together. "Thank you, Ben. I would like that too." She turned toward Misella, her face a deep shade of red. "Is…is that fine with you, Misella?"

"It seems I don't have a choice," Misella answered in a flippant tone of voice and with a flick of her wrist in Ben's direction. "Lead the indentured servant to your kitchen, Elinor. That, it seems," she said, with a withering glance at Ben, "is where I belong."

Chapter 43

Misella stared at the wide, airy kitchen in awe, at least ten times the size of Mrs. Dobbs' tight, narrow space where she barely had room to move from the box-like stove to the small table. Two long windows on either side of a huge mahogany sideboard invited in the afternoon sun that danced across the porcelain bowls scattered along its surface. A massive brick fireplace yawned against the far wall, its wooden mantle displaying Wedgewood china platters of varying sizes, while cast iron frying pans dangled from hooks attached to each side of the mantle. Against the wall next to the fireplace sat a black cast iron stove with a stove pipe thick as Logan's muscled forearm extending up through the whitewashed concrete ceiling. In the center of the slab stone floor, a long trestle table, covered with a flowered cloth, hosted six spindle chairs tucked underneath its edges.

An awkward silence ensued while Elinor fussed over a large cooking pot resting on the stove. She picked up a long-handled spoon and began to stir the pot, carefully at first and then with increasingly brusque strokes.

Elinor's rigid back, tight shoulders and pointed silence unnerved Misella. In the uncomfortable stillness, she gazed around the vast room and finally said, "It must be a pleasure to cook in this beautiful setting."

Elinor stirred furiously, stopping to whack the spoon a few times on the edge of the pot without saying a word.

"A far cry from our Portsmouth shack," Misella continued. "I remember how you would cough and sneeze from the burning bindweed as you struggled to cook the fish head stew in our tiny fireplace. I used to enjoy antagonizing you. 'Your face is redder than your hair, Torchy,'" I'd say. 'Watch out. Your head might burst into flames.' You called me a brat."

Elinor swung around, the dripping spoon in her hand, her face flushed. "You were a brat to me, Misella. And it seems you still are. I don't care if you spew your anger all over me, but Father does not deserve your wrath. He pined for you from the moment the carriage pulled away from our home—and mother did, too. All I heard from them morning and night, "Misella this....and Misella that," until I wanted to scream—but, of course, I never did. I watched them both write letters to you every single week, which you never bothered to answer. Your silence broke mother's heart—and father's too...," Elinor's voice cracked, "...because you were their favorite daughter." She turned her face away to hide the tears brimming in her eyes.

A sudden vision of Sir Richard pierced Misella's mind, as he stood on the threshold of their London apartment about to abandon her, pregnant and penniless. "Those letters from your home," he had sneered. "I intercepted them and burned them. To put an end to your mewling homesickness. What a lot of trouble you were for so little in return."

Misella swallowed hard and tried to speak, but the lump in her throat held her voice captive. When she finally managed to squeak out a few words, she didn't recognize her own voice. "I never saw the letters, Elinor," she rasped. She bit her lip, determined not to break down. She cleared her throat. "Sir Richard kept them from me." Her voice dissolved into a whisper. "He wanted me to forget about my home, to rely only on him, to need him...to love him." She raised her voice, thick with unshed tears. "And for a long time, I thought I did."

Elinor dropped the spoon, which clattered to the floor staining the stone and the hem of Elinor's gown, and flew to her sister's side. "Oh, Misella, please forgive my selfish blather, for not understanding how lost and angry you must feel. I was thinking only of myself, my own pain, forgetting about all the horrors that you have suffered. How terribly Sir Richard betrayed all of us, but most horribly abused you."

She threw her arm around Misella's thin shoulders, refusing to let her squirm away from the hug. "I was the one at fault when we were children. I caused your anger and name-calling, Misella, because I was jealous of you and I knew you would fight back…and pay some attention to me. So would mother or father then, if only to chastise me for being mean to you. All I wanted was to be noticed."

Misella rubbed her eyes and nodded. "It's what we all want as children, I guess, and we never seem to outgrow that need."

Sensing Misella's discomfort about reliving the past, Elinor released her shoulders, dropped her arm and stepped back. "Let's not dwell on our past faults, Misella. I want this to be a happy reunion, not a dredging up of old sins." She faced her younger sister with a shy smile. "Let's start over, shall we, and remember only the good things. I made a batch of the sugared oat cakes you always loved. While the beef stew finishes cooking, I'll make us some tea to have with the cakes."

She drew Misella to the table and pulled out a chair for her. "Please sit while I fix our tea."

"I'm supposed to help you, remember?" Misella said, refusing to sit. "I don't want you to wait on me. I can help myself. And I know how to make tea."

Elinor smiled again, hoping to lighten the mood. "All right. I won't fight with you. We'll make it together." She moved toward the stove, bending over to retrieve the fallen spoon and wiping the stained floor with a heavy cloth she grabbed from a wall hook. She set the spoon on the stove. With the cloth in hand, she lifted the stove door open.

When Misella leaned down to peer inside, a blast of heat struck her in the face from a bank of white hot ashes smoldering within. Misella backed away from the intense heat that made her eyes smart and water, reminding her of the sweltering conditions she had endured while imprisoned on the ship—forced to drink warm, tainted water from a scummed bucket. How she had yearned the entire time for a simple cup of English tea.

Elinor snatched a log from a stack of beachwood piled in a box on the hearth. She tossed the log inside and slammed the heavy door. A pewter teapot sat beside the log box.

"You can grab that teapot, Misella, and set it on the stove. I've already filled it with water from the well. We're lucky to have one just outside our back door. Remember how we had to trudge to the creek at home to fill our buckets? And in summer, we'd unlace our shoes, pull off our ugly wool stockings and go wading and splashing...and laughing together that time I tripped and fell? And you plopped down in the water next to me and said, 'I want to go swimming, too.'"

Misella rubbed her eyes and nodded. "I was very young then, and not afraid of anything." She looked pensive for a moment. "How long ago that was."

Elinor closed her eyes for a moment, unable to face her sister. "How badly we all failed you, Misella," she said. "I am so sorry. Mother was completely fooled by Sir Richard. She trusted him to give you a better life. And she convinced Father of that or he would never have given in."

Misella shook her head. "I wish I could believe that. But he knew what kind of man Sir Richard was. I heard Father call him a sharper when Mother first told him of her plan. He knew I didn't want to go. I tried to convince them to send you instead of me, Elinor. Did you know that? But Mother said no because she needed your help with the household."

Elinor squeezed her eyes shut and bowed her head. "I didn't know," she whispered. "But of course Sir Richard would want you, not me. You were beautiful and smart and spirited." She looked up at Misella with a weak smile. "And you still are. My heart breaks for you, Misella, for all the pain you have suffered...and for Father, too. He was devastated when Ben told us in great detail what happened to you. He blames himself, Misella, and he cannot forgive himself."

With her arms crossed in front of her chest and her hands tightened into fists, Misella did not respond.

Trying to ease the tension and change the subject, Elinor poured tea leaves from a porcelain jar into the teakettle. "A plate of oat cakes is on the sideboard if you want to bring them over to the table," she said to Misella, "while the tea steeps for a few minutes."

"Of course I will, if you stop apologizing, Elinor," Misella answered with a sigh. "We can't change what happened in the past, but we can choose how we move on from here. Now I am beginning to sound like Ben Turner." She laid the plate of oat cakes on the table. "I don't have much appetite for these any more. I've forgotten how they taste."

"Father won't eat any...he hasn't since you left home...and Ben dislikes them," Elinor said. She wrapped a cloth around the handle of the steaming teakettle and poured tea through a silver strainer into each cup resting on saucers in the center of a large silver tray. "In case you might remember how you used to crave them, I made plenty more." She set the tray down on the table, pulled out two of the chairs and positioned a cup of tea at each place. "Please sit, Misella."

Elinor waited until Misella sat down before she seated herself. "I thought we might be meeting your Jack Finn today, and I was sure that he, being an Irishman, would appreciate oat cakes. Ben has told us all about him. He plans to marry you, Ben says, as soon as Captain Barclay returns and you are free."

Misella hesitated. Before taking a bite, she set the oat cake down at the side of her saucer. "Let's talk about you and Ben first, Elinor," she said, her voice strained, her lower lip clamped between her teeth. She attempted a half-smile and cleared her throat. "I understand he has grown quite fond of you."

Elinor's face flamed. "Yes," she said. "In fact, he has asked me to marry him once he establishes his law practice here." She set her cup down carefully on the saucer. "Do you think me foolish, Misella, for agreeing to marry a man twenty-nine years older than I? I...I have come to love him dearly. I know that must seem strange to you with your young, handsome Irishman, but I do admire Ben so. I never thought I would marry, though I'm far from old age, only two years older than you. Yet, I believed that no one would ever want to marry me, and I would end up a spinster, as you always predicted." Her face lit up with a smile. "He and I just seem right for each other. He makes me happy."

Misella bit her tongue and held in the comment she almost blurted out, *"He wanted me first, you know."* Instead, she answered in a tight voice, "I don't think you foolish, Elinor. You could not find a better man anywhere than Ben. He is kind and compassionate and wise...and yes, a bit eccentric and opinionated, but that, to me, is part of his charm." She bowed her head. "I owe him my life," she said quietly, her eyes stinging. "And I can never repay him." Retrieving a white handkerchief tucked inside her sleeve, she blotted her eyes and said, without conviction, "I am happy for both of you."

Elinor noticed the embroidered initials on the corner of the handkerchief dangling from Misella's hand. Surprised and a little suspicious, she asked, "Where did you get that fancy handkerchief? Who is EB?"

Misella blushed a deep red. "From Captain Barclay," she murmured, "Eben Barclay. He loaned it to me at a time when I needed a kerchief. He told me to keep it until his return in the fall."

Elinor's eyebrows narrowed into a gentle frown. "Do you always carry it with you?"

Misella's back stiffened, and she sat up very straight in her chair. "Yes. Why shouldn't I?"

"No need to get defensive, Misella. I fear that if other people see you with it, they might assume you have taken it without permission. Ben has told me about some of the sad cases he witnessed in his London courtroom—destitute young women convicted and sentenced to transportation for merely stealing a handkerchief, consigned to a life of horror here for such a minor crime. He wants to defend poor souls like these when he establishes his law practice here. Father and I have offered to help him."

Misella tucked the handkerchief back into her sleeve. "I want to help, too, when I am free. And I might decide to live here then after you're married and take care of the house...and Father."

Elinor smiled and sipped her tea. "You don't need to worry about Father or delay your own marriage to Jack Finn in order to stay here with him. Father can hire a housemaid, Misella. He has plenty of money now. And Ben and I plan to settle close by and spend time with him."

Misella picked up the oat cake and nibbled at it. She set it down and fiddled with her tea cup, twirling it back and forth, some of the liquid spilling over the top and dribbling into the saucer. *I can't marry Jack*, she thought to herself. She wanted to confess the truth to Elinor, but she could not admit, especially to Elinor, that she had strong feelings for Captain Barclay. Elinor might leak the news to Ben who would feel obliged to tell Jack. She needed more time to make up her mind, time to find herself. *I don't know what to do,* she agonized. *I have lived a lie for so many years. I need time to find myself…who I am, what I desire.*

"I do want to try and start over with you and Father," she told Elinor. "Recapture the time and the family I lost when I was so young."

Elinor reached over and covered Misella's hand with her own. "I'm sure that Jack will give you all the time you need. If he loves you, he will wait for you. Think how long he has waited already; how hard he fought to be reunited with you. He will understand."

Misella closed her eyes and shook her head. That was not what she meant, but she couldn't expect Elinor to understand that she gave up the idea of becoming Jack's wife while on the ship. She didn't believe she would see him again. And then…when he showed up at Mrs. Dobbs pretending to be Margaret's brother, she was overwhelmed with joy and love and gratitude. But since that day, she had thought of him not as a husband, but as the brother she never had. And she worried that maybe she had always considered him that way because he watched over her, protected her like a brother would.

Elinor looked troubled. "You must tell Jack right away how you feel, that you need more time before you marry him. Be honest with him, Misella. He deserves that at least."

Misella wrung her hands together. "How can I tell him?" she moaned. "He's a man of action; he lacks Ben's patient wisdom." She hesitated for a moment. "He has suffered so much for me. I don't want to hurt him."

Elinor leaned closer to Misella and grasped her hands, stilling them in her firm grip. "Listen to me, Misella. Jack Finn is a wanted man in England. He needed to escape to avoid capture. You provided the incentive for him to leave and to fight his way here. You saved him as much as he saved you. You refused to marry Ben and save yourself because you didn't love him. You didn't want to live a lie. That took courage."

Leaning back, a surprised look on her face, Misella whispered, "Ben told you about that proposal?" She wondered if Elinor was taunting her as she used to do, reminding her subtly now that Ben no longer paid homage to "the spoiled one," as Elinor had often called her, "the vain one" who thought she was "so smart." The news that Ben had transferred his allegiance to poor, freckled, unschooled Elinor still rankled Misella and fueled her lingering distrust of her older sister.

"Yes," Elinor exclaimed. "Ben explained everything to me, and I am glad he did. I wasn't upset, Misella. I understood—and I appreciated his honesty. Jack will understand that you need more time if you are honest with him about your feelings."

Misella closed her eyes and bowed her head, distress evident in her face and the slump of her shoulders. "I will tell him when I see him next Sunday." She raised her head and pleaded, "Please don't say anything to Ben about this. I want Jack to hear it from me."

"Of course, I will say nothing to Ben about our conversation," Elinor said. "Be brave, Misella, as you have been throughout your long ordeal." She picked up her cup and took a long sip of tea before setting the cup down carefully on the saucer. "Tell me about this Captain Barclay," she said. "I am surprised that he would give you such a rich-looking handkerchief."

Misella's face softened, the frown around her eyes and the tightness of her lips disappearing. "I was surprised, too. I didn't expect such thoughtfulness from him. But he is kind and compassionate, though he often hides his sympathy behind a gruff exterior." She picked up her oat cake and devoured it, a faraway look in her eyes. "He is an honorable man."

"He sounds a lot like Ben," Elinor said, holding the platter of oat cakes out to Misella.

About to take an oat cake, Misella's hand froze in midair. She raised her eyebrows and stared at Elinor. "He is like Ben," she said, dropping her empty hand into her lap. "I never thought of him that way before—he is much younger, probably thirty-five or so, I'd guess, and quite handsome, especially in his Captain's uniform—the embroidered frock coat and gold-trimmed tri-corner hat." She hesitated for a moment. "He is a widower, too, like Ben. He lost his wife in childbirth and his only child. I was saddened to hear that."

She removed the handkerchief again, folding it in her lap, tracing the initials with her fingers. "I think about him often," she murmured. "I believe he is very lonely." She raised her eyes and stared intently at her sister. "I miss him. Do you think me foolish, Elinor, to remember my captor with affection and to long for his return?"

"Oh, Misella, if he was kind to you during your ordeal, I understand why you would cling to that idea of him—he seemed your savior at a dire time. And perhaps he was." Elinor arose from her chair and retrieved the teakettle from the stove. She poured more tea into both cups and replaced the kettle. When she sat back down, she avoided Misella's gaze, keeping her eyes on her cup as she continued. "But you were valuable merchandise to him, Misella; he needed to keep you safe and cooperative in order to complete his transaction with Ben and receive his payment. Does he really deserve your devotion?"

Misella bit her lip and sighed with exasperation, holding back the withering responses she used to fling whenever Elinor angered her in the past—idiot, red-haired witch. Instead, she said in a strained, quiet voice, "Perhaps not. I will have to see what happens when he returns in the fall."

* * * * * *

In the parlor, Johnnie Cross poured himself another glass of brandy. "You must allow me to help you, Ben. I have come across a small, empty store for sale that could easily be converted into a law office where you can see clients. If you'll agree, I want to buy it for you." He held the bottle out to Ben who waved it away.

"No more for me," Ben said. "I've had enough for now." He set his glass down on the cart before addressing Johnnie's offer. "I cannot accept charity, especially not from you, Sir. I might agree to a loan, but only if I can sign a promissory note." His face reddening, his head bowed with embarrassment, he admitted to his future father-in-law, "I have a debt in England that I must repay within the year. Otherwise, I would most certainly reject your kind offer, Sir. In any case, I would never accept it without a legal note of repayment."

Johnnie nodded in agreement, relieved that the two of them could reach an understanding. "We can do that if you insist," he said, "but you need to start your practice as soon as possible now that the court has licensed you in the county, and you have taken the oath. I have several wealthy acquaintances who will pay well for your services upon my recommendation, so repaying both loans should not be a problem for you. And these poor enslaved convicts need your help." He placed his half-empty glass on the cart next to Ben's and leaned forward in his chair, closer to him.

"I have one who needs assistance now," he said, his voice low, his eyes troubled. "Robby Benton, a young runaway who hid on board my fishing vessel while I was docked in St. Michael's. I discovered him late yesterday when I returned to Boston. A sad sight he is, and scared to death that I would turn him in."

Ben lurched back in his chair. "A danger for you, Sir. You could be seen as an accomplice. Does anyone else know?"

"No, no one else has seen him. He's still there, in the boat's cabin. I tried to make him as comfortable as possible; piled blankets on the floor for his bed, brought him some food, told him to stay hidden until I returned. The poor chap was half-starved, covered with sores."

He shook his head, pain darkening his eyes. "I never paid much attention to these indentures before. I'd see them sometimes when I'd deliver fish to the plantation at St. Michael's, toiling in the tobacco fields, lugging bales of leaves to the barns, emaciated men and women, even children no bigger than tobacco leaves themselves."

He picked up his glass and downed the remains. "I used to know what it was like to be poor and powerless," he mused, "but I'd forgotten. I'd grown smug with my newfound wealth, until you came and told us what happened to Misella. And I just can't look away any longer and do nothing."

Ben stayed quiet for a moment, his gaze shifting to the empty hallway, his attention drawn to the sound of voices coming from the kitchen. Assured that Elinor and Misella were still engaged in conversation, he asked Johnnie, "What do you want me to do?"

Johnnie Cross stood up and began pacing back and forth. He stopped in front of Ben, leaned in close, and muttered, "Come meet him with me, can you, when I take Misella back to the boarding house? I will tell the girls that I'm dropping you off at the inn before I return home. Then you and I will head to the harbor and board the fishing boat. I need your counsel about how to proceed and so does Robby Benton."

Chapter 44

Johnnie Cross swung a lantern jauntily in his hand as he led Ben Turner down the dark pier. The light from the candle bounced on and off each of the fishing boats as they moved down the line to the largest boat at the end of the pier. "Wait until you see the inside of this vessel of mine," he hollered, to warn Robby Benton of their approach. "I could throw a party in it. I've enough whiskey on board to keep us happy for a while."

He flipped the latch and opened the wooden gate that allowed entrance onto the deck surrounding the cabin house in the center. He drew a padlock key secured with a loop of twine from his pocket and raised his voice in case of any nearby listeners, "I always lock it when I leave because we often have stragglers hanging around, up to no good." He turned the key and lifted the lock open. "Come on in," said. "Welcome to my domicile when I'm on the water." He closed the door and set the lantern on a small table.

The cabin reeked of fish, unwashed bodies, and wet rubber. Ben detected a hint of camphor, too—an odor familiar to him from his Newgate visits to counsel destitute prisoners—and just as ineffective here as it was there. He noticed a blanket-clad ghost of a figure trembling in the corner, eyes blinking in the sudden candle light.

"No need for fright, Robby," Johnnie said, his voice low and calm. "Ben Turner here is a lawyer friend who wants to help you." He unlocked a cabinet next to the door and withdrew a jug of whiskey and three small glasses. "Come have a drink with us, and we will plan your escape." He uncorked the jug and filled the glasses, handing one to Ben and holding another out to Robby who huddled against the wall as if frozen in place.

Ben pulled a three-legged stool up to the table and sat down. He unbuttoned his jacket, removed his cap, tufts of graying hair springing up, and rubbed his hands together before lifting the glass and taking a drink. "Better come join us, Son," he said quietly without looking at Robby. "We have much to discuss."

Johnnie pushed two more stools up to the table and set Robbie's glass down in front of the vacant stool. He sat down next to Ben and lifted his own glass to his lips, ignoring as well the shaking figure in the corner. They sat in silence sipping their whiskey until they both heard the poor wretch drop the blanket and approach the table with shuffling footsteps.

Robby Benton dropped down on the stool, turning his face away from the lantern. Ben studied the bent head, shorn like a lamb at harvesting, the side of his gaunt face pocked with scars. The rank odor of the youngster almost made him gag. He would bring a bag of herbs with him on their next visit, along with a strong bar of soap and some borrowed clothes. The boy was so thin and stunted, a child's clothing would fit him, though Johnnie said the lad claimed to be eighteen. He had signed up for voluntary servitude when he was fifteen to escape his orphan's life in England, hoping to find promised riches in the New World.

Johnnie refilled Ben's glass and his own before addressing Robby, who hunched on the stool, his whiskey untouched. "Mr. Turner was a well-known barrister in London. He has come to Boston to seek justice through the court for indentured slaves like you. We want to help you."

Robby glanced up with surprise and stared at Ben. With a slow shake of his head, he picked up his glass and drained it. "Won't do no good," he said, his voice strained. He coughed and continued shaking his head. "Not here, anyways." He looked at Johnnie. "You know old man Jenkins, the plantation master, don't you?"

Johnnie nodded. "Delivered fish to him every month for years. Not very friendly or talkative, but he does pay me well."

Robby scowled. "Wish he paid us what we deserve. Instead, he beats us for no reason—and starves us, too. We don't never get any of your fish. Just grits and gruel, and hard bread once in a while."

Ben leaned forward, resting his forearms on the edge of the table. "What makes you think a lawyer can't secure better conditions and fairer treatment for you?" he asked. "If Jenkins isn't abiding by your contract, a lawyer might fight for that in the courtroom."

"Nope," Robby replied. "Jenkins changes the terms of the contract after you sign on. I know two people who have tried suing him in the county court—Jimmy Feeney and Mary Boyle, both runaways. They lost, and had hell to pay for trying. Feeney's dead now, beaten to death, and Mary will never complete her time cause Jenkins keeps adding on months. He does that to all of us for any little thing we do wrong or he doesn't like."

Ben sat up straighter. "Do you know if the two runaways were represented in court by counsel?"

Robby scoffed. "Doesn't matter if they were, they still lost because Jenkins is friends with the judge who always rules in favor of the plantation owners, or the merchants. Especially against runaways, the ones desperate enough to try getting away." Robby looked up at the two men, fear clouding his eyes. "Like me," he muttered. "Only I'm never going back. I swear I'll drown myself first."

Ben rapped his knuckles on the table. "No you won't, Son. We'll see to that. Mr. Cross has a plan to help you escape Jenkins and his twisted view of how indenture is supposed to work—and I plan to represent others like you in Boston's court of law to seek justice." He picked up his glass and sipped the whiskey.

Robby slumped down on the stool. "Nothing can help," he moaned, shaking his head like an obstinate child. "I'm a dead goose."

Ben snorted, slamming his glass down on the table. "Nonsense. We'll have no more whining. You're going to help us by staying alive and doing what we tell you. Understand? And maybe in time you can help others to gain their freedom."

Johnnie Cross spoke up before the lad had a chance to object. "Here's what we're going to do. You'll stay concealed here on board until next Monday when we leave to deliver fish to customers along the Bay, including Jenkins."

Robby jumped up, his stool slamming against the door. "No," he panted. "I'm not going back there."

"Settle down, Son," Ben ordered as Johnnie pulled the stool back in place. "Sit and listen."

Ignoring the boy's panic and waiting until he dropped back down on the stool, Johnnie continued, his voice low, "We'll have another person on board with us, Jack Finn, who will help me with the deliveries. You'll be well hidden and locked in here so no one else will see you or know of your presence. When we reach Annapolis at nightfall, you and Finn will exit the boat, and he will take over. He knows the area well; he has friends there who will help him sneak you into the woods where you will join a woodsman named James Logan, a deserter himself for many months. Logan will keep you hidden and safe."

Before the boy could protest or question the plan, Ben pulled a notebook and a fat pencil from his pocket and placed them on the table. "Do you know how to write, Son?"

Robby nodded. "My ma taught me—when she was still alive." He bowed his head and rubbed at his eyes. "That's how I qualified for free passage as an indenture. I thought I could get a job with a printer here, not planting tobacco for old man Jenkins."

"In the days ahead while you're waiting," Ben said, pushing the notebook toward him, "I want you to write down everything you know about Jenkins and the indentures who work for him, especially Jimmy Feeney and Mary Boyle. What all of you had to do, the hours you worked, the food, the punishments, what happened when you broke any rule. Everything. Can you do that?"

Robby hesitated for a moment and then picked up the notebook. "Yes, Sir, I can do that."

Ben leaned in close to the boy, holding his glass up near his nose so as to breathe in the whiskey vapors rather than the scent of Robby Benton. "You'll be my temporary law clerk, my eyewitness in *absentia*," he said, "and Jenkins is going to be my first courtroom case in Talbot County, Maryland."

Chapter 45

As soon as they reached the park the following Sunday, Misella released Jack's hand, dashing ahead to crouch by the pond, her shoes sinking in the marshy grass. "Oh look, the ducks are waiting for us to feed them. Hurry up, Jack. I need the basket."

"Okay, we don't want to disappoint the ducks, do we?" Jack plopped the basket down on a nearby bench and retrieved a slice of hard bread. "Catch," he said, tossing it to Misella and sitting down on the bench. He was glad to see her more animated. She had seemed distracted, much too quiet, when they left the boarding house. He wondered if she already knew about the boat trip he would take to Annapolis the next day with her father. Though he had intended to tell her after they reached the park, their private summer oasis, he hoped that somehow she already knew. He dreaded telling her that he would have to leave her again and didn't know how soon he would return.

Jack watched her breaking off pieces of bread, leaning over the water, her hand stretched out to the mother duck so that she could feed the ducklings lined up behind her. Misella seemed unaware of the water creeping up the hem of her skirt. "Don't fall in," he called. "I don't feel like swimming today, or rescuing maidens in distress."

She threw the rest of the bread into the pond, stood up, and swirled around, her hair coming unpinned and falling forward. "You won't need to rescue me again, Jack," she said, her face red, her voice rising with annoyance. "I can take care of myself now. I'm not the helpless little waif I was the last time you rescued me from drowning."

Jack jumped up. "Forgive me, Misella. I'm sorry for being thoughtless. I wasn't even thinking of that long ago time. I was joking, that's all. I did not mean to remind you of your past." He moved toward her to put his arms around her, but she pulled away.

She knew that Jack was only joking, trying to lift her spirits and dispel the foul mood that had plagued her all week—ever since the "happy homecoming" when she was expected to embrace her newfound family and let the past drift away like a dark cloud. But a hazy sense of anger and jealousy still soured her thoughts and filled her with an unshakeable despair. She wanted to erase her past and begin over, forget her innocent youth and how far she had fallen. Could she ever hope to do that if she married Jack? She worried that he might be a constant reminder of her stained reputation that she had to obliterate from her mind.

She thought, as she did often, about Captain Barclay who knew the worst about her, had witnessed her breakdown on the ship, her shame and degradation, and yet had treated her in the end with kindness. She had noticed more than once on the ship sympathy in his eyes when he looked at her, how they had softened with regret and longing, and perhaps love, as he left her with Mrs. Dobbs. How she yearned to see him again.

Leaning down, she gathered up her soggy hem and squeezed the water from it. When she let go, the hem swept the tops of her muddy shoes absorbing some of the grime. That she seemed unconcerned about her disheveled appearance as she headed to the bench worried Jack. She had been obsessed with cleanliness and neatness since her "slovenly Slammakin" days on the ship, as she described them, looking as if her "dirty clothes had been hung on her with a pitch fork." Setting the basket on the ground, she perched on the edge of the bench, ready to take flight, Jack thought. "I have something to tell you, Jack," she said without looking at him. "Please sit down."

Wary of upsetting her further, Jack took his place on the bench, careful not to sit too close to her. "What is it, Misella? You were distressed about something when I arrived at Mrs. Dobbs. Are you growing impatient to be done with her?"

Misella bit her lip and sighed in exasperation. "Yes, I'm impatient," she groaned. "Why wouldn't I be? I'm trapped there for another three months at least until the Captain returns and sets me free." She stamped her foot and kicked at the basket. "I'm sick of catering to the whims of that miserable crow and her doddering pack of blackbirds."

Jack reached out to take her hand, still damp with pond water. "I know how difficult this is for you," he said. "I hate this situation, too. Spending a few hours a week together, when I long to be with you every minute of every day. But take heart, Misella. It will happen soon enough and be all the sweeter when we marry because we have had to wait so long and endure so much to be together." He placed his hand gently on her cheek and turned her face to him. "All that matters is we love one another."

"Oh, Jack," she cried, her face contorted, her unpinned hair hanging limp over her ears. "I can't marry you. I've changed. I'm not that innocent young girl you thought you fell in love with. You don't really know me." Unable to look at him, she stared at her hands, twisting frantically together in her lap, as if they didn't belong to her.

Jack grabbed her hands in his and held them motionless. "Oh my darling, I do know you. You are still that sweet, brave girl I have always loved. Your past does not matter to me. We will both forget about our pasts and build our future together."

She closed her eyes and shook her head, her hair swinging from side to side, anguish evident on her face and in the unsteadiness of her voice. "How can I forget my past? My lost childhood does matter to me. I need to start over. I have to return to my father's house and begin again, to try to recover some of what I have lost."

Moving closer to her, Jack put his arm around her rigid shoulders and murmured, "How much time do you think you will need, Misella? I will wait. Six months? A year?

Because we will be separated anyway. I planned to tell you today that we'll have to postpone our marriage for at least that long. I have agreed to help your father and Ben rescue a runaway indenture, and accompany him to Annapolis to find Logan and seek his assistance. We leave tomorrow, and I am unsure when I can return."

Misella relaxed. "Ben's mission," she said. "Of course, he would want your help. He knows how brave and loyal you are. I know that, too. I've always admired your strength and courage." Removing Jack's arm from her shoulders, she held onto his hand, relief flooding her face and softening her voice. "I'll miss you, Jack. Very much. Ever since I saw you standing as my brother, my savior, in Mrs. Dobbs' parlor, I have pictured you that way when we are apart—as the loving brother I never had."

Jack dropped her hand and jumped up. "Brother!" he thundered. "That's how you think of me? No, Misella. Believe me, that is not how I think of you. As a sister? You must be joking." He raised his hands and raked his fingers through his hair, causing some of the dark curls to fall forward into his eyes—a gesture that evoked for Misella the sudden image of a young Johnnie Cross surrendering to his wife's demands, refusing to fight for the protection of his daughter.

From a dark corner of her mind crept the nagging fear that Jack might abandon her and leave her stranded alone as her father had done—as Ben did. How easily they both had forgotten their devotion and love for her when she had needed them most. She had to protect herself now. She huddled in misery on the bench beneath him. "I'm sorry, Jack," she said, her voice breaking. "I am lost and confused right now. I need to figure out what I want. I hope you can understand."

Jack took a deep, ragged breath and hung his head. "I'm sorry too, Misella. For both of us." He looked at her, the vivid blue of his eyes dulled with sadness. "I will try to understand. Perhaps we do need time. It may help us to part for a while."

Misella didn't answer. She leaned down to lift the basket onto the bench and opened the folded muslin cloth encasing their dinner. After spreading the cloth out next to her on the bench, she carefully placed wrapped pieces of cheese, sliced bread, and two bruised apples on the cloth. She withdrew two pewter cups and a small jug of sweet tea, setting the cups down first before uncorking and pouring the tea. "Please sit and eat now, Jack. We haven't much time."

Swallowing the lump in his throat and the words he wanted to shout at her, "I will never give up until you are my wife," he remained speechless. He sat down and forced himself to eat the dinner he knew she had scrimped all week to provide.

They ate in silence while the world around them thrummed with life and laughter: servant girls wheeling squealing babies in the warm afternoon sun, fathers lifting giggling children to their shoulders, shrieking toddlers flinging bread to the ducks while frantic mothers held on to them by the seats of their pants or the backs of their smocks.

They walked back to Mrs. Dobbs' boarding house in the waning sunlight, Jack carrying the picnic basket with both hands, Misella beside him lost in guilty thought about Captain Barclay's return. When they reached the steps to the house, Jack handed the basket to Misella. "Thank you for the victuals," he said and bowed with formality, as if she were a stranger he had recently met in the park.

Shocked by the coldness in Jack's voice, Misella struggled to hold back her tears. The memory of Jack's love and devotion, she realized, had sustained her through the years, even when she believed she would never see him again. During her early and most vulnerable years at Hawthorn Manor, Jack had tried to protect her from Sir Richard when he served as his coach driver; he had watched over her then as much as he could —like the brother she had yearned to have growing up.

Now, as he was about to leave her, she reached for his hand and held on. "Oh, Jack. I will miss you so. Whatever will I do without you here to raise my hopes and calm my fears?" Her voice caught in her throat. "To make me laugh?"

The stony look on his face dissolved. He squeezed her hand. "You know I'll be back, Misella. Like a weed you can't kill or a lost trinket you can't forget. Whatever happens, I'll always wait for you." He grinned, let go of her hand and saluted as he walked away.

"Jack," she called, her voice rising, tears beginning to fall. When he turned back, she placed her fingers beneath her chin. "Chin up; eyes to heaven."

Chapter 46

"Here it is, Sir," Robby Benton placed the battered notebook into Ben's outstretched hand. "I've included every violation against us I could remember since Jenkins bought my indenture and imprisoned me on his living hell of a plantation."

Ben opened the notebook and flipped through some of the pages, impressed with the detailed organization and neatness of Robby's list of violations, each category supported with significant documentation: names, dates, punishments received, final outcomes. He was also impressed with the new Robby—cleaned up and neatly dressed with a self-confidence that surprised Ben. "Thank you, Son," he said. "This will be a great help to me. I'll study it carefully and won't use the information to file a case until I know you are safe and cannot be threatened by Jenkins."

Robby nodded, his expression solemn like that of a judge. "You'll notice, Sir," he said, "that I have underlined Mary Boyle's information. I think you should use her as your first case—if you can find a way to meet up with her and get her cooperation. Lord knows she has suffered the most." He looked down for a moment, but not before Ben had seen the glint of tears in his eyes. When he raised his head, he was clear-eyed and continued addressing Ben in a controlled voice. "Tell her I made it to freedom, and she can too with your help."

Ben grabbed his hand and shook it vigorously. "I will do that, my Boy. You have my word. Maybe some day when all of this is settled, you can return and work with me on other cases of indentured servants who need protection by the courts."

Blushing, Robby seemed to stand taller and straighter, his voice strong and assured. "It would be an honor, Sir."

Johnnie Cross interrupted. "Time to go, Ben. Jack and I will take over from here. We'll try to make contact with Mary Boyle on our stop at the plantation, but may not see her on this trip. We don't want to raise any suspicions. If Jenkins should question why I've brought Jack along to help me, I'll say that my back is acting up again. I'll let you know what happened as soon as I return.

Ben shoved the notebook into his pocket. He shook Johnnie's hand and thumped Jack Finn on the back. "Godspeed, my friends." He shuffled to the doorway, the boat dipping gently, his cane steadying his gait. Before he stepped out into the gray dawn, he turned, his cane raised over his head. "Think like pirates, boys."

* * * * * *

Later that morning, Ben sat in his new office poring over Robby's notebook and scribbling on scraps of paper strewn across his desk. He'd organize his own notes and his thoughts about how to approach this case in good time. But now, he let the fire of his imagination lead his quill as fast as he could dip the point in the ink pot. He marveled at the boy's thoroughness. A week alone on the boat fighting for his slim chance of survival must have mightily concentrated his mind and fueled his memories.

When Ben read one of the underlined entries Robby had included about Mary Boyle, he dropped the quill and leaned closer, squinting his good eye to clear his vision.

After Mary and Jimmy Feeney ran away and then lost their lawsuit against Jenkins for his cruel treatment, Jenkins beat them unmercifully. Feeney died from his wounds, but Mary survived. As part of her punishment, Jenkins inscribed a tattoo on the inside of her left arm with his initials and the year she ran away—A. J. 1753.

He told her that her seven years of indenture would begin again from that date even though she had already served six years of her original agreement. Mary Boyle is not a convict but a free-willer—agreeing, like me, to the seven-year indenture as a way to pay for transportation to the New World.

Ben reeled back in disgust, not only at Jenkins' cruelty. The man had corrupted the meaning and the purpose of the 1720 indenture statute that allowed private sector individuals to help the British government dispose of convicts. The program had made merchants wealthy transporting undesirables to the Caribbean and America, where cheap, disposable labor on sugar and tobacco plantations was needed. And, of course, plantation owners benefitted as well. In time, non-convicts, who could not afford to pay for passage, signed on, agreeing to the terms of indenture to seek opportunity and eventual freedom from poverty.

A program begun with good intentions had devolved into nothing more than slave labor with little oversight or concern for the victims, no matter how cruelly or unfairly they were treated. Ben recalled a story he had heard at Newgate when he visited Misella there. An indentured convict, Elizbeth Briggs, sentenced to seven years for stealing a silk handkerchief, had written a letter home to her father from a plantation in Maryland. She pleaded with him to send her a few clothes because she was almost naked, without shoes or stockings, and she needed a blanket as she was forced to sleep on the ground. Fed little but salt and Indian corn, she was whipped like an animal. Fearing death if she didn't receive help soon, she begged him to forgive her transgressions and have pity on her.

Though skeptical when he heard that story and other rumors drifting around about the terrible treatment of indentures, Ben had dismissed them as hearsay until Misella was sentenced. And now that he was here in the Colonies, he had seen Robby Benton, heard his story, and read his detailed accounting. "This injustice must stop," Ben grumbled aloud, though no one was in the room to hear him. "And I intend to end it, beginning with Mary Boyle." He jumped up and began pacing the room without his cane, lurching back and forth from his desk to the window inscribed with large black letters, **Turner Law Office**.

When Elinor opened the door an hour later carting their lunch basket, she found Ben leaning over his desk, writing frantically and muttering to himself. He looked up, scowling at her as if she were an intruder. "Ben," she said, her voice sharp, her face red and damp. "You were supposed to come to the house first, hours ago, remember? But from the looks of you, I suppose you forgot. You worried me to death. I pictured you collapsed on some street corner near the dock, done in by this heat—until I came to my senses and deduced that you probably came here instead."

"Sorry, my dear," he mumbled, with a sheepish grin. "But I've found it. The hook upon which I will hang my first case, thanks to Robby Benton." He picked up the notebook and shook it in the air. "And I'm not going to lose. I know it!"

Elinor pushed some of the papers aside to make room and set the basket on the desk. "You can tell me everything while we eat."

Ben shook his head and, moving the basket to the floor, plopped down in his chair. "I'll eat later, my dear, not now. I'm not hungry." He picked up his quill and resumed writing, speaking out loud as he jotted down his thoughts. "Jenkins tattooed Mary Boyle, branded her after she ran away as if she belonged to him. She does not. He does not own her. He must abide by the terms under which the indenture program was set up—as a temporary work contract. Precedent may allow him to set the conditions under which she works to pay off her indenture, but he cannot hold her or her contract in perpetuity as the tattoo suggests. All that she owes him is seven years of just and fair labor."

He threw down his quill and grinned at Elinor. "Let them try to argue the intent of the law against me when I defend Mary Boyle in court."

Chapter 47

Albert Jenkins had inherited his tidewater plantation from his Puritan grandfather who emigrated from England to Maryland's Eastern Shore in 1644. After staking claim to a large plot of land along the shores of the St. Michaels river, his grandfather, with the help of his two sons, dredged and drained the surrounding fields and planted tobacco—killing himself from exhaustion in the process. Albert's uncle soon followed, depleted by the bare struggle to survive. The younger brother, Albert's father, however, managed to hang on and, in time, he and the plantation flourished, because of the 1720 indenture statute that brought several indentured convicts to work in his fields—and because of the increased demand for tobacco in the Colonies and in England.

As his father's sole offspring, Albert assumed control of the plantation in 1730 when both of his parents were murdered by one of their convicts. Nineteen years old at the time, Albert single-handedly captured the murderer as he tried to escape and hanged him from the oak tree next to his mother's garden. Small and wiry, thin as a ferret, Albert then turned his ferocious temper upon his remaining indentured servants. He trusted no one, became the lone overseer of his crops, and inflicted brutal punishments for the smallest infraction of his rules forcing several of his indentures, over the years, to try running away. None of them succeeded.

A sworn bachelor, Jenkins chose the most attractive female indenture from each new batch to work for him in his kitchen—and in his bedroom, until he tired of her and consigned her to the fields. Seven years ago, Mary Boyle had been one of his unfortunate choices. With an Irish temper to match his, she resisted him as much as she could and paid a severe price for her rebellion. He beat her repeatedly, starved her, yet she did not give in; she laughed at him, taunted him, and even addressed him as "Little Caesar." Determined to break her, Jenkins had kept her working inside, even after she ran away.

On Tuesday morning, when Johnnie Cross and Jack Finn dropped anchor and tied up the boat at Jenkins' dock, a punishing sun made the heat unbearable. Lifting the canvas sheet covering a sweating Robby Benton, Johnnie cautioned him to stay quiet. "I know you're beastly hot, but no matter how long we are gone, you must remain covered inside the cabin. When Jack and I return, we'll head to Annapolis to drop off you and Jack. We should dock there at nightfall. Don't worry. You'll be safe in here."

As Johnnie exited the boat, he motioned Jack to the packed nets hanging in the water off the back of the boat. "We'll need to move the cod quickly," he told him. "Usually, Jenkins is waiting here for me with a worker to carry the fish." With a hand shading his eyes, he scanned the grounds leading up to the house and the tobacco fields beyond where workers moved in slow motion as if treading in quick sand. "Better take them up ourselves. We can't leave them here on the dock in this heat."

Each of them grabbed a net flopping with live fish, unhooked it, and slung it over his shoulder, not minding the cool, wet slap of fish against his back. "Follow me," Johnnie said. "The gutting shed is off the kitchen. We should find somebody inside."

Finn nodded, too winded with the heat to speak as they trudged toward the house.

He was careful not to let any water drip on his shirt pocket where the note from Robby Benton to Mary Boyle lay. Not a note exactly, but a crude drawing of the British flag by which, Robby said, she would know he had escaped, but if Jenkins found it, the home symbol they both shared would not cast suspicion on either of them. If Finn could meet her, that is, and find a way to hand it to her discreetly. Maybe even talk to her for a moment and tell her about Turner's plan.

As they approached the house, a loud voice pounded through the open kitchen window and fractured the dead quiet of the yard. "You little slut. Stealing food again. Stuffing your ugly, back-talking mouth with my reserves." Several whacks and grunts followed.

Johnnie stopped. "That's Jenkins," he muttered. "Maybe we had better wait a few minutes before knocking."

"You don't frighten me," a woman screamed. "Your strutting and snorting makes me laugh. I think you were born in a barnyard and that's where you belong."

"I'm not waiting," Finn answered in disgust. "I'm going to stop the damned weasel. Especially if that's Mary Boyle he's abusing." Finn marched up and banged on the kitchen door, the bag of fish swaying behind him. Johnnie stood back and waited.

A strained silence ensued. "Who is it and what the hell do you want?" Jenkins hollered. "I'm busy."

Johnnie stepped forward and answered in a calm, sturdy voice, "It's Johnnie Cross, Mr. Jenkins. We have your fish order. Can we come in or put it in the shed? It's too hot to leave it out here."

After some stumbling sounds from inside, a panting Albert Jenkins flung open the kitchen door, one hand dragging a scrawny, wild-haired woman, welts evident on her reddened cheeks.

He does resemble a weasel, Finn thought, *shifting beady eyes, leathery brown face, sharp nose, pointy ears.*

Pointing a callused finger at Finn, Jenkins snarled, "Who's this? Never seen him before."

Johnnie Cross grimaced as he set down his bag of fish. "This is Jack Finn. Helps me when I need him. My back is acting up again. I can't dock the boat alone. Too old these days, I guess." He chuckled, but Jenkins didn't join in. Instead he kicked the door open, releasing his iron grip on Mary Boyle's arm.

"Take 'em to the shed," he snarled at Mary who stood back rubbing her forearm. "And gut all those fish right quick or I'll gut you."

Johnnie spoke up in a firm voice. "Finn here can help her with that. He's fast, an expert with a blade. You'll want to get those fish cleaned and salted before they cook in this heat."

Jenkins scowled and nodded. "I ain't paying for any spoiled fish." He motioned toward the shed. "Take 'em in there. The slut'll show you what to do." He shoved Mary out the door, and she stumbled down the steps.

Finn managed to grab her with his free hand before she fell to the ground and held onto her until she gained her footing. She felt lighter to him than the bag of fish he carried over his shoulder. She stepped away from him without a word or a glance at him or Jenkins, whom Finn heard mumble under his breath as she limped to the shed, "Clumsy bitch."

Finn grabbed both bags of cod and followed her while Johnnie drew the invoice from his pocket and said to Jenkins, "Can I come inside and settle the bill?"

"Okay," Jenkins grumbled, "but I ain't paying for any dead ones." He let the door slam behind him so that Johnnie had to let himself in to the dismal kitchen with its crude, hand-sawn furnishings and musty odor. A sack of walnuts, its contents strewn around a half-eaten apple lay atop the wooden counter. Johnnie sat down on one of the log chairs at the planked table and waited for Jenkins to retrieve his lock box of cash.

Meanwhile, Finn followed the silent Mary Boyle into the fish shed, wondering if she would speak or just chose not to in the oppressive heat of the reeking shed. The dead fish smell almost stole his breath and voice, too. A long slab of a counter, covered with dark stains, held a couple of dull-looking knives and a fish scaler. Two large tubs sat at the near end of the counter, one of them full of salt.

Mary Boyle picked up one of the knives and used it to flick back wayward curls of damp reddish hair from her bony face. Her moss green eyes glared at Finn as she held the knife aloft. "Don't get any ideas, Laddy."

Finn grinned in surprise at the familiar brogue. He pulled his blade from his belt and feigned a dueler's stance. "You needn't worry about me, Lassy. And it's a good thing because that broken, rusty blade wouldn't help you. How in Cork's sake do you skin fish with that sorry thing?"

Mary laughed, her eyes alight with relief. "It takes a long time, but "Little Caesar" is afraid to let me have a working weapon. He fears what I might cut off with it."

Finn moved close to her, his voice low. "Mary, I have a message for you from Robby Benton." As she dropped the knife and stepped back, he pulled the note from his pocket and handed it to her. "He said you would believe he was safe if I gave you this."

Mary opened the paper, gasped, and blessed herself before saying, "Glory be to God, where is he? I can't believe he made it." Tears flooded her eyes. "I prayed for him every day, missing him, and fearing his capture. He's so young, just a boy, an innocent; he was like a little brother to me. I tried to watch over him. He didn't tell me he was leaving. He knew I'd try to stop him."

Mary's words forced Finn to think about Misella and their final meeting in the park, how lost and confused she had left him with her talk of brotherly love. Her disclosure had stung his senses, wrenched his heart from its moorings, darkened his mind with despair. He shook his head as if to banish the troubling thought he had tried so hard to put aside because he had a job to do. "Mary," he said, "I have a proposition for you; you have a choice to make if you are brave enough to do it. And I feel certain that you will."

Finn told her everything about Ben Turner and the plan—if she could come undetected to the dock by midnight, Johnnie Cross would pick her up on his way back from Annapolis and take her to Turner who would file the lawsuit against Jenkins immediately. "He believes he can win this time. He knows the stakes are high, but Turner is a fierce defender; he will not let you down."

Mary agreed instantly. "I have nothing to lose but my life," she said, "and I have no life here anyway. I will be at the dock tonight or die trying." She grinned at Finn and raised the dull knife high, her eyes flashing. "Up the Irish," she whispered. "Now, let's tackle these fish."

Late that evening, Johnnie Cross drifted close again to the Jenkins dock where a dark heap, almost invisible this moonless night, huddled near the edge. This time he cast no anchor, tossing one of the heavy ropes to Mary Boyle, hoping she had the strength to pull the boat close enough to board. She missed grabbing the rope in the darkness the first time she tried. Johnnie held his breath as she tried again. He feared the boat slamming into the dock, the noise bringing a shotgun-toting Jenkins barreling down the hill. That would mean the end of Mary Boyle, not to mention the end of the Cross Fisheries.

This time, she grabbed the rope and hung on. Yanking the boat as close as she dared, she picked up her skirts with her free hand and leaped on board, landing with a thud. Johnnie whispered, "Well done, Mary Boyle," and handed her a long wooden paddle. "We will have to move the boat manually without a light until we are far enough down the river to pull over and anchor until dawn."

Afraid to speak or make a sound, her heart pounding against her chest, Mary grabbed the paddle, raised herself to her feet, steadied herself and began to paddle for her life.

When they had gained some distance from the plantation, Johnnie fired up a lantern to light their way. As they paddled in harmony, following the wavering yellow ribbon, he spoke aloud. "I'd like you to stay with my daughter Elinor and me at our Boston home until all of this is settled. Once you are freed—and you will be, that's certain—you can decide what to do next."

Mary emitted a long sigh before she spoke, her voice tight and strained, "I thank you for all of your help, Sir, what you did for me… and Robby Benton." Sniffling, her voice cracking, she continued, "God will reward you for your kindness…but I don't belong in your respectable, high class home." Her voice fell to a whisper. "An indentured slut like me."

Johnnie cleared his throat. "You are not a slut, my dear, and becoming an indentured servant is not a crime. You are not the criminal. We will work to convince you of that—Ben Turner, Elinor, Jack Finn and I…as we are trying, as hard as we can, to do with my other daughter, Misella.

Chapter 48

Johnnie Cross stood beside a subdued Mary Boyle in the parlor of his Boston home. Though she wore the same ragged, damp dress she had traveled in for three days, she had cleaned herself up as best she could aboard the fishing boat. She had tamed her flaming red hair into a scattered-looking bun and quieted her raging hunger with the bread, cheese, and apples Johnnie provided.

After introducing her to a beaming Ben Turner and Elinor, who sat forward expectantly in their chairs, Johnnie told them, "Mary is more than willing to testify against Jenkins."

Elinor jumped up and grabbed Mary's hand from her side. "We are so happy to have you here," she said with a smile. "Thank you for trusting us." When Mary frowned and failed to respond, Elinor blushed and dropped Mary's hand, embarrassed by her own lack of decorum. "I…I am sorry for being rude," she stammered. "I know that Ben and I will have to earn your trust. But I believe you have learned to trust my father and Jack Finn?" When Mary nodded, Elinor looked at Ben and continued, "We hope you will learn to trust us as well."

Mary stared with trepidation at the shabby-looking, bulky man Elinor had called Ben who sat hunched on the edge of his chair, squinting at her in seeming disapproval. If this was the brilliant lawyer Jack Finn had raved about, she began to question her decision. He hoisted himself out of the chair, leaning on the lion head of his cane, and stood next to Elinor.

"Welcome," he said. With both hands clutching the cane, he made no attempt to shake her hand. Squint-eyed, he stared at her for several seconds and then said in a gravelly voice, "You are a brave woman. I will count on your bravery continuing as we move ahead. The first thing you should know is that I will file the lawsuit tomorrow with a request that your case be moved to a Boston court because of judicial bias against indentures in Talbot County—based upon the outcomes of all the cases rendered in that district."

Mary was taken aback by the fiery determination in his gray eyes, though the watery left eye continued to blink and squint as if attempting to dislodge a foreign object. She had to admit to herself that she was flattered by the compliment he paid her and his seeming confidence in her strength and ability to keep going ahead.

"Of course, the change of venue will be denied," Turner continued. "The case will have to be judged in Jenkins' own county, but I will have established the idea of bias before we even enter Judge Crowley's courtroom."

Mary spoke, her voice low, the brogue softened. "I thank you, Sir, for your help. You can count on me. I won't let you down. I know how to fight."

Turner grinned. "I'm sure of it, my dear. I've learned a bit about redheads." He put his arm around Elinor and hugged her to him before he asked Johnnie about Jack Finn and Robby Benton.

"Let's sit in the kitchen before father shares that information with us," Elinor said. "I'll make tea and we can be more comfortable there." She smiled at Mary. "And when we are finished, I'll show you to your room upstairs. You must be exhausted. Or would you rather retire to your room now?"

Mary shook her head. "Oh, no, please. I want to hear about Robby. I need to know that he is safe."

"Of course," Elinor murmured, ushering the group from the parlor to the table in the kitchen. "Please sit, all of you, while I attend to our tea."

Mary waited for the men to sit down, startled when they remained standing. "After you, Mary," Johnnie said, pulling out her chair, treating her as if she were a lady.

Flustered, Mary blurted out, "I will make the tea so that Elinor can sit." She paused, her thin face reddening. "I'm the indenture," she stated firmly, "and I intend to earn my keep." She straightened her shoulders. "I don't like charity, and I will make the tea."

Whirling around from the stove with the tea canister in her hands, Elinor responded, "Yes, of course, Mary, as you wish. I will show you where everything is." She bustled over to the table where the two men stood in awkward silence. "Please sit down, gentlemen, but wait until we join you before you start your story, Father." She handed the canister to Mary. "Follow me," she said, with a wink at Ben and her father who remained standing.

When the tea was poured into the cups prearranged at each place, and the platter of honeyed scones laid on the table, the group sat down together. Johnnie proceeded to describe the drop off of Jack and Robby at the deserted Annapolis dock around midnight. "At first, I intended to pull farther down the dense shoreline and let the two disembark stealthily into the overgrown weeds. But the dock was empty, almost obscured in the moonless darkness, and Jack said he knew they could jump off there without detection."

Ben chuckled and nodded his head. "We don't need to worry about Finny's judgment or skill. He's a rascal with a pirate's head on his shoulders…and a patriot's heart." He turned his gaze to Mary Boyle. "You needn't worry. He'll protect your young friend and lead him to safety…or he'll die trying. He never gives up."

For the first time, she smiled. "Don't I know it, Sir." She bowed her head and crossed herself. "May good luck be their friend," she murmured, "and God's strength pilot them."

Chapter 49

When Ben arrived to pick up Misella one Sunday, a few weeks after her first visit to her father's house, she almost refused to go with him, claiming that Mrs. Dobbs needed her help. Although she yearned to escape the dreary, morning-long monotony of Mrs. Dobbs' Sabbath Day service, replete with Biblical readings and sermon, Misella struggled with her feelings of awkwardness in the new family setting and her continuing resentment toward her father and Elinor. She could not tolerate their fawning behavior, and she refused to pretend for their benefit that she was enjoying her "sublime homecoming."

"No, no, Margaret, dear," Mrs. Dobbs protested, with a tight smile and obsequious bow toward Ben Turner as he waited in the doorway. "Despite the illness of your brother, you deserve an outing with your distinguished mentor after working so hard all week. I wouldn't think of allowing you to miss out on your weekly trip to the park with the fine barrister."

Ben bowed in return, ignoring Misella's grimace. "I thank you, Mrs. Dobbs, in the name of King George," he purred, "for your generous spirit." He took Misella's arm and drew her to him. "Shall we go, Margaret?" he asked with a wink Mrs. Dobbs could not see. "Our carriage awaits."

Misella was relieved when Ben told her on their journey that Jack had made it safely to Annapolis with Robby Benton in tow;

she was happy for Ben that he felt confident about winning his case against Jenkins. Mary Boyle had been a surprise, he said, "a fighter determined to do whatever the case requires of her no matter the consequences."

"I believe you will like Mary Boyle," he added. "She will be staying at the house for awhile. You two have much in common. And soon you will both be free."

He reached for Misella's hand, giving it a slight squeeze. "She reminds me a lot of you," he stated, with a warm grin and a fond tap to Misella's cheek. "She is grateful for everything, especially to Jack for his bravery in standing up to Jenkins, and rescuing her and Robby Benton, at great cost to himself."

Leaning away from Ben, Misella experienced a sudden urge to defend her father. "Hmmm. What about all that father did? He's the one who started this rescue mission and put himself and his business at great risk to help. Does she mention him at all in her 'grateful' reverie?"

A look of surprise animated Ben's face. No doubt he was pleased by her unexpected display of loyalty to her father, Misella thought.

A smile hovered on Ben's lips as he responded, "Yes, of course she does, Misella. She reveres your father, too. But she considers Jack a kindred spirit because he is Irish, as she is, and they understand one another. She loves Robby Benton as if he were her brother, as you do with Jack, and she worries about him. She has a natural investment in his escape…and Jack's success."

Ben's words startled Misella. She stiffened and leaned forward, her eyes trained on his face. *He knows*, she thought. *Jack must have told him about the conversation in the park. He wants me to feel guilty about the way I treated Jack.* "What did Jack tell you…about our future plans?" she demanded, her voice hard.

Ben's face contorted into an exaggerated frown, his bushy eyebrows drawn together over his seemingly innocent gray eyes. "I don't know what you mean, my dear. Why would Jack confide in me about your plans? Especially when I have never asked him to?"

Misella moved to the edge of the seat, her back rigid with indignation. "Well done, Sir. Spoken like a skilled barrister in a hostile courtroom! Put the onus on the defendant with your pointed questions. Well, it won't work this time. I do not intend to joust with you…or listen to any of your lectures." She stood up, swaying a bit before plopping down on the seat across from him, folding her arms, and staring out the window.

"As you wish, my dear. I'm sorry if I have offended you. I'll keep quiet." Having planted the seeds of jealousy, he hoped, Ben was content to sit back and wait for Misella to come to her senses about Jack Finn, however long it took. He believed—no, he knew in his heart that they belonged together, but he could not lecture her about her mistake nor could he tell her how misguided were her feelings. She would resent his interference and accuse him of misplaced loyalty to Jack. He had learned in his long, troubled career and life that sometimes indirection works best, especially with the fairer sex.

Because she refused to look at Ben, Misella did not see the glimmer of a smile on his ruddy face and the twinkle of satisfaction in his eyes as he perceived her sudden misery.

For the remainder of the journey, they rode in silence, Misella brooding over her wounded sense of trust, feeling violated by both men—Jack for telling Ben about her rejection of marriage, and Ben for taunting her with that knowledge. How could Jack have defied her request to keep their discussion confidential? How could he have ignored her feelings so thoughtlessly? He didn't understand her. Maybe he would if she were Irish. As she prepared herself mentally to meet this usurper in her father's house, she honed her outrage.

When she met Mary Boyle, standing in Johnnie's immense kitchen as if she belonged there, Misella managed a curt, "Hello," but resentment seethed within her. She had expected a wrung-out, red-haired hag, an older woman, like Newgate's Molly Parsons, Flinty's doxie on the ship. Instead, Mary Boyle stood tall, almost Jack's height, slim as a reed, with the bloom of youth on her smooth, unfreckled face, her flaming-red hair pressed into a neat bun. Her moss green gown, clean but worn—no doubt a cast-off from Elinor—enhanced the color of her eyes. Standing shoulder-high beside her, Elinor provided a stark contrast.

"Misella," Elinor said, "you'll be pleased to know that Mary is an excellent cook and housekeeper who has taken over, for now, the management of the household, freeing me to assist Ben with her lawsuit. She is happy to do it as payment for our help."

Ben, with a sharp eye on Misella, cut in quickly. "Only until the fall, Misella, when the Captain returns and sets you free…we hope. . .and then you will inherit the job for as long as you please." He turned to Johnnie Cross, hunched slightly forward in the doorway, as if hesitant to step into the kitchen. "Don't you agree, Johnnie?"

"If that is what Misella wants," Johnnie said, his voice tender, his eyes focused on his lost daughter. "That is my fervent hope," he added, "for I have missed her terribly."

Distracted by her own dark thoughts and bitter feelings, Misella failed to answer or even glance at her father. She did not notice the slump of his shoulders or the shine of tears in his eyes as he looked down. But Ben noticed and spoke up with a trace of sadness in his voice."Haven't we all, my friend."

Chapter 50

Mrs. Dobbs' vegetable garden suffered end-of-summer fatigue: lettuce wilted; tomato plants withered; pepper plants died; green beans dwindled; cucumbers yellowed. Soon the pumpkins, squash and rutabaga would take over. Throughout the summer, Misella had spent long, sweating hours picking and chopping and canning until she feared she might end up forever a hunchback with cramped, crooked fingers.

Though the heat of August cooled with the arrival of September, Misella's anger and despair did not. Nor did the demands of Mrs. Dobbs and her black-clad flock of boarders. In addition to preparing all of their meals, washing their clothes and cleaning their rooms, Misella had to cater to their individual digestive issues.

Mr. Briar insisted that his humors had to be balanced, which required him to carefully assess his yellow bile, the color of his mucus, his water emissions and his daily movements. If any posed a problem, he gave Misella his list of remedies: ground liverwort from dried leaves found in the garden added to his nightly tea or brewed nightshade water from the berries and leaves Mrs. Dobbs provided.

Mr. Belmont required treatment for his inflamed bowels which meant scraping gel from the aloe leaves and adding that to his liverwort tea. Mrs. Dobbs had her own frequently needed remedy for insomnia: a few poppy leaves stewed in water with a generous dash of brandy.

Exhausted, disgusted with Mrs. Dobbs' constant demands, yet unable to relax and enjoy the Sunday afternoons spent at her father's house, Misella decided to suspend her visits. She could no longer abide Mary Boyle's presence or the dinners she provided or Elinor's raving about Mary's cooking or the constant discussions about Mary's upcoming trial or the talk about Robby Benton and Jack which seemed to pop up often, usually from Ben, or Mary's glowing comments whenever Jack was mentioned.

Misella expected Ben to be shocked at the news that she was stopping her Sunday visits when he arrived to pick her up. "I'm too tired to pretend any longer," she told him as they stood on Mrs. Dobbs' porch. "The moon-eyed hen keeps asking me when my brother will recover, and I have to keep making up excuses for why Jack doesn't show up with you." She frowned and leaned her back against the closed door, staring at the rented carriage waiting in the roadway so she wouldn't have to look at Ben. "You can just take me to the park on your way, and I'll walk home."

"Your father and Elinor will be very disappointed," Ben replied in a measured tone.

She expected him to reproach her or at least to try to reason her into compliance. But he remained silent. "Look," she said, her voice rising, "I know you want me to like Mary Boyle, but I don't." She waited, her arms crossed defiantly. When he failed to respond, she straightened up so she could face him, his damaged eye squinting at her with intense concentration. Anger flushed her cheeks and inflamed her voice. "The only thing Mary Boyle and I have in common is you and the family I used to have. . .and Jack." She wiped away a few wayward tears with the back of her hand. "That is funny, isn't it?" She attempted a laugh that sounded more like a snuffle. "I'm the outsider now more than she is."

"Only in your mind, my dear," Ben said quietly, "not in ours." He left her on the porch and inched his way down the steps. "I'll ask the driver to drop you off at the park," he called over his shoulder as he heaved himself onto the stool and into the carriage.

Feeling some remorse, the fight gone out of her, Misella hurried after him. She scrambled in and sat down next to him. "Ben, don't be angry with me. I'll resume the visits when the trial is over," she said, "and Jack returns."

He nodded silently without looking at her, and only spoke after they arrived at the park. As she exited the carriage, her lunch bucket swinging from her hand, he said, "I shall miss you today, my dear. I guess I won't see you again until after the trial, a few weeks hence, I believe."

"Thank you," she murmured, "...for the ride." She turned away, then swung back around. "And good luck with the trial. I'm certain you will succeed. You always do." Head down, she did not see Ben's pained expression as he watched her slouch through the wrought iron gate without a backward glance.

The park was less crowded now that fall hovered in the chilly, late-morning air. Misella tightened her shawl around her shoulders and headed to the empty bench where she and Jack always sat. She dropped the bucket onto the seat and plopped down, shivering in the slight breeze from the pond. A green slime, she noted, threatened to engulf the water lilies, and the ducks had disappeared.

She had never felt so alone and miserable, *trapped in a slough of despond,* she thought. She missed Jack. He would have tried to lift her spirits and make her laugh...or at least smile at his nonsense. She recalled the first time she had met him, on the journey to Hawthorn Manor, when he served as Sir Richard's coach driver—how the black curls bounced around his head when he bent to place the stepstool for her at the carriage door. His green coat, a bunch of red posies springing from the lapel, had swirled open revealing britches tied at each knee with multi-colored strings, emblems of his happy-go-lucky nature. When he noticed her staring at him, he grinned and winked one startling blue eye, and somehow she had known that she could trust him.

He had proven that trust when he saved her from drowning after Isobel, Sir Richard's jealous daughter, shoved her from the boat into the sea. With a bone-deep shudder, Misella relived that moment—struggling against the waves, the thick water filling her nose and mouth as she sank, the sky darkening around her as Jack grabbed her in his iron fists and hauled her to shore. "Can you sit up, Miss?" he had asked, bending over her, wet curls falling into his dancing eyes, water dripping from his britches, their colorful strings drooping around his ankles like Maypole ribbons. "Ye'll be alright now, Miss," he said. "Keep your chin up, and your eyes to heaven." And she had been alright whenever he was near.

Even during the darkest days of her trial for murder, Jack, at great risk as an escaped convict himself, had shown up in disguise. Even before she saw him, she had felt his presence in the courtroom, and when she finally recognized him from those blue eyes drilling into her, she gained the strength to keep going—because she knew he believed in her.

But she was not alright now. Jack was gone, and she had no one. She was, to quote Mrs. Dobbs, "nothing but a useless speck of dust in this wide, cruel world."

The wind picked up, the clouds thickened overhead, and the air smelled like rain. Misella looked around, wondering how much time had passed during her reverie. The few people in the park when she arrived were leaving, no doubt heading home to their loved ones and a hot dinner. She dreaded returning to Mrs. Dobbs' too soon, for then she would have to join the others in the parlor for the boring Sunday services. And Mrs. Dobbs would expect her to take over cooking their late dinner. Choosing to remain where she was, she huddled into her shawl, determined to outlast whatever storm might descend upon her.

Chapter 51

Though Judge Crowley had delayed the proceedings as long as he could, Mary Boyle's trial date was officially set for October 2nd, 1754—the trial would be held in the Talbot County Courthouse in Easton, Maryland, known as the "Colonial Capital of the Eastern Shore."

"The journey will be long, the trip arduous," Ben Turner warned Mary Boyle as they sat together at the desk in his office. "I have booked passage for you and me on the *Sealark* docked today in Boston Harbor, and leaving tomorrow for Annapolis to load tobacco before returning to London. We will disembark in Annapolis and secure lodging for a day or two at Reynolds Tavern until I can arrange for a coastal vessel to take us up the Bay to Easton in time for the trial."

Mary glanced up from the documents spread across the desk. "What about Elinor? Is she not coming with us?"

Ben shook his head. "Sorry to say, she cannot. We cannot afford to pay her expenses, and she has rejected the idea of asking her father for more funds. Though I have tried to talk her into it." He swung his torso around with a grunt to look up at Elinor who stood behind them, the office as yet lacking an additional chair.

Elinor frowned, impatient with him. "We're done with that discussion, Ben. As I already told you, father will need me at home with Mary gone…and Misella not there yet." A veil of sadness spread across her face.

Ben reached for her hand and held it for a moment. "Give her time, my dear. Things will improve." He turned back to Mary. "Are you concerned about traveling with me as your only chaperone?"

Mary chuckled, her green eyes dancing with amusement. "Not unless you're planning to ravish me. Are you?" She laughed aloud as Ben blushed fiery red. "Maybe you intend to extract payment from me for your services," she continued. "But fair warning, Mr. Benjamin Turner, I will have a weapon with me." She grinned with delight at his shocked expression, and glanced up at Elinor. "What do you think, Elinor? Should I be worried?"

Elinor smiled, enjoying the unusual spectacle of Ben redder than a bowl of Mary's beet soup and speechless as a bumpkin, his lawyerly demeanor diminished. "Well.l.l…," she drawled, "I do believe he is a rather randy fellow. Not that I would know, of course, but you will have to insist that he act with propriety at all times. It may not be easy, but I'm sure you can manage him."

The two ladies giggled as Ben sputtered, "Elinor, I'm surprised at your lack of decorum. Not so much at Mary's loose talk, but yours…and you not yet a married woman."

"I expect you'll not mind so much then, Sir," Mary said with a grin. "There's a bit of the devil in all of us, you know. In my homeland, there's a saying: 'Me darlin' was sweet, me darlin' was chaste; Faith, an' more's the pity.'"

Ben laughed in spite of himself. "There's more than a bit of the devil in you, Mary Boyle," he said with a sheepish wink at Elinor, "and plenty of spunk. You'll need both in the weeks ahead."

Mary's manner and voice turned serious. "I'm ready, Sir, and I pray my Irish luck continues. How blessed I am to have been found by all of you." She stood up, her hands folded together as if in prayer, and addressed Ben who leaned forward in his chair to face her. "You're a lucky man, Mr. Turner, to have found a partner like Elinor. I will miss her, and Mr. Cross while we are gone. I pray I return a free woman, thanks to all of you." She crossed herself, kissed two fingers and laid them for a moment on Elinor's cheek.

Chapter 52

The Talbot County Courthouse looked rather puny, Ben Turner thought, compared to his previous professional domain: the sprawling, intimidating Newgate court building attached to the prison in the center of London. All city trials were held in one of its three cavernous courtrooms. Not that he had expected much in this rustic corner of the Colonies, its crooked fingers of land grabbing the waters of Chesapeake Bay. But he was surprised when he entered the narrow, whitewashed courtroom with Mary Boyle.

The courtroom had the appearance and feel of a primitive, backwoods church. At the front of the room, an altar-sized mahogany table, elevated on a low platform, stretched between double-paneled, lattice-work windows, uncurtained, allowing sunlight to shine upon the judge. To the right of the judge's table, a smaller table without a platform accommodated; the presiding lawyers. Facing the judge's table were three backless benches precisely aligned, one in front of the other, along the wooden floor boards. Three additional pew-like benches rested against the back wall. On the far left, a massive white stone fireplace held a few unlit logs; a large, metal clock on its mantle showed the time—10:45 a.m. The trial was scheduled to begin at 11:00. A faded Union-Jack flag dangled from a stand in the corner beside the fireplace.

The defendant, Mary Boyle, and her lawyer were the last to arrive. A well-dressed crowd, all men, filled the benches. All chatter ceased when the two visitors entered the room. A black-robed Judge Crowley bent forward in his chair and straightened his wig, pushing aside the pile of documents on the table. Lowering his glasses, he frowned at them as if displeased by the interruption. "You will please take a seat," he said in a gravelly voice. "The defendant in the front row," he pointed to a vacant spot in the middle of the first bench, "and Mr. Turner, if you are indeed her lawyer, at the table next to our Mr. Prendergast."

Mary inhaled a deep breath and hesitated. Grabbing Ben's arm, she leaned close and whispered, "That's the place next to Jenkins. What shall I do?"

Ben whispered back, "Ignore him. Stand tall as I take you to your seat. Think of Robby Benton." He bowed to the judge, took Mary's hand and led her to her place, glaring at the stunted creature baring his teeth at Mary as she sat down beside him and stared straight ahead.

Instead of his black robe and wig, Ben wore his usual brown serge jacket and britches, a ruse, he had explained to Mary, to disarm the enemy. Before shuffling to his chair, he bowed to the judge. "I apologize, your honor, for my inappropriate attire, but I'm afraid I inadvertently left some of my baggage on board the ship from Boston when I departed in Annapolis." The judge shook his head; the audience chuckled. "But I do have my notes with me," Ben added, holding up and waving his leather folder.

Judge Crowley grimaced. "May we continue, Mr. Turner, before we run out of time? If you don't mind! Please take your seat."

"Yes, Sir," Ben said, moving to his chair and dropping the folder on the table. He smiled and nodded, with seeming good will, to the smirking barrister he recognized from the Newgate court, disguising his surprise at finding in this courtroom an enemy lawyer from London. Of course, Ben considered many of the barristers he had known then unworthy of the name, especially Prendergast who had advocated for the nobility. He had earned his dazzling reputation among them by successfully prosecuting forgery and inheritance cases against bastard sons and other greedy, debt-plagued relatives. Ben wondered what had driven him to depart such a lucrative position to end up here in this backwater setting.

Grunting, his bad knee aching, Ben lowered himself carefully onto the armless, wooden chair awaiting his arrival. With a scowl, he stared for a moment at Prendergast's padded armchair. "The pretender's seat of honor, I presume," he muttered under his breath.

Prendergast flinched, color flooding his face. He glowered at Ben and deliberately moved his own stack of documents out of Ben's line of vision. He shifted his chair a little to the right, as well, as if he feared contagion.

But he remained silent as Judge Crowley gaveled order and intoned, "Let us begin." He called Mr. Prendergast to come forward and present the facts supporting Albert Jenkins' position in response to the lawsuit filed on behalf of the runaway indentured servant, Mary Boyle.

Prendergast stood with a flourish, the hem of his black gown swirling around his patent-leather pumps as he scooped up his documents from the table and stepped before the judge. He bowed his head, the side curls of his wig lifting slightly before settling back in place. "Your Honor, what we have before this court is a sham lawsuit without merit. A flagrant waste of your time and that of Mr. Jenkins. Mary Boyle brought these same charges against Mr. Jenkins last year, the first time she ran away and was caught. Her case at that time was thoroughly adjudicated by you and settled.

"Her second escape has caused Mr. Jenkins to sustain significant financial losses once again, not only from the suspension of her work service, but also his cost to run another ad in the local news bulletin." Prendergast flipped through the documents and pulled one out. "May I read the ad for the record, Your Honor?" When the judge nodded, the lawyer continued:

> Ran away from the Subscriber, in Talbot County last month, a servant woman named Mary Boyle, a tall, well-set Irishwoman, red-haired, with an impediment in her speech. 'Tis supposed she is gone away in company with another runaway known by the name of Robby Benton. Being whipt last court, she may possibly have the marks on her back. Two pistols reward besides what the law allows.

Ben glanced at Mary to gauge her reaction, but she remained grim-faced and stoic, leaning as far away as she could from the scurrilous Jenkins who appeared to be cursing her under his breath.

In fact, Jenkins could hardly contain his fury, which had escalated when Mary, clean and well-dressed, entered the courtroom with her unbound hair flaming down her back. "There's the cunning hussy and her pettifogger lawyer," he growled over his shoulder to the fellow plantation owners gathered in support on the benches behind him. When the lawyer led her over, she primly sat down, leaning away from Jenkins as if she feared catching a disease, ignoring him as if she had never met him before, never gone down on her knees to him. He had to grip his hands together in his lap to keep from whacking the swank right out of her.

Prendergast continued. "Now, your honor, Mr. Jenkins, as in his previous case against Mary Boyle, does not dispute the charge that he at times took the whip to her when she needed it—as certainly she did after running away the first time. Whipping a servant is not a crime here or in England, our mother country, if servants refuse to obey or fulfill their duties. Mary Boyle willingly entered into this indenture agreement, signing a contract to work for Mr. Jenkins for seven years in exchange for free transportation to America, food and lodging. He was well within his ownership rights to add time to her exit date for any infractions of his rules—and certainly for running away."

Several of the men in the room called out in agreement, "Hear, hear." One man dressed in a fitted linen jacket, rose to his feet. "Why are we here again? Enough of this nonsense. We planters are running out of patience with these cheaters who take from the Crown and us and renege on the bargain they've made. Put an end to this nonsense, once and for all, Judge. No more lawsuits allowed. No more catering to the whims of the lazy, criminal whiners." The room erupted in applause and the stamping of feet. Jenkins smirked in agreement. He leaned toward Mary and whispered, "Me thinks your luck is running out."

Mary drew back from the rancid smell of his breath, cringing in horror at the intimacy of his voice in her ear once again. Though she tried to maintain a calm demeanor, her heart hammered in her chest and fear clouded her thinking. She looked in desperation at Ben who appeared battle-ready, sitting at attention, his hands clutching his folder. He smiled at her and winked his weak eye, appearing to onlookers as if it were giving him trouble.

Judge Crowley struck his gavel half-heartedly on the table. "Settle down now, gentlemen. Remember where you are. I hear you. We've heard from Mr. Prendergast." Giving a cursory nod in Ben's direction, he added, "We shall allow Mr. Turner to have his say."

Ben waited for the room to quiet down. He scraped back his chair and arose with an air of brisk confidence. He moved in front of the judge, blocking his line of vision to Jenkins. "Your Honor," he began, "I wish to remind the court that Mary Boyle was not a convict when she signed on as an indenture. She was a free-willer. Your esteemed colleague, Mr. Prendergast, has justified the whipping of indentured servants here by falsely comparing this non-criminal treatment, as he calls it, to that used on servants in England. Let me remind him and this court of the differences:

"1. In England, if a servant contracts for a year or several years, the employer has no power to force an extension against the servant's will. Mr. Jenkins, however, has added time to Mary Boyle's contract terms, without her permission, for the least infraction of his arbitrary rules:

   - for disobedience—3 months;
   - for complaints about the food, or lack thereof—3 months;
   - requests for decent clothing—2 months;
   - for running away—1 year.

2. In England, servants tend to be treated as members of the household, not as livestock forced to survive on gruel unworthy of pigs and in some cases sleep outside on nothing but the bare earth. While obliged to survive on mere scraps, Mary Boyle did not have to sleep outside. Instead, she was forced to share her master's bed…against her will.

3. Though it is true in England that masters do occasionally whip recalcitrant servants, they would not so easily be allowed to whip them to death without paying the consequences. England enforces the law against murder. Mr. Jenkins, however, whipped his runaway indentured servant Jimmy Feeney to death last year with impunity."

Ben raised his voice. "I ask the court to consider these questions. Why does the estate owner in this far-off land with a whip in his hand have the legal right to demand unquestioning obedience? And why is he allowed to go so much further than his equivalent in England?"

The agitator in the linen jacket jumped to his feet again. "I've a question for you, gimlet-eyed old toast. Why don't you go back to England?" Some of the planters laughed and yelled, "Hoa, hoa," in agreement. Others applauded and stamped their feet.

Amid the chaos, Judge Crowley pounded his gavel to no avail, forcing him to hoist himself up to a standing position and bark, while pounding away on the table, "Cease your squalling in my courtroom until we're done here."

When the noise diminished and the men ceased their grumbling, the judge sat back down and looked pointedly at the clock on the mantel. "You have ten more minutes, Mr. Turner. I intend to finish by 11:30 sharp. You may continue."

"Thank you, Your Honor." Ben had faced the judge throughout his testimony and during the raucus disruption that followed. He continued to keep his eyes trained on the judge, refusing to look at Jenkins or Prendergast or Mary Boyle. He needed to preserve his concentration and prevent any distraction, such as Prendergast's sneers or Jenkins venomous expression or Mary's increasing fear.

Focusing all of his attention on Judge Crowley, Ben continued, "Mr. Prendergast also referred to Mr. Jenkins being within his ownership rights to add time to her contract for any rule infractions. I beg to differ here, as well." He raised his voice and thundered, "Mr. Jenkins does not own Mary Boyle. He owns a temporary work contract for her, and he must abide by the terms of the indenture program, a program intended to benefit all those involved: the ship owners in England who contract with the Crown and are paid to transport prisoners and free-willers to the Colonies; the ship owners who also receive payment for each indenture sold upon arrival; and the planters and merchants here who pay a small fee to acquire able-bodied workers whom they promise to support in return for their labor."

Ben swung around and faced the disgruntled but attentive audience. "Though planters have reaped the rewards from a cheap and compliant workforce, the contract does not allow them to coerce or con their servants into longer terms of service—to reduce them to chattels whose freedom exists only at the discretion of their masters."

Red-faced and seething with anger, Ben turned back to Judge Crowley. "And they surely do not have the right to brand their indentures as Mr. Jenkins has had the audacity to do to Mary Boyle after her last escape."

Dead silence prevailed in the courtroom until Mr. Prendergast arose and shouted, "Where is the proof for Mr. Turner's absurd accusation? Can the defendant produce such a branding?"

Mary Boyle hunched on the bench, beads of moisture evident on her colorless face. Jenkins furiously pumped one leg up and down, causing the bench to rattle, and Mary to rock back and forth.

The judge ordered, "The defendant will step forward and reveal the branding…if it exists."

Ben held his hand out to Mary, and as she grasped it, he lifted her to her feet. "Don't worry," he muttered under his breath. "We're almost done. You need only show the judge, no one else." He put his arm around her shoulders and led her to the judge's table. "Mary, please pull up your sleeve and show Judge Crowley the inside of your left arm."

Mary nodded, unbuttoned the cuff at her wrist, and rolled up her sleeve to reveal the tattoo.

Ben gently held up her arm. "You can see, your honor, that Mr. Jenkins has permanently inscribed his initials and the year that Mary Boyle ran away, A.J. 1753.

He branded her as if she were nothing more than livestock that permanently belonged to him. And then," Ben turned to point at Jenkins, "this sharper declared, like some unholy prophet on the

Mount, that her seven-year indenture would begin from this date even though she had already served six years of her original contract." He turned his fierce glare upon the entire audience. "A travesty of justice," he boomed, "that must not be allowed to stand."

Prendergast jumped up, his voice and outrage matching the level of Turner's. "This woman broke faith with Jenkins by failing to fulfill the terms of the bargain she agreed to, not once, but twice. He had the God-given right to indemnify her compliance and her obedience by whatever means necessary."

The audience of planters in the courtroom broke out in cheers and loud applause, and Judge Crowley did nothing to stop it.

"He did not have the God-given right to mistreat her as he did or to rape her," Ben answered in a loud voice, though he knew the cause was lost. He had no other choice; he would have to play his trump card. He approached the judge with Mary at his side. "There is time left on the clock, your honor, and I have one more point to raise."

The judge, looking annoyed, raised the gavel and called for silence. "Mr. Turner has asked for a few minutes to wrap up. In all fairness, we will give him that time."

Ben kept Mary with him as he made his final argument, addressing Albert Jenkins directly. "Mary Boyle deserves to have her contract with you dissolved immediately for all of the reasons I have provided. But allow me to offer you one more. I am close friends with Andrew Dunning, the merchant who holds the contract on every transportation ship that arrives in Annapolis from England. As a matter of fact, his son, Charles, was my law partner for years in London. I'm sure Mr. Prendergast can verify the accuracy of this.

"If you do not destroy her contract today and withdraw any claims you may have against her in this courtroom or any other, I will ask Andrew Dunning to blacklist your name with all of his ship captains so that none of them will allow any indenture to be purchased by you or for you in the future. And believe me, he will do it!" Ben doubted that he could ever convince that skinflint Dunning to cooperate, to have a heart, but Jenkins wouldn't know that, and neither would Prendergast.

Jenkins reeled back as if he had been struck, the color draining from his bony face. He looked panic-stricken, his beady eyes darting to his lawyer.

Prendergast arose and asked the judge, "Your Honor, may I have a moment to consult with my client?" The judge agreed.

Jenkins knew that without a steady stream of cheap, indentured labor, his tobacco plantation would never survive, nor would any belonging to the planters gathered here. Their deafening silence confirmed their fear about Turner's threat. When Jenkins stumbled, as if in shock, to his table, Prendergast muttered, "Do it. You have no other choice."

Jenkins nodded, and Prendergast told the judge, "Your Honor, my client wishes to withdraw his complaint and will comply with Mr. Turner's demands." Removing Mary Boyle's contract from among his papers, he said, "I have Mr. Jenkins' permission to destroy the contract." With that, he tore the contract in quarters, approached Mary Boyle, and thrust the pieces into her hand.

Mary stared in disbelief at the soiled remnants of the contract she had signed with naïve exuberance so many years ago. With tears in her eyes, she held the pieces out to Ben as if she feared they might dissolve in her hands. "Thank you," she whispered.

Prendergast scrubbed his hands across the front of his robe, as if to dispel contamination from a foreign pestilence. "I hope this is the last we see of both of you," he snarled. "By the way," he added, leering at Mary, "my client wishes me to tell you that he knows you will never forget your time with him because of the mark he left upon you."

Mary's back stiffened; wisps of her hair flamed across her face. "Please tell your client, little Caesar, for me," she said, in a quiet voice laced with scorn, "that he was so unremarkable, I have forgotten him already."

Ben eased the gripped contract from her fist and placed the crumpled pieces inside his folder. Turning his back on Prendergast, he grasped Mary's arm. "You have your freedom, Mary. That's all we need. Let's go home."

Chapter 53

After her lonely, wet Sunday in the park, Misella spent the next Sunday trapped for the entire day in Mrs. Dobbs' oppressive household. With Ben in Chesapeake Bay, and Jack gone to Annapolis for more than a month, she had no one to rescue her, and no family to provide temporary refuge. She felt lost, as if imprisoned at sea once again, on a ship without a rudder. After spending a few more Sundays alone, wallowing in self-pity, she began to regret rejecting the very people who loved her the most, seeking to punish them for her pain.

As she knelt bereft in the parlor one Sunday morning, struggling to keep her eyes open during the long service, Mrs. Dobbs droned on with the readings until she glanced up and suddenly stopped. Her sharp eyes drilled into Misella, and she rapped her knuckles rapidly against the wooden Bible stand. "Straighten up and pay attention, you," she screeched. Misella nodded, threw back her shoulders, opened her eyes wide and tried to focus on the next reading.

Mrs. Dobbs scowled at her before she continued, her voice softening with reverence:

> *"Matthew 18: 21-22: Then Peter came up and said to him, 'Lord, how often will my brother sin against me, and I forgive him? As many as seven times?" Jesus said to him, "I do not say to you seven times, but seventy-seven times.'"*

Misella had to bite her lips to keep from smiling at the sheer hypocrisy of Mrs. Dobbs who could solemnly advocate forgiveness and yet never practice it. The passage, however, also ignited Misella's conscience, causing her to dwell upon her own inability to forgive. She wondered if she could ever forgive the worst offenders from her past: Sir Richard, the wealthy predator, who had tricked her into believing he loved her; or his vicious daughter Isobel, who had tried to drown her; or Lady Marian Bentley, Sir Richard's surrogate, who had forced her to become a prostitute to avoid debtor's prison. Surely, they did not merit forgiveness, did they?

She had to admit to herself, however, her conscience squirming, that she had been cruel to her father and Elinor, unwilling to forgive them for past betrayals. An incident from childhood sprang into her mind: when she and Elinor had fought viciously because Elinor had yanked the starched ribbon, along with a fistful of hair, from Misella's head, calling her, "Mum's little, curly-haired doll," and Misella had bloodied her nose. She recalled with stark clarity her father's words in admonishing her. "Forgive your sister, Misella," he'd said, "because each time we can't forgive, our spirits die a little." She banished the uncomfortable thought from her mind.

She managed to keep that unwelcome thought and her nagging conscience at bay during long days of repetitious chores and Mrs. Dobbs' constant criticism. When guilt overwhelmed her, keeping her awake far into the night, she began to help herself to some of Mrs. Dobbs' remedy, a cup of brewed poppy leaves and brandy to blot out the memories of how, after meeting her father for the first time in eight years, she had slapped his book of psalms into his hand, willing him to feel her guilt and pain, and turned her back on him like a petulant child. She had driven Elinor to tears by insinuating that, richly housed in comfort and love throughout Misella's dire ordeal, she somehow had shared responsibility for Misella's fate.

Mrs. Dobbs' concoction put Misella to sleep immediately, and, at first, comforting childhood dreams followed: images of her father showing her how to craft a quill from a goose feather; holding her in his lap as they read the psalms together; teaching her to gut a fish; lifting her to his shoulders on market day. She woke up on those mornings feeling joyful, renewed by the idyllic dreams of the two of them together, until the day's drudgery began bringing with it the slap of reality—the glowering face and punishing hands of Mrs. Dobbs. Misella would spend the remainder of these days longing to see her father again.

At times, Elinor entered her dreams: playing games with her when they were very young; curling up close to her side at night on a single pallet in the loft; splashing barefoot together in the creek. During the daytime when Misella relived the early days with Elinor, she remembered that those happy days together had ended after the younger sisters were born, and Elinor, as the oldest child, had to become the family cook and child minder. "Keep your sisters occupied, Elinor," their mother would call to her, and "feed the baby while Misella and I do our lessons." Thus would begin the hours devoted each day to teaching Misella to read and write. Whenever Misella complained or asked why, her mother would say, "Because you're the smart one, and I want more for you." She'd smooth Misella's curls off of her face and retie the ribbon in her hair. "You, sweet girl, will make me proud one day." A red-faced Elinor, in her faded brown gown and damp head scarf, glowered at them as she burped the squirming baby.

To discourage unpleasant childhood memories and insure restful sleep, Misella continued the nightly doses, in time adding more brandy, but gradually, the dreams turned to nightmares: in the carriage leaving home with a grinning Sir Richard, her father allowing him to take her away; the horror of her attic room at Hawthorn Manor, a rag doll on the narrow cot to welcome her, stabbed through the chest with a sacking needle; the sneering faces of Lady Sarah, Sir Richard's sickly wife, and his cruel daughter Isobel, creator of the rag doll; running through the maze in torn clothing after Sir Richard had raped her. One night she witnessed her baby daughter Lily's death scene in its entirety: the child lying in the road, ground to stillness by the horses' hooves; herself slumping to the cobbled street, the stones rough and hard against her cheek; the sour smell of milk and sweat and horse manure; the crowd shouting "murderess" at her; the rough hands of her captors dragging her to the constable.

Panting for breath, she bolted upright, her heart pounding, her face wet, her throat clogged with fear. For a few minutes, as she peered into the darkness from her straw mat, she imagined that she was in her prison cell. She forced herself to breathe deeply, drawing in the pungent smells of the pantry: drying herbs, forest mushrooms, the basket of apples, and soon remembered where she was. She spent the remainder of the night, lying rigid as a corpse on her mat, reviewing the terrible choices she had made: placing her complete trust in Sir Richard; never wondering why he preferred her company over that of his own daughter; believing she deserved his attention, his gifts, his devotion because, as he often told her, she was prettier and smarter than Isobel; ignoring Jack Finn's warning about Sir Richard until it was too late, and Jack was gone—and worst of all, becoming Sir Richard's willing accomplice, his live-in mistress, the mother of a baby he did not want and had ordered her to abort, though she had finally refused to go that far. Not because of any ethical awakening or moral outrage, but only because she feared the consequences of committing a capital crime.

Could she ever forgive herself? She knew she needed to forgive that lost, young girl for the mistakes she had made. Ben, dear Ben, had tried to convince her so many times before the trial that she was not to blame for what had happened to her or to Lily. "You are a victim," he used to rant, "of a vicious, immoral system that has made a mockery of justice and decency." Yet, at that time, she could not forgive herself because she believed she did not deserve exoneration. She had blamed herself even though she did recognize how naïve she had been to believe Sir Richard and his self-serving lies.

Despite all of the adversity in her life, or maybe because of it, she had become stronger, able to think for herself, to survive, and she did pride herself on how far she had come. A well-earned pride, that she could admit now needed to be tempered with a little humility and a lot of forgiveness.

She determined to do better, if given another chance. She prayed that her family and Ben and Jack had not given up on her, that Ben would initiate another visit to her father's soon after his return from Annapolis. Having decided to pursue a reconciliation with all of them, most especially with Jack, she devoted her bedtime thoughts to achieving that goal, and soon discovered she could fall into a peaceful sleep without the tea.

One Thursday, Ben sent her a note, delivered by Mr. Briar who handed it to Misella instead of giving it to Mrs. Dobbs first. He confronted Misella in the kitchen as she was preparing supper. "The barrister insisted that I place this directly in your hand, Margaret," he said with a sniff, his wild gray eyebrows raised to meet his hairline.

Misella was taken aback. "Where did you encounter him, Mr. Briar? I did not know he had returned from his trip."

Before answering, Mr. Briar removed his long, black coat and pancake-sized hat and thrust them into her arms, as if hanging them up himself on the hooks beside the front door posed too much of a strain for his feeble arms. With a frown, he said, "The man lumbered, uninvited, into the narthex of St. Giles where I had just sat down at my desk to continue writing the pastor's sermon. He must have followed me on my way back from dinner. He demanded I give the note to you. It was not a polite request." Mr. Briar sniffed again and stared accusingly at Misella.

She bowed her head in seeming gratitude, laying his coat and hat on the lone kitchen chair. "Thank you, Mr. Briar," she said. "Very kind of you." She slipped the note into her pocket, determined not to read it until Mr. Briar left the room. She turned away, picked up the chopping knife and began slicing the cabbage.

Mr. Briar coughed a few times and waited. When Misella ignored him and continued working, he mumbled something under his breath and left the kitchen.

As soon as he left, she wiped her hands on her apron and retrieved the note, relieved to see that Ben had remembered to use her fictitious identity:

To Margaret,

I'll be by at 10:00 this Sunday morning to pick you up. I have much to tell you. Please be ready.

Your humble servant,
Attorney-at-Law

Misella controlled the urge to sing "Hallelujah."

She pressed her lips together as Mrs. Dobbs swept into the room. Her beady eyes darted from the note in Misella's hand to the coat and hat bunched up on the chair. "What did Mr. Briar want?" she snarled. "Give me the secret correspondence he gave you behind my back." She snatched the note from Misella's hand. "I spied him creeping past my door, sneaking in here to see you."

Stepping away from the wrath of Mrs. Dobbs and any slaps she might decide to administer, Misella grabbed the coat and hat from the chair. "I'll just hang these up for Mr. Briar while you read the note he gave me from Mr. Turner, who happened to run into Mr. Briar on his way here to drop off the note. I'll be right back to finish the cabbage." She dodged around the irate woman and hurried to the vestibule, hoping to dispel the gathering storm of Mrs. Dobbs' suspicions.

When Misella returned to the kitchen, Mrs. Dobbs' anger had subsided somewhat, though she still sputtered about Mr. Briar. "He should have given this to me," she said, tossing the note onto the table, "instead of ignoring my instructions." She squinted at Misella. "And you, Miss Lightfingers, should have reminded him of my rule and directed him to give the note to me first." She raised her chin and looked down her nose at Misella like an empress forced to address an underling. "You have my permission, for now," she grumbled, "to entertain Mr. Turner on Sunday. If," she stressed in a loud voice, "you behave appropriately before the time arrives. Do you understand me?"

"Yes, ma'am," Misella replied, her head bowed, her hands gripped together behind her back, striking a submissive pose that belied the venom in her heart. For a moment, she thought perhaps she should find room in her heart to forgive Mrs. Dobbs for her cruelty, but that challenge, she decided, required the fortitude of a saint, much too difficult for a novice like Misella. She needed a lot more practice in the art of forgiveness.

On Sunday morning, Misella paced back and forth on the porch as she waited for Ben to arrive, her nerves rattling with anxiety. This time she suffered a different kind of dread—fear that she might have waited too long to reconcile graciously with her family. Their patience may have run out. Maybe not Ben's, for he was coming to see her, but she feared what he would tell her. If he had gained freedom for Mary Boyle, would Mary move permanently into her father's home, into his kitchen? That would free Elinor to marry Ben and leave without any worries. No need to wait for ill-tempered Misella to make up her mind. And what about Jack? Had they met up with him in Annapolis? Was he happy to see Mary and to discover that she would be waiting for him in the Cross home? As soon as she saw the carriage turn the corner at the end of the road, she dashed down the stairs and waited on the patch of withered grass in front of Mrs. Dobbs' house.

When the driver pulled the horses to a halt, she yanked open the carriage door and told a startled Ben, "No need for you to exit; I'll just hop right in." Before he could respond or the driver could jump down to place the step stool, Misella grabbed hold of the far side of the opening with one hand and clambered in, her skirt drawn up to her knees with her other hand. Landing with a thump on the carriage floor, she looked up and panted, "I'm so happy to see you, Ben." Taking a deep breath, she stood up, pulled the door closed, and plopped down beside the stunned barrister. Leaning sideways, she kissed Ben's cheek.

"Misella," he gasped, "what has happened to the dejected waif I left at the park three weeks ago? I do believe a sprite has taken over the girl I used to know."

She took his hand and held on tight as if she feared he might pull it away. "Oh, Ben," she cried, "I've been so miserable here all alone since you and Jack left. Not able to sleep, reliving the past, dreaming about my childhood days when Father and I did so many things together, when Elinor and I used to be friends." She stopped to take a deep breath, a shadow of fear darkening her face. "But then the nightmares came, terrifying me, the terrible days at Hawthorn Manor with Sir Richard—Lily's death and the trial," she panted. "And you, Ben, you saved me from hanging. . .and from myself. I've been such an ungrateful, unforgiving ninny. I need to start over, with my father and Elinor and Jack and you. I…I don't want to live another day without all of you in my life." She looked down, afraid of finding blame or anger in his eyes or worse, doubt.

Ben placed his hand under her chin and raised it up so that she could see in his eyes and on his face the intensity of his affection for her. "My dear," he said, "I am overjoyed, and I know the others will be as well. We all would have waited until the close of this century and beyond, if necessary, for you to embrace us again."

Misella grinned with relief, and squeezed his hand. "Well, Mr. Turner," she said with a lilt in her voice, "I sure hope I don't have to wait that long to hear what happened at the trial, and if you saw Jack in Annapolis."

As the carriage veered forward into the dusty road, Ben leaned back with a satisfied smile. "A complete and welcome success at the trial," he said, with more than a little swagger in his voice. "Mary's contract was justly destroyed, her enemies demolished, and her freedom obtained. A day of justice for her and for indentures in this country. But I don't believe the next case will be easy for me nor can I guarantee such a positive outcome. The path ahead will be treacherous and uncertain."

For me as well, thought Misella. "Wonderful news about Mary," she said with feigned excitement. She tried to sound sincere when she congratulated Ben on his victory and asked, her voice wavering, "So Mary is back home to stay?"

Ben shook his head. "No, I don't believe so. Her stay will likely be temporary until you have your freedom. She told me that she plans to return to London then and seek employment as a housekeeper there."

"What?" Misella exclaimed, her voice rising with disbelief and excitement that she willed herself to suppress. In an effort to appear nonchalant, she gazed out the window and asked, without looking at Ben, "Why would she do that?"

"She came here as a free-willer," Ben said, "not as a convict. So, unlike you and all the other unfortunate convicts, she maintains the right to return without facing the penalty of death. Why she is choosing to do so, she did not say. You should ask her when you see her."

Shocked but elated, Misella murmured, "Oh, I will. And Jack?" she asked anxiously, hoping that perhaps an unsatisfactory meeting with him had influenced Mary's decision. "Did you manage to meet up with him anywhere in Annapolis?"

"No," Ben said, with a note of sadness in his voice. "Though I asked at the Reynolds Tavern where Mary and I spent a few nights, but Harry, the barkeep, had not seen Jack or heard anything about him. He checked around for us at some of Jack's old haunts while we were in Easton but without success. I was not surprised because I'm sure Jack would cover his tracks well to protect Robby Benton's identity. They are both probably holed up somewhere in the woods with Logan. Don't worry, Misella. He'll be back soon, kicking up his heels. You know Jack!"

"Yes," she said with a hint of a smile, her voice trembling. "Indeed I do."

Upon arriving at the Cross residence, they both exited the carriage in a buoyant mood, Misella stepping down first and extending a hand to Ben. "No need for help, my dear, I can manage," he said with a chuckle, anchoring himself on the step stool with his cane and hopping down onto the graveled driveway. Taking her hand and tucking it into the curve of his elbow, he bowed and said, "Let us begin anew," as they proceeded up the walkway to the front door.

Elinor reacted with a guarded look of surprise when Misella reached out to hug her as soon as she opened the door. Over Misella's shoulder, she widened her eyes and raised her eyebrows at Ben, who stood back grinning. "We've missed you these past weeks, Misella, haven't we, Ben?" Elinor said hesitantly, returning the hug without much enthusiasm.

Misella leaned back and, studying her sister's wary expression, realized that she probably expected some cutting remark, as usual, from Misella. Instead, as if seeing her sister for the first time, Misella said, "Elinor, I am truly happy to be with you again. I have a lot to share with you, if you agree to listen, beginning with my apology for my past behavior."

The last of Elinor's reserve disappeared. She seized both of Misella's hands. "No apologies, Misella, please. We will all do better and move forward together."

"Right," Ben said. Placing a hand on Misella's back and clasping his other arm around Elinor's waist, he pushed them gently through the door. "Forward we go."

Johnnie Cross leaned against the door frame at the parlor entrance, waiting to see if the group chose to join him in the parlor or if Misella preferred to bypass him and head straight to the kitchen. He seemed surprised when she disentangled her hands from Elinor's and approached him. "Hello, Father," she murmured, her solemn eyes trained on his face. "I hope you will welcome your wayward daughter back home again, for she has yet to master some of the lessons you tried to teach her long ago—about kindness and neglecting to cast the first stone—and forgiveness."

His eyes aglow, his voice hoarse with emotion, Johnnie responded, "Dearest Misella, yes! I will always welcome you with wide arms and an open heart." He glanced toward Elinor and Ben, who hovered in the vestibule, she with her eyes shining and Ben wearing a self-satisfied grin. "Have faith, Ben told us, and be patient." Raising one hand in a kind of salute to Ben, Johnnie said, "You were right, my friend. Through the grace of God, we have been granted another chance to help one another." He closed his eyes and bowed his head for a moment as if saying a prayer of thanksgiving. Opening his eyes, he stared at Misella with pure joy. "You and I can work together once again as we used to do." When he reached out to draw her close to him, she did not turn away.

Johnnie finally released her from his arms when Misella said, "I have an apology I also need to give to Mary—and my congratulations on her freedom. I want to ask her how it feels. Where is she?"

Elinor stepped forward, tucking her handkerchief into her sleeve, and grabbed Misella's hand with both of hers. "Mary insisted on fixing our dinner to celebrate her liberty—and yours, which should be coming very soon with the Captain's imminent arrival," she said, leading Misella toward the kitchen. "The men can entertain one another in the parlor until we call them."

With silly grins on their faces, Ben and Johnnie watched the sisters disappear into the kitchen before Johnnie turned and entered the parlor with Ben strutting happily behind him.

Mary Boyle, a flowered apron tied around her slim waist, leaned over a large pot on the stove stirring vigorously. She turned around with a wide smile when Elinor said, "Here we are, Mary, the Cross sisters who are anything but cross at the moment!"

Mary set the stirring spoon down on a side plate and glided over to join them, her hand extended to Misella. "I am glad to see you," she said, grasping Misella's hand and holding on, "and hope you will soon join me as a freed woman."

"Thank you," Misella murmured, "I pray every day for Captain Barclay's return, but I want to sincerely congratulate you on your victory." Her face reddening, she looked away for a moment before continuing, "I have been unkind to you in our past encounters; I am sorry about my rude behavior. I was thrilled to learn of your success, to discover that you have achieved what I can only hope to accomplish soon."

Mary grinned and released Misella's hand. "You will," she said. "I wish for you that Irish angels may rest their wings right beside your door, as they have done for me, and brought your father and Jack and Ben and your dear sister into my life." She gave Elinor a quick hug and glanced around the kitchen. "And you, Misella, will soon take my place here after I am gone."

Misella, seeing the sadness in Elinor's face, said to Mary, "Ben told me that you plan to return to London. I hope that is not because of me or my actions toward you."

Mary smiled. "No, of course not. It's a decision I made long ago, soon after I arrived at the Jenkins plantation and discovered that my dream of America had turned into a living nightmare. If I ever managed to escape from there, I promised myself that I would return and start over in the country where I belong."

Elinor interrupted before Mary could continue. "Let's sit down at the table," she told Mary, "and we can share more of your plans with Misella." She pulled out a chair and directed Misella to sit while she poured tea from the tea pot already steaming on the table. She and Mary took their seats and Elinor proceeded to explain more to Misella. "When Captain Barclay arrives and frees you from your contract with Mrs. Dobbs, Ben will arrange with him to provide passage for Mary on his return trip to England. Father and I will be giving Mary letters of recommendation as an exceptional and experienced housekeeper or cook. We have also written to our sister Annabelle," she said looking directly at Misella, "who, as father and I told you, lives in London now with her wealthy husband. We have encouraged her to help Mary in any way she can. Perhaps even hire her to work in her home."

Mary hummed a few bars of her favorite song, *The Shamrock Shore*, and said, "I'm the luckiest lass in the Kingdom for finding the likes of all of you. I bless this family, and Misella, I pray the angels soon settle you here where you belong."

Chapter 54

Throughout the first week of October, after reconciling with her family, Misella floated through her chores, humming to herself, ignoring Mrs. Dobbs' recriminations and waiting confidently for Captain Barclay's arrival. She had marked off the days on a crude calendar that she had scrawled on the backside of an early market list from Mrs. Dobbs. According to Misella's calculations, he should arrive in Boston no later than mid-October, even if the ship encountered unexpected weather delays. She knew well that the Captain would not allow any storm to divert him from his schedule for very long.

On Tuesday afternoon, the 10th of October, while Misella was cleaning the upstairs rooms, Mrs. Dobbs summoned her to the parlor by furiously ringing the hand bell she kept on the mantle. The sound startled Misella as she sat down to rest for a moment on Mr. Briar's chair and to daydream about rekindling her relationship with Jack. Mrs. Dobbs had never before rung the bell except on Sundays as a warning that services were about to begin. Like an obedient postulant, Misella bolted from the room, leaving her cleaning supplies behind. As she descended the stairs, Mrs. Dobbs' screeching replaced the ringing of the bell.

"You must think I'm a crazy, old fool," she screamed. "I have no intention of abiding by your wishes. Oh, I warned Grace long ago about you, but she wouldn't listen." The veins in Mrs. Dobbs' scrawny neck pulsed with fury. "I was not surprised that she was driven to her death by a scoundrel like you."

Misella stopped short at the open doorway of the parlor. Mrs. Dobbs, her face scarlet, panted behind her altar table, the cast-iron bell clutched in her hand like a weapon. A bare-headed Captain Barclay, his back to Misella, loomed over the table in his dress uniform, his tri-cornered hat tossed on the chair in front of the empty fireplace. In the far corner of the room, a thin, poorly dressed, young woman huddled against the wall as if hoping to disappear.

Mrs. Dobbs, her eyes darting to the doorway, silenced the bell. "There you are, Margaret. I want you to bear witness to Captain Barclay's outrageous proposal. Your esteemed Captain has no respect for signed contracts or the indenture laws."

Captain Barclay swung around to behold Misella, a familiar shock of dark hair falling across his broad forehead. The tightness of his face relaxed, and the fierce anger in his eyes dissolved. He smiled at her. "Hello, Margaret," he said in his booming voice, "you look well, I'm happy to see. I must say I have worried about how you were being treated here."

Misella's heart lurched when he greeted her; she felt a sudden flush of heat in her face, an unexpected wistfulness in the presence of this strong, handsome Captain, who had protected her on his ship, especially in the aftermath of the storm and her breakdown in his cabin. He had lifted her up, held her in his arms and listened to her lament with such concern. Her reaction to seeing him again confused her. She thought she had made up her mind, that she wanted to spend the rest of her life with Jack. Didn't she?

The Captain, in an effort to collect himself, it seemed, retrieved his hat from the chair before approaching Misella. "Do come in, Margaret, and meet your replacement. Mrs. Dobbs has already met her." As Misella stepped into the room, Mrs. Dobbs emitted an exaggerated snort but held her tongue.

Her head down, the young woman in the corner stared at the scuffed tops of her brown shoes, their knotted laces drooping to the floor beneath her dark gray skirt, abloom with mismatched patches. Her hair, the same color as her shoes, fell across her ruddy face like a shield. When the Captain called, "Come here, Rose," her head snapped up, and she moved forward to stand before him.

The poor girl looked like a scared rabbit caught in a snare, about to be skinned alive. Which she soon would be, trapped here at the mercy of Mrs. Dobbs. Knowing what the future would hold for this unlucky substitute, a strain of sorrow invaded Misella's joy. She remembered the utter hopelessness she had felt on her first day here, and her heart swelled with pity for the girl.

"Margaret," he said, "this is Rose Halliday from London. Rose is a free-willer who seeks indenture here for a five-year term. I was just explaining to Mrs. Dobbs that Rose will take over for you starting today, and she will not have to pay for the exchange. Your brother, Jack, has arranged with me to buy your contract. I am using the payment I have secured from him to cover Rose's contract which I will turn over to Mrs. Dobbs."

"Oh, no, you won't," Mrs. Dobbs roared, "not unless I say so." Her voice increased to a screech again. "And I don't!" Slamming the bell down on the table, she picked up her copy of Margaret's contract and shook it in the air. "My name is on this contract, signed for me by Mr. Briar, and paid for by me, with my signature added on the day she arrived in my house." She squinted at the contract before continuing, "July 5th, 1754, for a period of seven years, Margaret MacDonald's indenture to be completed on July 5th, 1761."

Mrs. Dobbs looked up at them with an ugly grin. "Margaret has completed only three months and five days of her contract. I refuse to relinquish her contract to you or release her until she has satisfied the terms of her indenture to me. I certainly do not intend to spend my time training a new one of your blockheads after all of the effort it has taken to teach Margaret how to do things properly."

Misella's knees collapsed. She slumped against the Captain who put his arm around her and held her upright. She closed her eyes, clenching her teeth to keep from pelting Mrs. Dobbs with a string of obscenities she had learned on the ship. She knew that remaining here at the mercy of this malicious woman would break her spirit and end her life long before her contract expired.

"Take a deep breath," the Captain murmured in her ear, "and hang on to me. The old witch hasn't won yet." He withdrew his arm from around her waist and addressed Mrs. Dobbs in a calm and measured voice.

"You might wish to reconsider your decision, Gretchen, if you want to maintain your current situation. I know it has been quite some time since you left England, but you do remember, I am sure, that you convinced Grace to loan you a significant sum of money so that you and Deacon Dobbs could set up your little congregation here in Boston."

Mrs. Dobbs squinted at the Captain with suspicion as she swung the metal cross hanging around her neck back and forth with one hand, the other hand clutching the contract.

"Your preaching and pleading must have cast a spell over Grace," the Captain continued, "for she cleaned out our bank account without telling me until you and your new husband had already sailed." Shaking his head with a deep sigh, he added, "So uncharacteristic of my timid Grace. Needless to say, I was dumbfounded when she told me. I was livid with her. . .and with you."

Mrs. Dobbs sniffed dismissively, but stopped moving the cross, holding it immobile against her flat chest.

"However, some of my anger with Grace diminished when she showed me the note she had you sign with your promise to return all one hundred and twenty pounds as soon as possible." Captain Barclay's demeanor changed. He thrust back his shoulders, freed his arm from Misella's grasp and stepped threateningly closer to Mrs. Dobbs. He whipped a folded sheet of parchment from an inside pocket of his navy jacket, the tassels of his shoulder insignia swaying. His voice surged with anger. "Ten long years, Gretchen. I think it is time for you to pay up."

Mrs. Dobbs gasped, her face blanching to match the roots of her hair. "Where…how did you get that?" she sputtered. "I thought that bargain died with Grace."

"It wasn't Grace's money, you fool. It was mine, and you are still indebted to me. I can by law bankrupt you, if necessary, to collect what you owe me." He let that knowledge sink in for a moment before he continued. "Unless you come to your senses and accept my offer—a contract of indenture for Rose Halliday in return for Margaret's contract. I am willing to destroy this promissory note if you agree."

Overwrought, Mrs. Dobbs jiggled Misella's contract in her hand, her beady eyes darting from one girl to the other. "That is not a fair exchange," she whined, "a fiver for a seven-year term. And I will have to start all over again, training this one." She nodded at Rose.

Disgust evident in his voice and on his face, the Captain lashed out. "For the love of God, woman, have you no sense in your grizzled head nor a spark of gratitude in your shrunken heart? Make up your mind right now or I will walk out the door and procure a barrister." He slipped the note back into his jacket before the agitated Mrs. Dobbs could ask to examine it, donned his hat and turned toward the door.

"Wait," Mrs. Dobbs screeched. She ducked around the table. Grabbing Captain Barclay's arm, she thrust Margaret MacDonald's contract into his hand. "Take it, and good riddance. Leave the other one's contract on the table before you go. And cease all contact with me in the future." She sniffed and looked down her nose at Rose Halliday. "Come along, Miss Rosey Gills," she sneered. "To the kitchen. You'd better know how to cook." Before she left the room with Rose trailing slump-shouldered after her, she turned back to look once more at the Captain. "Poor, little Gracie," she said. "She deserved better."

Captain Barclay shook his head, the shock of dark hair springing from beneath his hat and falling across his forehead again. He carefully balanced Rose's contract on top of the Bible resting upright on its wooden stand. "Maybe the old bat will get the message, but I doubt it. Get your things, Margaret," he said with a self-satisfied smirk, "and let's get out of here."

To avoid any chance of a last encounter with Mrs. Dobbs, Misella waited in the dining room until Mrs. Dobbs opened the back door to lead Rose into the garden for further instruction. When they were well out of sight, she hurried to the pantry, collected her few belongings and stuffed them into her worn canvas bag. She placed the Captain's monogrammed handkerchief, newly washed and ironed, on top, before tying the strings. Without a backward glance, she exited the pantry and dashed to meet the Captain waiting for her at the front door.

Overwhelmed by the precariousness of her final release from servitude, Misella could not yet comprehend that she was a free woman. Nor could she manage to carry on a conversation with Captain Barclay at the moment. She sat tongue-tied next to him in the waiting carriage, their shoulders touching, her heart hammering against her chest as she sought to understand her confused reaction upon seeing him again. As the coach headed away from the Dobbs' house toward her own, she allowed the Captain to do all of the talking.

He was ecstatic about what he had accomplished. "I knew I could do it," he gloated. "Fool the old reprobate into accepting my terms." At first, Misella thought he meant Ben Turner, but as the Captain continued, she realized he spoke about Mrs. Dobbs. "She never even asked to inspect the fake promissory note. I would have been pilloried if she had, and you would have been trapped in her web for years."

He pulled the folded parchment from his pocket and opened it to show her a blank page from his diary. "My wife did tell me about forcing Gretchen to sign a note, but her guilt over that 'godless transaction,' as Grace called it, impelled her to destroy the note before she died. She confessed to me on her death bed. 'Neither of us,' she rasped, 'should take that money out of the hand of God.'"

Not from God, Misella thought, *but from Mrs. Dobbs who is certainly not the hand of God, although she acts as if she is.* As she inhaled her first breaths of freedom, Misella realized that God had been on her side throughout her ordeal, bringing help from Jack and Ben when she needed it most. She remembered Mary Boyle expressing similar feelings about her own freedom, and her wish for Misella that had miraculously come true. Mary's Irish angels had rested their wings right beside Mrs. Dobbs' open door.

Misella had to admit to herself, however, that help had also come from Captain Barclay—for a price. Nevertheless, she owed him thanks as well, though she was struck by his nonchalant dismissal of his wife's dying wish that he not take the money from the hand of God's surrogate, Mrs. Dobbs.

The Captain chuckled. "Well, I won't have to, will I? I'll soon take the money instead from the willing hand of your mentor, Mr. Turner, who met me on the dock this morning per my orders. I must say, I was mighty suspicious when I went to his law office in London, only to discover from his partner, Charles Dunning, that he had already departed for America, to find you. Dunning told me that Turner planned to set up a law office in Boston. So after we docked early this morning, I sent a crew member, Evans, to locate the Turner Law Office and give the barrister my note."

Though the Captain brimmed with pride and boasted about his cleverness, *something Jack would never do*, Misella thought, his smile at her seemed warm and sincere. "A most favorable ending for both of us," he exulted. "You have your freedom at last, thanks to me, though many might believe you don't deserve it given your past record and your imprisonment for prostitution."

Ignoring Misella's sharp intake of breath, he continued, "Anyway, I will soon have my money back. Your Mr. Turner knows how to drive a hard bargain. I expected him to bring the money to me this morning, but he insisted I bring you to your father's house first. He told me the whole background story about finding your father and sister. An extra benefit for you, eh Margaret?" he added, tapping her arm with the fake note. "Oops, I mean Misella. The barrister directed me to tell Mrs. Dobbs that I would deliver you to your brother, Jack." With a puzzled expression, he asked, "Who is Jack? You never mentioned that you have a brother."

Misella closed her eyes and bowed her head for a moment before looking up at him. "I don't, but Margaret had a brother, three actually, named Danny, Malcolm and Michael, but not a Jack. Jack is a friend of Ben Turner's…and mine." She expected him to offer some tribute to the memory of Margaret, a brief prayer or perhaps an apology for what happened to her, but he didn't. How could he have so completely forgotten about her, the only prisoner to ever die on his ship?

Holding her hands together in prayer, Misella murmured, "We give thanks to you, O Lord, for Margaret; may she rest at peace in Your loving hands. *The Lord is my shepherd; I shall not want. In verdant pastures he gives me repose; beside restful waters he leads me; he refreshes my soul.*" Barclay bowed his head and said, "Amen." With a sheepish glance at Misella, he admitted, "You are right; we can't forget Margaret. We are here because of her, and so is Turner, whom we will meet at your father's house.

"Turner told me that in order to receive the entire balance of one hundred pounds, in addition to the fifty pounds he had given me to secure the deal, I must provide free passage back to London for Mary Boyle, a guest at your father's house. I must say I have to admire the audacity of the old barrister. Well, I won't quibble about the loss. I'm still ahead—150 pounds from him, minus 30 pounds for her passage, and I replace the entire amount that Grace gave away."

Though Misella remained silent, her thoughts and emotions churned. She remembered when Elinor had queried her a few months earlier about the Captain's handkerchief, and Misella had tried to explain her feelings for the Captain. Elinor had dismissed the relationship as a mere "business arrangement." Misella recalled the sting of her painful words: "You were valuable merchandise to him, Misella," Elinor had warned. "He needed to keep you safe and cooperative in order to complete his transaction with Ben and receive his payment."

At the time, Misella refused to listen, attributing the advice to Elinor's usual jealousy. But now, after the recent awakening of her conscience, and listening to the Captain brag about recovering his money without any mention of Margaret's sacrificed life, she had to reconsider her answer to Elinor's question, "Does he really deserve your devotion?"

Misella recalled that after describing the Captain's appearance to Elinor that day, his marital status as a widower, and his kindness, Elinor had thought he sounded a lot like Ben. Misella had agreed, but she could see now that the resemblance was merely superficial. She realized that the Captain could never measure up to Ben or Jack and the sacrifices they had made, without remuneration, to keep her safe and to love her no matter what she had done. If anything, Captain Barclay had briefly served, during her imprisonment, as a substitute for Ben and Jack. . .and perhaps for her father, as well.

As the carriage stopped in front of her home, Misella untied the strings and opened her canvas bag. She removed the monogrammed handkerchief and placed it in the Captain's hand. "I am grateful," she said, "for your kindness and help throughout my long ordeal on your ship."

He looked at the handkerchief with surprise. "I forgot all about giving you this. I thought I had lost it or left it somewhere." He folded the handkerchief neatly into quarters and tucked it out of sight inside his jacket pocket. "Are you ready to start your new life, Miss Cross?" he asked, as he swung open the door of the carriage and stepped out.

"Yes," she murmured, though the Captain didn't hear her as he had already reached the front door which stood open waiting for them.

The family, gathered in the vestibule with Mary Boyle, cheered as Misella joined the Captain on the porch. Johnnie Cross came forward and thrust a bouquet of wildflowers into Misella's arms. Hugging her, he whispered, "Welcome home at last, my dear Misella." He drew her inside first and then invited the Captain in, introducing himself and thanking him, while the others, one by one, embraced Misella, congratulating her on this first day of her freedom.

Ben handed the Captain an envelope and thanked him before introducing Elinor and then Mary Boyle. "I know you must return without delay to your ship for your early departure," he said, "so we won't dawdle. Mary is ready."

The Captain, speechless with surprise, stared at Mary, regal as a queen, eyeing him back with quiet confidence. "I. . .I'm sorry," he sputtered, "for staring. I was expecting to meet an elderly aunt."

Mary laughed. "Well, Captain Barclay," she said, her brogue thick and deliberate, "'tis true, I am an old soul, but I am young in mind and spirit."

And body, thought Misella, noticing the way the Captain's eyes traveled over Mary's trim figure in her eye-matching green woolen suit.

The Captain turned to Ben and asked, "Is she traveling alone?" When Ben nodded in response, the Captain lowered his voice, although Misella could still hear him. "This is not a good idea, Sir, for a young female passenger traveling alone at sea among my crew for more than six weeks. When you made the arrangement with me, I assumed that Mary Boyle was an elderly woman, at little risk of being bothered by the crew."

Ben shook his head, answering in a hearty tone of voice, "You needn't worry, Captain. Mary can take care of herself. She'll have a weapon with her, and I imagine your crew will quickly learn to leave her alone. I would not have asked this of you without being quite sure, from experience, mind you, that Mary is not easily intimidated—by anyone."

Mary picked up her valise, and stepped before the Captain. "Shall we go, Sir? I have already said my long good-byes to my friends here and wished them thoughts glad as the shamrocks in the days ahead. For me, God's help is nearer than the door, and your ship will bring me where my heart is."

Chapter 55

Elinor's bedtime prayers extended longer than usual on the first night of Misella's freedom. Kneeling beside her bed, a wool shawl draped around her shoulders, logs smoldering in the fireplace, she finished her litany of thanksgiving prayers for Misella's safe return home. About to extinguish the candle flickering on the night stand before climbing into bed, she heard scurrying footsteps outside her bedroom door, the sound of pacing in the hallway.

Picking up the candle holder, Elinor glided to the door and opened it to discover the ghostly figure of Misella, wandering up and down the hallway in the billowing white nightgown Elinor had left for her in Mary's old bedroom. Assuming Misella was sleepwalking and hoping to avoid frightening her, she kept her voice low. "Misella," she called softly, "would you like to come join me in my room?"

Misella stopped pacing and stared at the image of her sister outlined in the doorway, her unpinned red hair drifting across her shoulders. "Do you really want me here with you in father's house, Elinor?" she asked, her voice unsteady. She shook her head back and forth, her hands twisting a fold of the nightgown. "Why would you? I deserve to be isolated from good people like you and Ben. . . and father. I'm not worthy of your company."

"Please, Misella," Elinor pleaded. "We need you here with us; we're your family; we love you; you belong here." She swung the door all the way open. "Come in, won't you, and share my bed as you used to do?"

Hesitating for a brief moment, Misella hurried to the doorway. "I would like that very much. I…I have spent so many nights all alone in the dark, afraid." Thoughts darted into her mind of the first time she began to fear the darkness closing in around her, choking her, as she lay, terrified and alone, in her attic room at Hawthorn Manor. Never again had she felt safe. "I never used to be afraid of the dark. Remember, Elinor?"

"Yes, I do remember," Elinor said, taking Misella's cold hand and leading her into the bedroom, "and I was jealous of your fearlessness."

Misella snorted. "My fearlessness disappeared when I lost my home, my family, my dignity, my virginity, my daughter," her voice wavered, but she swallowed and continued, "my self-respect and my freedom. I have nothing left for you to be jealous about, Elinor."

"You will be safe here with us, I promise," Elinor murmured, closing the door quietly while still gripping Misella's hand. Leading her to the bed, she set the candle on the side table and drew back the bed quilts. "Hop in, Misella, as you used to do when we shared our skimpy pallet in the loft. There's plenty of room for both of us here."

Unable to resist, Misella climbed between the lavender-scented sheets, squirmed to the far edge of the feather mattress and lay on her side, stiff as a broom, her back pressed against the wall.

"Would you like me to leave the candle burning until you fall asleep, Misella? Elinor asked.

Misella sighed deeply. "No, I'm fine now, Elinor. You don't need to coddle me."

Elinor folded her shawl, placing it on her rocking chair and blew out the candle. She lay down on her side of the bed, careful not to crowd Misella. Drawing the quilts up, she tucked the edges around them both.

Misella remained quiet for a moment before choking out an apology. "I'm sorry, Elinor. I don't mean to seem ungrateful. I'm just not used to kindness yet."

"I understand," Elinor said. "Sleep well, Misella."

But Misella lay sleepless in the chilly darkness consumed with guilt. Why had she survived and Margaret hadn't? Not because she was fearless. No. In truth, she had lived with fear ever since she was a child—a mute, little pawn caught up in a powerful game of adult chess which her mother had won against her father, and delivered her, the prize, to Sir Richard who had trained her, convincing her to give up her values, her reputation, her very soul, and had almost destroyed her.

Hadn't she played that same cruel game with Jack, betting against him when he tried to warn her about Sir Richard's intentions and again when she rejected him because of a silly infatuation with the undeserving Captain Barclay? Had she learned nothing from her miserable past? What if she loses again and Jack doesn't return? He might decide to live in the woods with Logan and Robby Benton. He likes adventure. He used to be a highwayman and a pirate. He thrives on danger. Why should he return to a used-up thornback like her, an old maid, a miserable mopsqueezer?

Shame and regret overshadowed the joy of her freedom. "Elinor," she whispered, "are you still awake?"

"Mmmm, yes," Elinor responded, her voice muffled with sleep. "I'm here. What is it?"

Misella leaned away from the wall, clutching the top quilt in her hands. "You were right about Captain Barclay," she blurted out, her voice no longer a whisper. "I was valuable merchandise to him. That's why he wanted to save me, not because he cared about me. He wanted to collect on his investment. It was the money, not me that he really wanted." She began to rock back and forth, the movement dragging the covers askew. "I've been such a fool," she said. "The way I've treated Jack. Why couldn't I see that I was choosing the wrong man again? What if Jack no longer wants me either?"

Elinor sat up as well, reached in the dark for her shawl, and wrapped it around Misella's quivering shoulders. "Nonsense, Misella. Jack will come back," Elinor said, her voice firm." She smoothed the covers and lay back down. "I've only met him once before he left for Annapolis, but I liked him very much, especially after Ben told me how determined Jack was to find you."

Twisting knots in the shawl's fringe, Misella continued to rock. "But I turned him away. He will never forgive me for rejecting him. It's too late."

Sitting upright again, Elinor reached out to still the frantic twisting of Misella's fingers. "That is not true, Misella. Jack loves you, and he will come back to you. Ben told him before he left that we will not marry until he returns. He is very fond of Jack, as you know. Jack would never abandon Ben ...or you. He never has; he never will."

Realizing that Elinor was waiting for a response, Misella murmured a hesitant, "I want to believe you," as she eased her hands away from Elinor's and slouched against the wall, "but I'm just so worried about him."

Hoping to distract Misella from her negative thoughts, Elinor repeated the request she had made of her earlier in the evening, asking, "Are you sure you don't mind my leaving you alone tomorrow while I help Ben at the office?"

Misella sat up straighter. Rubbing her eyes, she sniffed a few times. "Of course not, Elinor. I am anxious to start forgetting about the Dobbs' household and devoting my time to this one...and spending time with father if he feels I am worthy and able to live up to his expectations."

Chapter 56

The next morning, in the habit of rising early in the Dobbs household, Misella awoke at four o'clock after a few hours of restless sleep propped in a sitting position against the wall. She folded back the covers on her side and scooted quietly to the foot of the bed without disrupting Elinor. Hugging the shawl around her, its fringed edges in sad disarray, she crept to the door, opened it without a sound, and slipped into the dim hallway to return to her new room. Ignoring the array of colorful gowns Elinor had provided for her in the mahogany wardrobe, she dressed in the clothes she had arrived in—the drab, cotton gown, donated by a local charity, that the miserly Mrs. Dobbs had given her to replace her ragged prison garb.

Extracting her old, stained apron from her canvas bag, she tied the apron around her waist and headed down to the kitchen to prepare breakfast. After spending most of her life cramped in narrow quarters—her childhood home, the garret at Hawthorn Manor, the prison cells at Newgate and on the *Seaflower*, Mrs. Dobbs' pantry—this house with its enormous kitchen overwhelmed her. As she hesitated in front of the massive black iron stove, sudden images of drowning flooded her mind—Isobel shoving her, a non-swimmer, into deep water; Sir Richard removing her gown as she lay drugged in the hermitage of Hawthorn Manor's maze; the First Mate, Amos Bristol, imprisoning her in a closet on the *Seaflower*—a victim again at the mercy of circumstances she could not control.

Determined, however, to earn her keep, to pay retribution for her damaged past and her recent lapses in judgment, she set about making the morning tea. Elinor had assembled the necessary breakfast items the night before, as if she doubted Misella's ability to handle the chores: filling the teapot with water from the well; measuring the exact amount of tea leaves into a container; arranging the place settings on the table; leaving half a dozen uncracked eggs in a bowl; and setting the greased iron skillet on the stove to fry the plated ham slices and the eggs. The only thing Elinor hadn't done was slice the bread, to prevent it from drying out, Misella assumed. . . like my life, she thought in despair. Unable to shake the black mood that hung over her despite Elinor's attempts to build her confidence, Misella felt lost and disoriented. Without an adversary like Mrs. Dobbs to keep her wits sharp and her doubts at bay, her fighting spirit shriveled.

Listless, she fired up the stacked logs in the fireplace, the flare of heat providing little warmth to her chilled limbs. She lit the flame under the tea kettle, mindful that the breadth of the stove top with its three additional burners put Mrs. Dobbs' ugly two-burner stove to shame. The luxury of such excess space reminded her again of the abyss between her old lives and this one. She wondered if she could ever truly belong here.

Heavy footsteps on the flagged stones behind her followed by an audible intake of breath impelled her to whirl around in fear, expecting to see the frowning face or the raised hand of Mrs. Dobbs.

"Did I startle you, Misella?" Her father, dressed in a jaunty fishing outfit—dark wool britches and a colorful plaid shirt—stood before his place at the table. Clutching a matching plaid cap in his hands in the pre-dawn gloom, he added, "I'm sorry if I did. I was just shocked to see you standing there instead of Elinor or Mary. I forgot for a moment that we have you home with us at last."

Misella grimaced. In an effort to control her confused emotions, she focused her attention on her father's heavy fishing boots, like the kind he used to wear, though not scuffed and stained with split seams along the sides. These sturdy replacements, she thought, could withstand the elements and last for a long time. "I find myself shocked to be here, too, father," she mumbled. "I'm not sure I should be."

The pained expression on his daughter's face surprised him, reminding him of his own guilt and uncertainty about their renewed relationship. Unsure of Misella's true feelings toward him, he hesitated, controlling the impulse to rush over to her, grab her in his arms, and reassure her that she did belong here. He wanted to tell her he loved her, this was her home, and to think otherwise was sheer nonsense. But he feared she might reject him again as she had on the first day of their reunion. Though she seemed to have grown more comfortable with Elinor on subsequent visits, her attitude toward him had remained cool and distant, as if she did not yet trust him. Instead of acting on his impulse to embrace her, he took a moment to set his cap down on the table before answering her. "Why do you think you don't belong here with us, Misella? Is it because of me?"

"No, Father, not because of you," she blurted out, exasperation elevating her voice. Her chest heaving, she bit her lips to hold back the tears that threatened to erupt. "It's. . . me," she panted, short breaths distorting the staccato tumble of her words. "I can't do it . . . pretend that everything . . . is n-normal now. It can never…never be the same." Her voice rose higher as she gripped the apron in her hands and twisted it. "I'm different now. . .my stupid mistakes. . . I don't deserve to live here. . . I deserve to be punished."

Holding onto the back of his chair, Johnnie Cross willed himself to remain where he was and to reply calmly, "Don't you think you have suffered enough for your sins, Misella? I think you have." He raked his hands through the graying curls on his bowed head, a familiar gesture he often used, Misella remembered, whenever he was flummoxed by ignorance or obstinacy.

His hair in curly disarray, his eyes drilling into her, willing her to believe him, he asked in a quiet voice, "How much more punishment would suffice, Misella, before you can allow yourself to denounce fate and accept good fortune?" He shook his head as if unable to understand her resistance, but then he stopped. With the hint of an apologetic smile, he said, "I sound like Ben now, don't I? I don't mean to lecture you, Misella. I guess what I do mean is that in trying to help you, I hope to atone for my own sins."

Unable to trust her voice and respond to his confession without sobbing, Misella remained silent until the whistling of the tea kettle saved her. She swung around to the stove and began preparing the tea. "The tea will be ready in a moment, Father," she said, her voice hoarse. "Why don't you sit, and I'll bring it to you. Milk but no honey, right?" She raised the end of her apron to wipe her cheeks.

"Yes, that is one thing about me that hasn't changed. Come sit and have your tea with me, Misella, and we can talk as we used to do before I trudged off to my boat on those early, foggy mornings in Portsmouth with my nets thrown over my arm. You would call to me as I went out the door, 'Catch the best fish, Father!' Remember?"

Misella carried the two brimming mugs to the table and set them down intact before seating herself in the chair her father had pulled out for her. "And do you remember what you always said in return?" Looking puzzled, he shook his head. "Nothing," she said with a slight grin. "Instead, you'd stick your thumbs up through the netting as a signal that you heard me and would do your utmost to comply."

"Ah, that's right, my dear. I do remember now." Puckering his lips, he blew on the tea, as he always did, before he risked a first sip. "Perfect," he said, "now that you are here with me." He stared at her misty-eyed, unashamed to show the depth of his feelings. "There is something I want you to know, Misella. Through all of our family tragedies—the loss of you, your mother and your two sisters—I have learned to accept the mystery the psalms have tried to teach me—punishment that can drive us to the breaking point can also allow us to know and accept ourselves, to have faith in the future." He raised his cup to his lips and took a long, slow drink before setting the tea down. "The psalms have shown me the path back to my life. That can be a gift, my dear, not a curse."

She sighed as she picked up her own mug of tea and took a tentative sip. "I'm afraid, father, if I am ever to reach that point of acceptance, I will need more help understanding your psalms. Unlike you, I am not yet able to forgive all of the punishment I incurred because of Sir Richard and the life he forced upon me—the death of my child, a trial for murder, my sentence, my transportation here as a prisoner." She thumped her mug of tea down on the table, slopping a little over the top and staining the lace placemat. "How was any of that fair? Why did I deserve that pain?" she asked, her cheeks aflame.

"Can your hallowed psalms explain that to me?" She closed her eyes, trying to ignore the guilt and sadness that dulled her father's eyes and spread across his face.

"I'm sorry for all you have endured, Misella," he murmured. "You did not deserve such pain, but that, I fear, is the mystery of human existence we must somehow learn to accept. You know what Ben always says about human motivation." He continued despite her exasperated sigh. "'We are all deceived by the same fallacies, animated by hope, obstructed by danger, entangled by desire, and seduced by pleasure.'" He nodded his tousled head. "I believe he is right. Yet we never seem to see the truth or the dangers of our choices in advance. I know I didn't."

Misella reached out and covered his clenched fist with her hand. "Oh, Father, I no longer blame you for my mistakes and the curse I brought upon myself. I can admit that much, at least, so maybe I have finally gained some knowledge. But I need more if I am ever to accept my good fortune without guilt. Perhaps I may if I devote my time to exploring those psalms again with you—and less attention to Ben's lectures. Let Elinor handle those."

Johnnie chuckled. Opening his arthritic fingers with a grimace, he grasped Misella's hand in his. "It's a plan, he said. "We can begin tonight."

Over the following months and throughout the bitter winter evenings, the two of them sat before the blazing fireplace reading and discussing, and sometimes arguing over, the psalms. Psalm 37 in particular raised Misella's ire. "Let's skip that one, Father," she said, sitting up straight, no longer leaning in close to read along with him. "I don't need to hear ever again how the 'wicked shall perish.' That verse was used by so-called religious men, the prison Ordinary and even Captain Barclay, to chastise me for my sins. The Ordinary would chant the words in his dreadful monotone whenever he entered my cell, drilling them into my brain.

Noisome and festering are my sores because of my folly,
I am stooped and bowed down profoundly; all the day
I go in mourning, for my loins are filled with burning pains;
There is no health in my flesh.

"I have mourned my past behavior long enough." She stood up, grabbed the poker resting on the hearth and jabbed the burning logs into a fiery heap before replacing them with fresh logs from the firewood box.

When she sat down, Johnnie retied the covers of the little book of psalms and set it on the floor behind his chair, away from any wayward sparks. "We'll continue with these readings later then, Misella," he said. A frown deepened the wrinkles around his eyes. "I fear you have not yet removed your sackcloth," he murmured. He raised his eyebrows as if inspired by a sudden idea. "Perhaps we might read the Book of Job first before we continue with the psalms."

Misella exhaled with disgust, flicking her hand in the air as if to dismiss a pesky gnat. "I know that story well, Father. I've lived it. I don't need to visit the suffering of poor Job again."

Johnnie nodded in seeming agreement. "I know it well, too, Misella, but I've learned something new each time I read about the testing of Job. He is a vivid example of what the psalms teach—acceptance of God's will."

Misella shook her head. "No, Father. Job can teach me nothing because a human monster, not a mystical God, caused my torment, and I gave in to his will. I cannot change what I did."

"Ah but, my dear, your tormentor, Sir Richard Maltby, is dead, yet your guilt keeps him alive in your mind. You give him mystical power over you, and he does not deserve that—nor do you." He smiled at her with a look of palpable tenderness in his eyes. "You may not appreciate my saying so, but you remind me of Job, Misella. Despite all of the misery and anguish you suffered, you never gave up. Like you, Job lost everything—his home, his family, his wealth. Though he despairs and wonders why he must suffer, he accepts his fate because he has faith. He illustrates the power of faith over doubt."

Misella could not control her temper. She lashed out in anger at her father's simplistic comparison. "Nonsense, Father. Job is not like me at all. He is driven by faith, not guilt. He has done nothing wrong, so he has no need to make amends for sinning. Job is not a logical comparison for someone like me."

"He's not meant to be. His is a spiritual journey, not that different from your own. You were selected because you were young and innocent, a victim deceived by someone who had power over you, thrust into circumstances you could not control. But you took action to remove yourself from Sir Richard's control when your spiritual instincts intervened."

Hunched over in her chair, her head bowed in shame, she confessed the truth to her father that she had concealed from everyone else, including Jack and Ben. "No, Father. It wasn't spiritual faith that impelled me to refuse Sir Richard's demand that I abort our child, conceived in sin. It was my guilt and fear of punishment if I committed that capital crime." She looked up at him, expecting to see revulsion in his eyes, surprised to see tears instead. "Isn't it ironic," she asked, her voice thick with her own unshed tears, "that in the end, my baby daughter died anyway? My ultimate punishment. Job's situation cannot compare. His loss is temporary; his daughters return to him."

"Oh, my dear," her father whispered, one hand resting on his heart, reaching out to her with the other. He cleared his throat. "Perhaps you have suffered more than Job. I didn't mean to upset you or cause you more pain. I only want you to believe in yourself, as I do, as I always have." Her doubtful expression increased his frustration not only with her for not believing him, but with himself for having failed to protect her. He stood up, grimacing as he straightened his back and shoulders. With the fierce gaze of a prophet, suggestive of Ben Turner, he raised his voice. "Job has taught me to understand the redemptive power of suffering and repentance. I pray that his story can help you accept, without guilt, your new life here with all of us who love you." He slumped back down to his chair. "That is my hope," he murmured, red-faced with embarrassment at his outburst. It was not his way to be loud or confrontational. Subdued and apologetic, he said, "I'm sorry, Misella. I don't mean to lecture you. I only hope you can indulge me by rereading Job with me in the coming days."

"If you insist, Father," Misella sighed, not wanting to disappoint him or risk ending their treasured evenings together.

Over tea in the following weeks, during their early morning chats, they continued their discussions of Job and the psalms, Misella insisting, "Job is too passive, Father. He does nothing to change his situation. He doesn't ask questions; he takes no action."

"You take him too literally, Misella, instead of seeing him as God intended—a spiritual example to illustrate the value of fortitude, tenacity and faith." He smiled at her. "Values you have learned well, my dear."

"I'm not so sure about faith," she mumbled.

During Sunday dinners they tried to share their conclusions about Job with Elinor and Ben, but Ben only wanted to discuss their wedding plans. "Spring," he bellowed exuberantly one February afternoon during a pause in the conversation. "When Shakespeare's 'darling buds of May' blossom, so will our vows," he exulted, flinging his arm around Elinor's shoulders and drawing her into his embrace. He gazed fondly at her, squinting his bad eye into an exaggerated wink. "If my blushing bride hasn't grown tired of me by then."

Elinor patted his ample mid-section, covered with a well-fitted, brown wool vest she had knitted for him to match his tailored britches, cream-colored shirt and wool hose. He was far better dressed these days, thanks to Elinor's subtle efforts. "No, not quite yet, dearest," she said with a smile, "though I must put up with you and your banter, not to mention your lectures, every day at the office." She winked at Misella who, wearing a worried expression, failed to smile. "But I think I can manage until our wedding day."

Ignoring Elinor, Misella laid down her fork and turned to Ben, her voice tense. "Do you think Jack will come home before then? What if he doesn't show up?" She pushed her unfinished dinner aside and crossed her arms over her chest as she often did whenever she felt threatened.

"Oh ho," he said merrily, "I can assure you, my dear, he'll keep his promise to attend our wedding. He'll show up as he always does, with his devilish grin, his dashing flair, and scold us for doubting his return—which I've not done since Pirate Jack appeared like a phantasm before me on the *Mary Anne* leaving me speechless in dumbfounded amazement. Nor must you doubt his return to you, Misella." With a stern look at her, he asserted, "We can trust Jack to do what he says he will do, though I can guarantee he'll arrive with plenty of far-fetched yarns to test our patience about meeting fairies and leprechauns in the woods. And he'll dare us to disbelieve him."

Her expression softening, Misella relaxed her arms and nodded. "And I will believe him," she said with a wistful smile. "Well, at first anyway."

Ben's certainty about Jack's return eased her mind enough that she could enjoy the spring thaw and the warming rays of sunlight that illuminated every room and lightened her mood. She didn't complain about the tracks of mud left by her father and Ben that kept her scrubbing the flagstones in the kitchen and vestibule. She prepared the Sunday dinners with heartfelt enthusiasm and welcomed the increasing intensity of Ben's and Elinor's wedding discussions.

On Easter Sunday, balmy and bright, with the promise of new growth evident everywhere in the garden, Misella picked enough dandelion greens, baby sprigs of lettuce and radishes for a salad to accompany the baking ham, candied yams and peach cobbler for their dinner. She had plenty of time to finish her work before the others returned from church. They hadn't pressed her to join them, respecting her disdain for Sunday preaching instilled in her by months of listening to Mrs. Dobbs. "For now," she told her father and Elinor when they asked her to join them for Sunday mass, "I will draw all of the spiritual help I need from the psalms." They seemed to understand, even Ben who managed to forego lecturing her about the importance of observing the Sabbath.

Later after the church-goers returned and had gathered for a pre-dinner glass of wine in the parlor, Misella remained in the kitchen to finish up dinner preparations. Hearing a commotion in the hallway and a loud, "Oh ho," from Ben, followed by a burst of laughter, Misella, dressed in a sky-blue dimity gown, wiped the lemon juice from her hands onto her new print apron and hurried to the kitchen doorway.

In the crowded vestibule stood Jack, his chin hidden under a dark beard, an untidy mustache drooping from his upper lip. A mass of black curls covered the open collar of his over-sized burlap shirt; a red, polka-dotted scarf encircled his head. Brown leather britches, held in place with a rope belt, ballooned to his ankles, each one tied with a matching piece of rope.

"Finny, my boy, welcome back," Ben hollered, clutching him in a fierce hug and giving him a hearty whack on the back. "You look like you've just escaped from a pirate ship again. In Logan's cast-offs, I reckon."

Jack grinned, his sapphire blue eyes alight with joy as he returned the hug. "You're right, old man, Logan is responsible for my dapper appearance." He looked around, his eyes darkening with anxiety, his voice heavy. "Where is she? Is she here?"

Misella flew from the doorway. Pushing Ben aside, she leapt into Jack's arms. "I'm right here, Jack Finn, where I belong," she said, breathless with happiness. "And you may kiss me—but not like a brother."

Chapter 57

"Let's make it a double wedding, Misella," Jack declared, as the two snuggled on the settee in the parlor a week after Jack's return, his pirate garb replaced with a sensible pair of britches and a fitted green linen jacket, his curls trimmed above the neckline. His face appeared clean-shaven except for a neat mustache which provided a more serious demeanor. "Everything would already be in place," he said, his eyes ablaze with excitement as he clasped his arms around her and drew her close for another kiss. "We'll serve as witnesses for Elinor and Ben, and they can do the same for us. Make it easy for everybody, including your father."

Misella wriggled out of Jack's arms and jumped up. "No, Jack," she exclaimed, crossing her arms over her chest. "We can't interfere with Elinor's plans, and divert attention from her on her special day. I know how much her wedding means to her, especially because she believed she was destined for spinsterhood." The fierce shaking of her head unleashed blond curls from the clasps holding them in place so that they flounced into her eyes and along her inflamed cheeks. She ignored them.

"Furthermore, Elinor and Ben would not approve of me abandoning father," she continued, shaking her head, her curls flying back and forth in agreement. "Leaving him all alone. I cannot do that. We must wait."

Jack stood. He brushed the curls from her eyes, anchoring them behind her ears, grasped her around her waist, and responded in a soft voice, "My dearest, I don't believe Elinor would mind sharing her day with us. She would be happy to do that. Also, we would not leave your father, now that you have found him. We will live right here with him. There is plenty of room for us, and now that he has offered me a job, we can both devote ourselves to helping him."

Misella turned away, averting her eyes. "You're not hearing me, Jack. Elinor should not have to share her wedding day. I will not ask that of her. . . or of myself. It's…it's too soon for me. Perhaps father wouldn't mind, but I do. I need more time. I'm not ready." When he released his hands and stepped back, she glanced up at him.

"More excuses," he said, his face dark with despair. "Making Elinor the scapegoat." He raked his fingers through his hair, upending the curls he had earlier smoothed into compliance with a dab of goose grease. Profound sadness dulled his eyes and altered his voice. "I fear you may never be ready, Misella," he sighed.

He fell silent for a moment, a grimace uplifting the corners of his mustache, before he spoke again. "You seemed overjoyed when I returned, ready to love me, with all your heart, you told me." He raised his left hand to flick a few wayward curls from his eyes, exposing the branded thumb with the bold **F** that labeled him a felon from his highwayman days. He usually hid the thumb under his sleeve, but lost in thought, a faraway look in his eyes, he seemed to forget about it and her.

"When I was young," he murmured, as if talking to himself, "I hated to lose at anything. I'd run to Granny Finn for comfort . . . and, I realized as I grew older, her words of wisdom. I remember a time when I was distraught about losing a championship boxing match, and she told me, 'Ah, lad, ye found the bees, but missed the honey. Ye'll have to wait til next time. Chin up; eyes to heaven.'" He shook his head. "I'm afraid there will never be a next time for us, Misella, no matter how long I wait."

His words stunned her, triggering fear, more virulent than ever, that he would leave her again and not return. "I'm sorry, Jack," she cried out, clutching his hand and hanging on tight as if she could not bear to let go. "I'm afraid . . .to marry you because...because I don't feel I deserve you." She inhaled, squeezing her eyes closed as she fought to control her voice. "I'm afraid that in time you will want to be rid of me." She hung her head. "I'm no good, Jack," she whispered. "I'm damaged, a worn-out prostitute."

Jack unfastened his hand from her grasp and grabbed her shoulders, shaking her. "Look at me, Misella," he said, his voice stern. "You are not a prostitute. You did what you had to do to survive. So did I. I stole money; I terrorized innocent people. To avoid hanging, I agreed to work for Sir Richard, a man I despised, but I accepted his help, and he sent me to prison anyway. I'm ashamed of my past, too, of all my mistakes, but because of them, I met you." His voice softened, and his grip on her shoulders relaxed into a caress as he hugged her to his chest, murmuring into her hair, "I fell in love with you years ago, and I have never stopped loving you. I'm here because of you, and I always will be. Please believe me. I...will...never... leave you."

She broke away from his embrace. Despite Jack's promises, she could not control her doubts. "You love adventure, Jack—as a highwayman, a pirate, you thrived on danger and excitement. I know that is why you volunteered to escort Robby Benton on the dangerous journey to seek out Logan. I could tell from the stories you told us around the dinner table how much you enjoyed your rendezvous in the woods with them, reenacting, as Ben jovially pointed out, your Robin Hood days. You can't," she exclaimed, "deny what was so obvious to all of us."

Jack snorted. "I admit I weave stories, Misella, to entertain, to make people laugh. That's the Irish way to cover up sorrow and uncertainty." With a familiar gesture, so like her father's, he raked his hands through his hair again. "Those days in the woods were painful for me—missing you, worrying about you, wondering why you had forsaken me, and if you could ever return my love. . . or marry me." His voice broke and he swallowed a few times before continuing.

"If I crave adventure in the future, I will find it right here in Boston with you." He hesitated, searching for the right words to convince her of his determination. "Logan and I believe that a big fight with England over taxes is on the horizon. We both think that Boston, as the major port in the Colonies, will become the cradle of that conflict with the Crown."

At first, Misella was dubious, afraid Jack was manufacturing another story to placate her, but then she recalled hearing about the Molasses Tax while indentured with Mrs. Dobbs. Her voice rose with excitement. "I think you may be right, Jack. Whenever I shopped for Mrs. Dobbs at Fanueil Market, I heard grumbling about the unfair Molasses Tax. People complained because they had to pay an extra six pence a gallon for molasses imported from England when the Indies offered a fairer price, but imports from elsewhere were banned. It didn't make sense to me either—England imported molasses directly from the West Indies, but the Colonies could not. I was surprised that Mrs. Dobbs, that skinflint, agreed with the tax. She paid it without complaint, insisting we must remain loyal to the Crown; our Christian duty demanded it." Misella shuddered. "How I detested that woman. I'm thankful every day to be rid of her—and of the country that so cruelly mistreated me."

Jack drew her closer for a tentative hug. "I'm thankful too, Misella, because I need you by my side as this fight grows when taxes on goods to and from the Colonies increase to offset England's national debt. The Crown, with Parliament's help, will continue to punish us. We both know how expert they are at cheating the poor: ignoring press gangs who kidnap hardy citizens like Logan and force them into years of service on merchant ships; luring desperate people like Robby Benton and Mary Boyle into the indentured servant program, promising them a better life and eventual freedom in America, but ignoring the abuses of that fraudulent system; ridding their crowded jails of convicts by consigning them to that same abysmal program with the added insult that, under penalty of death, they cannot return.

"That includes us, Misella. As ex-convicts, we can never return to England, nor would we want to. The tax fight that we know is coming is a fight we will want to join—because we're fighters, Misella, you and I. We belong together in this place."

Grasping Jack's hand, her eyes trained on his branded thumb, she traced the black **F** with her fingers. "I am learning to leave my past behind, Jack, I promise. As my Bible-quoting father keeps reminding me, I'm no longer a broken dish." She lifted his hand to her lips, kissed the branded thumb and raised her eyes to look at him. "I don't know if Ben has told you how he tried to save me from transportation here."

Though Ben had told him everything, Jack shook his head, not wanting to silence her. He knew she needed to tell him in her own words.

"He would have married me," she said, "though I told him I didn't love him that way. He arranged with the Archbishop to convince the Judge about changing my sentence to give me the benefit of clergy, as you received to keep you out of prison the first time you were caught—until Sir Richard sent you back to prison. A simple branding of my thumb to label me as a felon—and, like you, I could have avoided my fate." She sighed and turned away, still gripping his hand. "I could not deceive Ben or myself, though I was sorely tempted to accept his offer. But I needed to redeem myself, to find a new life and become the strong, honest woman I yearned to be.

"I'm almost there, Jack, and if a fight with England is coming, as you predict, I want to pursue that new life with you—because I love you." Facing him, she raised her hand and caressed his jawline. "Chin up; eyes to heaven, Pirate Jack. This time we will find the honey together. Elinor can have her day in May. We'll make ours a June wedding."

Chapter 58

"I don't want a Church wedding," Misella declared emphatically to her Father and the newlyweds as they gathered around the kitchen table to plan the special day, a bottle of Irish brandy sitting in front of Jack. "I've had enough of Church scripture from hypocrites like the Ordinary of Newgate, Mrs. Dobbs and her Mr. Briar. We will marry here, in the parlor—in two weeks, on the 15th of June."

Elinor stepped discreetly on Ben's foot, signaling him to hold his tongue, as she responded to Misella's troubling demand. "You'll need to marry in the Church, Misella, to fulfill the three-week requirement to publish the banns. You cannot marry legally without doing so to insure that no one objects to the marriage. There's still enough time if we postpone the ceremony until the end of June. Don't you agree, Jack?"

Before Jack could open his mouth, Misella lashed out at her sister. "Elinor, stop treating me like a ninny. I know that we can buy a marriage license in a few days, without publishing banns, since Jack and I are legally old enough to marry. We don't need the Church." When Elinor drew back, a hurt look on her flushed face, Misella softened her tone but not her criticism. "I didn't interfere with your wedding plans, so please respect mine."

Frowning, Johnnie spoke up in a quiet voice. "Perhaps you don't need to marry in the Church, my dear, but you will need a minister of the Church of England to conduct the ceremony for the marriage to be recognized in the Colonies. We are still bound by England's laws here."

"Faugh!" Misella hissed. "Am I never to escape the greedy clutch of English law?"

"I'm afraid in this case you cannot, my dear," her father answered, "but I suppose the minister could marry you here in the parlor." He nodded his head and smiled at Misella. "I think I would like that since Elinor's wedding was more traditional. I could arrange it easily—a wedding here, by the fireplace."

Misella's anger dissolved. "Thank you, Father," she murmured. "That would be perfect—and you could recite one of your psalms, something celebrating love and marriage. I know that Jack agrees because we've already decided what we want." She reached for Jack's hand before turning to Elinor with a forgiving smile, ignoring the rebuke in Ben's eyes, though he held his tongue and remained hunched over in grumpy silence. "Elinor, I hope you will agree to bake our wedding cake, the same one as yours, although you don't need to insert a piece of nutmeg for our small group. We won't have any unmarried young people to surprise with that predictor of the next to marry. I know you made sure at your reception that I received the slice with the hidden piece of nutmeg. That was fun, and I appreciated the gesture, not to mention your delicious cake."

Her good humor restored, Elinor smiled back. "Of course I will make your wedding cake, Misella."

A shadow of sadness crossed Misella's face. "A much smaller cake, though, because we will have only us at the ceremony—and the minister. How I wish Logan and Mary Boyle could be here . . . and Annabelle, too. But I know that is not possible.."

Jack squeezed her hand. "Chin up, Misella, we'll see them all again sometime in the future. I know we will." He picked up the bottle of brandy and poured Ben another draught. "The cat got your tongue, old man, or has marriage worn you out already?"

"You sly dog," Ben countered. "I outdanced you at our reception, without my cane, and drank more tankards of hard cider than young whippersnappers like you could manage." He drained his glass and thumped it on the table. "Ask Elinor how worn out I am."

Elinor blushed and turned his glass over. "That's enough bantering you two. And drinking. This is not a competition—nor is marriage. I hope you and Misella will be as happy as we are, Jack. And Misella, I'd be glad to loan you my brocade wedding dress, if you'd like. I'm sure it will fit."

"Thank you, Elinor, but I have decided to wear my simple blue gingham with a ring of lilies of the valley on my head instead of a veil. I want vases of rainbow-colored day lilies strewn throughout the parlor, and I'll carry a bunch in my arms. Jack plans to wear his favorite outfit. Mine, too. His loose-fitting sapphire blue jacket and comfortable cream-colored britches instead of the fancy suit he wore last month to your wedding. We don't need fuss or fashion, just each other." She rested her head on Jack's shoulder as he put his arm around her. Sitting up suddenly, she added, "And all of you, of course." Her voice wavered, and she had to swallow before she continued, "All of you who helped me reclaim my life."

The morning of June 15th dawned clear and bright, the sun rising like a promise in a cloudless sky. Misella had chosen early morning to take their wedding vows. They gathered together in the parlor surrounded by the brilliant colors and soft fragrance of trumpet daylilies: the portly minister in a severe, black wool suit with a starched white collar; Elinor and Ben dressed in their past wedding finery; Johnnie Cross beamed before the fireplace in a new linen jacket and britches, his outfit similar to Jack's; Misella, a garden nymph adorned with a crown of lilies of the valley, a cluster of daylilies in her arms.

Simple gold bands would seal their vows to one another, but first Misella asked her father to recite excerpts from the Old Testament Psalms 57 and 117 that he had chosen.

Determined to keep his emotions under control for Misella's sake, and his own, he intoned in a strong, clear voice:

Your word is a lamp to my feet
And a light to my path . . .
For great is your love,
reaching to the heavens,

your faithfulness
reaches to the skies.

How perfectly those words describe Jack, Misella thought. *From the day I first met him he has watched over me and loved me. And never gave up until he found me again. How lucky I am.*

She realized then that those words defined Ben Turner as well, and her father, although her father would probably insist it wasn't luck so much as God's grace that had brought her back to them. Whatever the cause, she knew, as she murmured, "I do," and Jack slipped the gold band on her finger, she would embrace her new life in this new world with fierce devotion, trust, and undying love.

Author's Note

Slavery in America has a sordid, cruel history. The first 19 or so African slaves to reach the English colonies arrived in Jamestown, Virginia, in 1619, brought by English privateers who had seized them from a captured Portuguese slave ship. The early African trading companies had developed English trade and trade routes in the 16th and 17th centuries, but it was not until the opening up of Africa and the slave trade to all English merchants in 1698 that Britain began to become dominant.

As early as 1618, however, England had begun its policy of white indentured servitude described by Don Jordan and Michael Walsh in their extensive study, *White Cargo: The Forgotten History of Britain's White Slaves in America.* At this time, "authorities in London began to sweep up hundreds of troublesome urchins from the slums." Despite protests from their parents or guardians, the children were shipped to Virginia. Promised a new start as apprentices in this developing New World, they were instead "sold to planters to work in the fields and half of them were dead within a year." This inhumane practice provided a template for the long, callous history of slavery that followed.

By 1720, the British government officially developed its program of indentured servitude and promoted it as a path to freedom and opportunity for the disadvantaged. However, the policy quickly devolved into a systematic method of enslaving the poor and ridding Britain's overcrowded jails of petty criminals. Providing cheap, disposable labor for tobacco plantations and other merchant classes in the newly developing Colonies, the system thrived until the American Revolution ended that program but not the appetite for slave labor. Instead, America continued the criminal plunder of Africa to supply the slaves needed for its fields and homes—and the exploitation and cruelty persisted.

While Jordan and Walsh conclude that "black slavery emerged out of white servitude and was based upon it," they also concede that "black slavery had hideous aspects that whites did not experience." Black slaves and their offspring had to serve their masters for life, without hope, whereas indentured servants, like Misella Cross, Mary Boyle, and Robby Benton, were at least promised a time limit to their enforced labor, though their well-being and subsequent freedom depended upon their Masters or the kindness and courage of others. If white slaves managed to escape or completed their time with an honest master, the color of their skin helped them to succeed and rise above suspicion, unlike black slaves who, even when they gained their freedom, faced discrimination and constant fear of retaliation. Though the indentured servant program ended with the Revolutionary War, the repercussions and effects of black slavery, despite emancipation after the Civil War, continue today. Perceptive and sympathetic about the issue of slavery, Samuel Johnson recognized in the eighteenth century that "Slavery is now nowhere more patiently endured, than in countries once inhabited by the zealots of liberty" (*Idler #11,* June 24, 1758).

The Journey of Misella Cross resumes the story begun in my first novel, *The Trial of Misella Cross*. In this sequel, I wanted to explore the immoral past history of servitude in America, especially through Misella's experience as one of these poor, indentured slaves. I have included many of the same characters introduced in that first novel: Ben Turner, Jack Finn, Johnnie and Elinor Cross, and Captain Barclay. As noted in the previous novel, Ben Turner is modeled after Samuel Johnson, the well-known eighteenth-century curmudgeon, who was a writer, not a lawyer—though he could have served as one.

Acknowledgements

Thank you to my talented writing friends who have read several versions of the manuscript and have improved my work with their comments, suggestions and questions. I am indebted to Debbie Carlson, Dr. Vesna Neskow and Maureen Stack Sappéy for their dedication, insights and encouragement.

Several works informed my research—I have once again borrowed from James Boswell's portrayal of Samuel Johnson in his remarkable *Life of Johnson* to develop the character and philosophy of Ben Turner. I have also learned so much from the following helpful sources: Don Jordan's and Michael Walsh's *White Cargo: The Forgotten History of Britain's White Slaves in America*; Anthony Aver's *Bound with an Iron Chain: The Untold Story of How the British Transported 50,000 Convicts to Colonial America;* James Michener's *Chesapeake*; Barry Unsworth's *Sacred Hunger*; Barry Clifford's and Kenneth J. Kinkor's *Real Pirates*; Robert Robson's *The Attorney in the 18th-Century*; R. Kent Lancaster's *Indentured Servants* from the online Hampton National Historic Site; *Talbot County*, Maryland Courts online site, and the *Maryland Courier* online.

A sincere thank you to Our Lady of the Mississippi Abbey for providing space, time and inspiration for me to write in their beautiful, peaceful setting.

My heartfelt gratitude to Bridget Hassan who created the exquisite water color of an 18th-century sailing vessel that graces the cover of my novel.

Thanks to my loving family for their continuing support and encouragement, and especially to Hank, my love, for keeping me grounded and making me laugh.

Made in the USA
Columbia, SC
15 January 2024